The Virgin River Series
WILD MAN CREEK
PROMISE CANYON
MOONLIGHT ROAD
ANGEL'S PEAK
FORBIDDEN FALLS
PARADISE VALLEY
TEMPTATION RIDGE
SECOND CHANCE PASS
A VIRGIN RIVER CHRISTMAS
WHISPERING ROCK
SHELTER MOUNTAIN
VIRGIN RIVER

The Grace Valley Series
DEEP IN THE VALLEY
JUST OVER THE MOUNTAIN
DOWN BY THE RIVER

Novels
A SUMMER IN SONOMA
NEVER TOO LATE
RUNAWAY MISTRESS
BLUE SKIES
THE WEDDING PARTY
THE HOUSE ON OLIVE STREET

Watch for
BRING ME HOME FOR CHRISTMAS,
*the October 2011 Virgin River Christmas book
from Robyn Carr*

ROBYN CARR

HARVEST MOON

MIRA®

ISBN-13: 978-1-61129-326-5

HARVEST MOON

For Nancy Berland, a writer's best friend and ally.
Thank you for all you do!

One

"I need to see you," Phillip said. "My office."

Kelly Matlock, sous chef, threw him an incredulous look. She was literally holding apart a big Italian and a big Swede; the Italian line cook had a spatula and the Swedish one was wielding a metal spoon as they fought over stove-top territory. The request that she go to the restaurant manager's office right now was so absurd, she almost laughed. "Really too busy here, Phillip," she said. "Not only are we having a brawl in the kitchen, but it's seven o'clock. Prime dinner rush. Check with me at ten."

"It's urgent," he said. "Otherwise, believe me, I wouldn't ask."

"Where's Durant?" Kelly asked, speaking of the chef de cuisine, the head chef.

"Making his rounds in the front of the house, gloating. Let these two morons kill each other—we're short on meat anyway."

That suggestion did far more to separate the line

cooks than Kelly had. "I'll be right there," she said to Phillip. He liked to be addressed as *Philippe,* although Kelly had learned he didn't actually have a French cell in his body. His accent was entirely for show. She went to her locker, removed her apron and exchanged her soiled white jacket for a clean, crisp one and left her senior line cook in charge.

It never crossed her mind that it might be a real emergency; Phillip loved his melodramatic displays. His second favorite thing was making passes at the female staff and his third, screaming matches with Durant.

One day, when Kelly finally became chef de cuisine, there would be no Phillip; she would never tolerate a manager with such annoying, socially unacceptable behaviors.

She gave a couple of taps on Phillip's office door and then pushed it open. Her heart almost stopped. Seated there, in a chair facing the restaurant manager's desk, was Olivia Brazzi, wife of the world-famous master chef Luciano Brazzi. Although Kelly crossed her path regularly—at charity events and in this very restaurant—they didn't know each other at all. Luca owned a controlling interest in this restaurant. Olivia was tight with Durant and her presence here was not unusual. But Olivia had always ignored Kelly, treating her as if she were a mere cook, not worthy of her time.

Olivia smiled at her with such warmth and kindness, Kelly wondered for an insane moment if she were dreaming and Olivia had come to turn Luca over to her.

While Mrs. Brazzi was stunning in her elegant black

crepe dress, shiny textured stockings, three-inch heels and strategically placed diamonds, she did not look her fifty years, not by twenty. She looked like a girl. A sophisticated girl with ice-blue eyes.

Kelly's stomach flipped. *What in the world could she want with me?* she thought. *Could she expect me to cater a special dinner party or event?*

Olivia glanced at Phillip. "A moment, Philippe? May I have the room?"

Kelly became light-headed. On her list of most unexpected events, a private meeting with Olivia Brazzi was up there with alien abduction.

"Of course, Olivia," he said and paused to kiss the back of her hand before leaving. It made Kelly want to gag.

"Ms. Matlock, please," Olivia purred. "Sit down a moment." She gestured with a small, delicate hand to the chair beside her.

Kelly said a brief prayer. *Whatever this is, please let it be over quickly!*

"I'm sorry that our first meeting is so awkward, Ms. Matlock, but I've come to ask you to stop sleeping with my husband."

Kelly's eyes grew large in spite of her desire to remain poised. "Are you serious?" she asked, mortified.

"Oh, my, yes," Olivia said.

"Mrs. Brazzi, I'm *not* sleeping with Luca!"

"Perhaps there's not that much sleeping… Now, let's get it sorted out quickly and quietly. Shall we?" And she lifted a brow.

Whew, at least Olivia was quick and to the point. And that sounded suspiciously as if Olivia and Luca were not as separated as Luca claimed.

Of course, Kelly *wasn't* sleeping with him! But best to say nothing further, she decided, because her feelings for Luca would probably show all over her face. She swallowed those emotions with an effort.

Kelly was pretty; she knew she was pretty. But Olivia was *beautiful*. And chic. And seasoned; experienced. Her sophisticated and contained self-assuredness was a bit overpowering. Kelly had been up against the most diabolical chefs in the world, yet the soft spoken Mrs. Brazzi had her completely intimidated.

"Luca told me everything. How you met, how long you've been seeing each other, etcetera. It's a familiar story. Of course you're not the first," Olivia said. "I imagine you know that by now. My husband seems to have a particular taste for blondes. Please, will you break it off?"

She knew she shouldn't say anything *at all*. But this was a bit too crazy to leave alone. "With all due respect, Mrs. Brazzi, I don't know what you're talking about."

"Your affair with Luca has been going on for about three months now. Maybe four? You met at a charity event—in fact, I was present. You love to exchange food. It leads to all the other things—for Luca, food equals passion. Your number was all over his cell phone, so I confronted him. It's not the first time we've gone around about something like that. The messages, the texts, the pictures, all that. Please, it's out now. I just want it to end."

Kelly stiffened. "Really, Mrs. Brazzi, I've known your husband much longer than three months. I've been sous chef here for three years! We've had professional contact, sometimes frequent—this *is* his restaurant, even if Durant thinks he owns the place, but—"

Olivia smiled indulgently. "Please, do call me Olivia. After all, we have so much in common. And my dear, you really don't want to pursue this. If it's not already obvious to you, allow me to enlighten you—Luca has a short attention span. Has he told you about the other children? The ones he's fathered outside our marriage?"

If her intention was to shock Kelly, it certainly worked. "Ah, Mrs. Brazzi, you have me at a complete disadvantage. This is sounding more and more like personal business between you and your husband. I wouldn't know anything about—"

"We've managed to keep those unfortunate liaisons inside the family and company, but if you're really close he would have told you. Luca has many conquests on his record. For all I know, there could be a dozen children. But not on the books—I keep a close eye on the finances. I'm sorry if you're hurt, but the sooner you move away from this mess with Luca, the better, I promise you. It won't come to a tidy end. And there's no money in it."

Kelly shot to her feet. "Money? You can't possibly think—" And then she could have kicked herself. How's that for sounding like a confession? But the suggestion that she was a gold digger was somehow even more offensive than the accusation that she was fooling around with Luca!

"I'm truly sorry," Olivia said. "I meant no offense. I'm sure you probably love him madly. You should know that while Luca supports his children, their mothers haven't profited. They're forced to live simply. And sadly, my children haven't been welcoming to them. As you might imagine, it doesn't please them that their father has such a wandering eye. They're very loyal to me."

"Mrs. Brazzi, I wouldn't know about things like children outside your marriage because I don't believe I'm a confidante. I speak to Luca about recipes and menus, about dining venues and career opportunities. He's been a mentor and friend. But really—"

"Just save it, Ms. Matlock. I couldn't possibly have stayed with Luca this long by being naïve. You call or text him several times a day!"

"Those are replies," Kelly insisted. It was the truth— if there were several texts or calls in a day, it was because she was answering him. She never initiated *many* calls; she didn't want to appear needy or desperate. "I wouldn't want to bother him! He's a very busy man!"

Olivia leaned closer. "I've seen the records, dear. I know you're in love with my husband and we have to end this here. Now."

Fair enough, Kelly thought. The relationship, such as it was, would hereby end. But she bristled at the way she was being misjudged, as if *she* had gone after *him*, perhaps for profit. Luca had told her that he and Olivia lived separate lives under the same roof, that for over twenty years they'd had separate bedrooms, that they were together for their children and important social events that led to business success. Kelly had *never* been his lover!

All that being said, Kelly had long ago admitted to herself that her relationship with him wasn't completely innocent. Luca romanced her with food and words, claimed to have fallen for her, professed to love her. And although she had said she wasn't getting involved with a married man, she'd lapped up his praise and adoration like a thirsty puppy.

Still, she couldn't imagine what Olivia Brazzi had seen that would lead her to assume some sexual liaison!

Kelly could play along with this until she spoke to Luca and found out what was going on. "Seriously, Mrs. Brazzi, I would never disrupt your family. Luca should have saved you the trouble of coming here. In fact, if he said it would be best to have no friendship at all, I would understand. I'm not holding him hostage."

But what Mrs. Brazzi had said—preference for blondes, many conquests, children born outside his marriage? None of this reflected anything Luca had told her.

Of *course,* she chided herself. Big surprise.

Olivia actually laughed. "Who do you think sent me, darling? It's not the first time I've had to clean up after him."

"Are you out of your mind?" Kelly nearly shouted before she could stop herself.

"I know rudeness runs rampant in the kitchen." Olivia frowned. "Believe me, I've witnessed that for myself on many occasions, but it's not charming. Yes, Luca sent me to talk to you. He thought that coming from me, you would understand."

"That's the thing I *don't* understand. Why would he do this to me? I'm certainly no threat to you." She shook her head. "He had only to tell me that you were uncomfortable with our friendship, and that would end all communication between us."

"Nice try, darling," Olivia said. "While he was in the lavatory last night, I looked at his phone. I found a couple of weeks' worth of recent calls, a couple of very sultry voice mails from you, some texts he hadn't deleted. We fought. We negotiated. He made me an offer—if I would ask you to kindly move on, he would stop taking your calls and instruct his staff to make polite excuses. I agreed. As I have before. Can we consider this over now?"

Kelly frowned. Then she really laughed. Sultry? Not likely. "Mrs. Brazzi, you've got the wrong girl. I can't imagine I've ever left him a sultry message!" And the Luca Kelly knew was more likely to explode in anger than whimper a confession and beg for help from his estranged wife to end a relationship over what might've been on his cell phone! Kelly was paranoid and nervous enough to never leave a suggestive text or voice mail. She couldn't count the number of assistants Luca employed.

She had believed Luca, that he and his wife had an understanding and their legal separation and divorce was being negotiated. There was an occasional text: *I'll be in the restaurant office at five. I want to see you.* Couldn't he be sending that sort of text to any chef he wanted to speak to? Any colleague? To Durant? To Phillip?

Was it possible Olivia was a little nuts? Was she exaggerating, or was it possible she was a little crazy?

Frankly, it surprised Kelly that Luca was still around. Most men with the good looks, money and power of Luca Brazzi would move on to a woman more willing to throw caution to the wind and succumb to that full-blown affair Olivia apparently thought they had had.

It was irrelevant that Kelly longed for that; it was beside the point that Kelly adored him, that she believed herself to be in love with him. She'd managed to keep him at a safe distance because he was married. And… because she was woefully inexperienced with men.

"I think you need to work this out with Luciano," Kelly said, shaking her head. "I'm not sure what's really going on here."

"If that's the case, dear, then you won't be at all upset when you can't reach him."

"Mrs. Brazzi, if he's such a philanderer and cheat, having children with mistresses and spoiling your good name, why in the world are *you* with him?"

"That's a fair question. Because we married for life, we have a very large family together, we're business partners and breaking up an international company as large as ours would be dreadfully complicated. And you may rest assured, my name is on every document that matters. All that aside, despite his flaws, I do love the man. He's a genius, a gifted and complicated man, and he couldn't manage without someone like me. He has a habit of telling his women that there's nothing between us, but of course it's not true—we sleep together every night. We're husband and wife, dear. Now, here's what will happen," she explained. "He has given his word he won't contact you again. The romance dissolves here and now and you're on your way to the next available man. Thank you for your time."

She turned, and before Kelly could even speak, Olivia's hand was on the office door to leave.

Kelly lost her head and blurted out her feelings before she could stop herself. "I can't imagine running off alleged girlfriends for a man I loved! Why do you do it?"

Olivia turned toward her. She smiled patiently. "Trust me, I have my reasons. Billions of reasons, really. Good evening, Ms. Matlock."

Kelly went back to the kitchen, which was hot, steamy and alive with action, shouting and chaos typical of seven-thirty in the evening. In something of a daze, she quickly replaced the perfectly white, starched coat with her slightly soiled one and wrapped her apron around her waist. Of course Luca could have lied to her; perhaps he was just trying to consummate the very fling Olivia suspected.

Or, Olivia could be lying about Luca sending her to ask Kelly to go away, for a billion reasons.

She wasn't going to find out soon, so she got back in there and started directing traffic, checking the orders, moving dishes along to the waitstaff, observing the line cooks at work, stepping in whenever her assistance was needed.

Luca owned many restaurants, was a controlling partner in dozens if not hundreds worldwide, had a commercial food line and appeared regularly on a nationally syndicated television program, and yet it was not surprising Kelly knew him. He had a special fondness for French American cuisine and partnered up with Durant to open *La Touche* several years ago. Since Luca kept one of his large, family homes in the Bay Area, he liked to frequent his local investments. While his wife and her friends might dine, the true beauty of Luca was that cooking was still the most important thing to him, all other business or TV shows aside. And Kelly loved it when he was here—everyone held back a respectful distance, and the entire kitchen came under control like at no other time. That was probably because Durant, smart enough to step lightly around his betters, behaved like a professional when Luca was in the house.

She had adored him immediately but never imagined he'd return the emotion. That had been fairly recent, but he'd been promising her a chef de cuisine position since long before he made a romantic overture.

She tried to ignore the fact that Durant and Phillip were chatting near the freezer. When had they *ever* chatted? They fought like junkyard dogs over control of the restaurant. She assumed if they were talking, it had to be about her.

That light-headed feeling returned, and she ignored it. Kelly yelled that the salmon was up, the crème brûlée was ready for the flame, the filet was out of time.

She had a little trouble catching her breath, and her heart raced. Then suddenly, a burning ache in her chest. *This is probably what happens when a man's wife comes to tell you to end the affair you're not quite having yet,* she thought. *This is probably what I deserve! I always knew I should have said, "Great, let's talk again when the divorce is final!"*

But the worst pain came from imagining Luca selling her out like that—admitting they were close, perhaps too close, and sending his wife to shut it down.

She was panting, couldn't catch her breath. She grabbed her chest. A scary bit of heartburn; she never had heartburn. She broke out in a sweat.

Durant's cruel smile appeared before her, which was easy—they were both five-five. "You slept with Luca Brazzi didn't you, you stupid cow?"

Kelly's eyes rolled back in her head and she went down. Lights out.

When Kelly awoke, a man in a navy blue T-shirt smiled into her eyes as he wheeled her toward a vehicle with red-and-blue flashing lights. There was a mask over her mouth and nose. She realized she was on a gurney or stretcher; she felt the motion of it as it slid into the back of an ambulance. "Well, hello," he said after he'd closed the doors. "Feeling okay?"

She clawed away an oxygen mask. "Where… What…"

"You passed out, got a little cut on your head. Your EKG looks okay at first glance but has to be checked by a cardiologist. Your blood pressure is way up there and you were out a little on the long side." Then he asked her a series of questions—who is the president, what year is it, where do you work? He listened to her heart, checked her blood pressure. She lifted her hand and saw the IV. "We started the IV in case we need to administer drugs. Do you have asthma? Allergies?"

It was pure instinct that prompted her to struggle to sit up. "No, I'm fine, I'm just…"

He pushed gently against her shoulder. "We'll be there soon, Miss Matlock. Trust me, you need a little visit with the doctor." She watched as he tinkered with the IV, then pushed something in with a syringe. Then he laughed uncomfortably. "That kitchen," he said with a snort. "I might never eat out again…"

"Huh?"

"Seriously," he said. "We have paramedics in the kitchen and people are yelling about spinach sides and they're stepping *over* us! Don't they take a little break when a chef could be having a heart attack?"

She put her hand to her chest, and her eyes were panicked. "Am I having a heart attack?"

"Nah, I don't think so. You're stable now. But you had some noticeable symptoms. One of the cooks said you grabbed your chest and had trouble breathing. You have to see the ER doc before you go anywhere. Seriously, that kitchen is a nuthouse."

She fell back onto the gurney, suddenly very tired. "Yeah. Tell me about it."

"You under that kind of stress all the time?" the paramedic asked.

She nodded, but what she thought was, *Except for Luca's wife confronting me, it was a pretty average night.*

He chuckled humorlessly. "Unbelievable. I had to clear out the kitchen…"

"Huh?"

"I told them to turn off the stoves and get the hell out of the kitchen or I'd have the police do it," he said. "Thing is, a lot of people have high-stress jobs—surgeons, stockbrokers, pilots. But I'd never work in that kitchen."

"Don't like to cook?" she asked tiredly.

"I love to cook. I bet I'm the best one at the house." Then he grinned. "Firehouse. And of course there's stress in being a paramedic. But I saw a difference the minute I was in that kitchen. We work as a team. We can count on each other."

Kelly was fading; she could hardly hold her eyes open. "Did you give me something?"

"Valium," he said. "The ER doc ordered it. It'll calm

you down a little. You're anxious, which could account for the rapid pulse and high blood pressure."

"We work as a team, too. We have to in a five-star kitchen…"

"Yeah, but on your team, they kick the injured to one side. That can go hard on your nerves."

"Hm. Well this Valium certainly fixes that."

He smiled. "Have a little nap. We're almost there."

"Do you have my purse?" she asked. "Can I have my cell phone?"

"Let's get you to ER and let the docs have a crack at you first," he said. "We'll dig out your cell phone later. You're too groggy to make good use of it right now anyway."

Apparently she wasn't going to die. At least not yet. And she didn't have her cell phone. It must have fallen out of her purse when she was taken to the ambulance.

After five hours in the ER, she was released to go home. She had follow-up appointments with a cardiologist for a stress test and an internist to give her a physical and deal with her elevated blood pressure, which could be stress-related. Blood work indicated she was also anemic; her head CT was negative—no concussion.

But the first thing she did in the morning was go to the restaurant in search of her cell phone. When she couldn't find it, she called Phillip at home, waking him. "Who got my purse for the paramedics?" she asked him.

"Me," he said with a tired groan. "I'm the only person

who can get in all the lockers. I figured you'd need ID and your insurance card."

"But my cell phone is gone. I don't even have a land-line in my flat, and all my numbers, address book, calendar and appointments are in that phone!"

"I'll look around when I open up, but it didn't turn up when we were shutting down."

"I'm at the restaurant now," she said. "I know the alarm code!"

"Listen," the manager said, sounding as if he came awake slowly. "You need to take a couple of days to figure out why you crashed. That disruption cost us money. What did they say at the hospital?"

"No big deal," she reported. "I'll be fine. But I will take a day or two. I have follow-up appointments to get some…vitamins… And I obviously have to buy a *phone*."

"Look under all the equipment, lockers, etcetera. Maybe it got kicked out of the way or something."

She sighed. "I *have,* Phillip."

"Sorry, then," he said and hung up.

She continued to talk into the silence. "Thank you, I'm feeling fine, Phillip! I'm sure I'll be all right, but it's so sweet of you to ask if there's anything you can do to help!" And then she clicked off the phone and slammed it down onto the desk.

She wasn't feeling so fine; she was still a bit groggy from the effects of the Valium. The ER doc had pointed out that not only was her blood pressure too high, but her molars were flattening out from grinding her teeth. The light-headedness and heart palpitations had probably been due to an anxiety attack—that should be verified if possible. Stress, anemia and exhaustion all added up to her fainting spell.

"Is it going to kill me?" Kelly had asked. Perhaps she could blow off the follow-up appointments.

The ER doctor had shrugged and said, "It will at least seriously affect your quality of life. You should really consider slowing things down if you can."

There was the little matter that her heart was broken; talk about a fatal injury to quality of life.

Fortunately, she could remember the most important numbers stored in the lost cell phone—her sister Jillian's and Luca's. To her supreme shame, she called Luca's phone first. His voice mail came on. Her message was, "I lost my phone and have a new number. This new number should be recorded on your phone directory, but just in case it's not, it's the same area code, 555-7604. Please call me, I've had quite a shock. If I don't hear from you, I'll have to assume your wife was telling me the truth—that you sent her to speak to me, to inform me that we can no longer have a friendship of any kind—personal or professional." Then she sent a text to his phone with the same message. Then she attempted to send him an email with the very same message, but she had to create a new account first. Losing the phone on which she carried all her information and email accounts was incredibly complicated.

But to her complete frustration, she didn't hear from Luca all day.

After seeing both the internist and cardiologist, she placed a call to one of Luca's personal assistants, Shannon. "Hi, Shannon, it's Kelly Matlock, sous chef at *La Touche*. I seem to have misplaced my cell phone and have a new number and new email address. I'm trying to reach Luca. I have a business matter to discuss. Will you please pass on my new number, email, and ask him to call or something?"

"Absolutely, Ms. Matlock! I'd be happy to. I should see him in an hour or so."

But the new cell phone didn't ring.

Kelly called Jillian in Virgin River, but all she said was that she'd lost her phone and had a new number. She'd tell all when the doctors had had their say and the crisis had passed, but she didn't want to worry her sister. Besides, Jillian had just gone through her own difficult time and was barely reunited with her man. Instead, Kelly holed up at home, waiting for that new cell phone to ring. She betrayed her pride by making a few more attempts on Luca's cell, but to her credit she was as professional as ever with the messages she left.

The second day brought the results of tests, which, thankfully, were far from catastrophic. She was given a shot with an iron booster. Prescriptions were called in to the drug store for blood pressure and low-dosage antianxiety medications along with the name of a good over-the-counter vitamin with extra iron. Kelly was going to be just fine; all doctors recommended a better diet—better than what a five-star chef could provide?—more rest, less pressure, reduced stress.

She laughed to herself. *Yeah, right.*

She had kept her flat darkened so she'd rest, but sleep eluded her. She realized she hated the apartment. It was a small two-room efficiency that cost a fortune because it was in the city, but she had only leased this particular one because it was so close to the restaurant and she rarely had to use her car.

Loved the city, hated her place. But hell, she didn't spend much time there anyway. It seemed her life had revolved around the restaurant for three years. She had friends, good friends, but rarely saw them; hardly ever made time to play or relax with them. She couldn't remember the last time she'd gone to a movie. Work, work, work—and much of it was just to keep her position safe, not out of sheer joy. Even her love life seemed to begin and end at *La Touche.*

She returned after two whole days off. A couple of line cooks had beaten her to the kitchen and were slicing and dicing; they didn't ask her how she was feeling. She got about the business of checking her inventory and the contents of the freezer while slowly the kitchen began to fill up with employees. She heard arguing and recognized the voices of Phillip and one of the cooks and resisted the urge to check it out; she wished Phillip would mind the front of the house and stay out of her territory, but he was always in everyone's business. Before long Durant began verbally abusing a couple of cooks, then telling Phillip he was a useless idiot who should stay out of his kitchen.

Soon the kitchen was fully staffed; the noise escalated and the temperature rose along with the tension. Everyone had their territory, either vegetables or pasta or meat or fish or pastry. Durant saw something he didn't like and poured the contents of a saute pan into the sink, calling the cook a stupid, incompetent bitch. It was a young female line cook he loved to berate because he could make her cry. "Matlock!" he yelled. "You watching this or just playing with yourself?"

She ignored him and brought out the filets and the salmon from the cooler.

Criticism poured from Durant; everything he saw sucked. Kelly felt her pulse pick up and her forehead bead with sweat. God, she hoped she wouldn't pass out again. She was pretty sure she couldn't afford another ambulance ride.

Her phone, which she was now keeping in her pants pocket, gave a short chime that announced a text had just come in. In spite of her good sense, she prayed it was Luca, texting her that the whole thing with his wife was untrue and that he loved her. She couldn't imagine how that could be, but she hoped anyway. In this hot, packed, mean kitchen, she felt so alone. So alone she wanted to cry.

Funny, she hadn't cried in the forty-eight hours since Luca's wife had broken her down and ejected her from Luca's life. Shouldn't she have cried her heart out?

There was a picture in the text. A massive pile of pumpkins all tangled up in their vines came from Jillian. The message said, *The leaves on the trees are changing as we watch! The pumpkins and melons are ripe and still growing! We sit on the back porch with lemonade and just soak it in—I've never seen such beauty. Wish you were here! xoxoxo*

"Matlock!" Durant shouted. "No phones in the kitchen! Put it away or I'll shove it where the sun don't shine."

She smiled and enlarged the photo of the pumpkins. *I've never seen such beauty. Wish you were here!*

"Matlock, you stupid cow, I said—"

And just like that, she'd had enough. She was done.

Kelly slipped the phone into her pocket and turned her back on Durant. She carefully slid her personal knives into the leather case, then she went to her locker. She never kept much there. She stuffed her large satchel with a couple of extra chef's coats, a spare pair of kitchen pants, her second pair of clogs, printouts of the schedule and the menu. Her purse fit inside the satchel, though barely.

I have nothing here, she thought. *I have no one. Luca isn't going to find me my own restaurant. Durant is never going to let me get any farther ahead. Every day is going to be sheer abuse. Quality of life? Ha! All I have is high blood pressure, flat molars, anxiety attacks and no one.*

She put the strap over her arm and headed through the kitchen toward the back door.

"Matlock, if you walk out of here, I'll make sure you never work in this city again!"

She smiled over her shoulder. "Can you promise that?"

She walked out the door.

Applause and whoops of laughter coupled with Durant's screaming and name-calling followed her exit. It was impossible to know if the line cooks were cheering because her position was opening up or because they admired her guts.

It didn't matter. She went home to the apartment she hated to pack up her life.

Two

All Kelly really wanted was to be less lonely, relax enough to stop grinding her teeth and get away from that hellhole that was her kitchen! She looked at that picture of the pumpkins twenty times; she transferred it to her laptop so she could get it nice and big. She fantasized about sitting on the porch, watching the leaves turn.

Of course, being a chef, she envisioned hot soups, warm soft breads and a blazing hearth to go with the fall colors.

Her sister Jillian had gotten rich during her ten years with a software manufacturer, allowing her to buy a big old Victorian on ten acres of land in Virgin River, but sous chefs who didn't have their own restaurant, trademark food line or TV show earned only decent salaries. Kelly had a little saved; she was far from flush, however. But while recuperating from Durant and company, Kelly knew Jill would be glad to give her a room and a bed. She thought she could scout around on the internet and through contacts for calmer chef's positions. At the moment, money and prestige were far less important than a little peace of mind.

Without saying a word to Jill about all she'd just been through, Kelly packed up her place, leaving the boxes inside. She didn't have much; it didn't take long. With her in the car she took some clothes, her spices, recipes, knives and, because Jill wasn't much of a cook and her kitchen not well-appointed, some of her favorite pans and table linens. She left the key with her neighbor so movers could be let in to load it all up, phoned her landlady to say this was her last month and hit the road. There was usually a long waiting list for city apartments in San Francisco; the landlady would have no trouble filling the space.

It was on her drive to Virgin River that Kelly started rehearsing her explanation for showing up without notice, without asking, without having told her sister of her circumstances. She felt the pressure build the closer she got. Of the two girls, Jill had always been the impetuous one while Kelly usually had firm, practical, long-term plans. Jill had been the one to leap into a job she'd had no training for because it intrigued her. Jill had been the one to fall in love with a man she barely knew. Kelly had always been the solid one, not the flighty one. Oh, Jill was brilliant in PR, marketing and business, no question about it. But Jill took chances. Kelly did not.

And yet Kelly had found herself working for an abusive, lunatic chef, lusting after a man who was married rather than separated, and flying off to a small town to escape before having a nervous breakdown. Kelly, who had been the one to get Jill through every trial from starting her period to starting college, had ended up acting like a flake. Kelly wasn't sure if Jill would pity her or have a really good laugh.

By her estimation, she'd arrive in Virgin River by around six. She decided it would be a good idea to stop off at that bar in town, Jack's, and bolster herself with a glass of wine, or something, before heading out to Jillian's house. She had barely slept the last two nights and hadn't eaten all day. How could she with the surprising turns her life had taken?

Lief Holbrook entered Jack's and took a seat up at the bar. It being October and hunting season, the place was full of men in khaki shirts with red vests and hats enjoying that end-of-the-day brew. They were all in groups; however, he was the only guy in the place flying solo.

Not for the first time, Lief thought about how he fit in better here than in L.A. and definitely better here than in Hollywood. Originally from a big farm in Idaho, he was more likely to dress in jeans, boots and chambray than pleated slacks and Italian shoes.

But then, he was a writer, not an actor. Most of his work was either done at home and sometimes behind the camera, never in front of it.

He was also an outdoorsman as he was raised to be—a hunter and fisherman. It was while doing those things, either hunting, fishing or working with his hands, that the stories would come to him. Lately Lief had been doing more fishing than writing, more introspection than outpouring. His stepdaughter, Courtney, required a lot of mental energy. She had just turned fourteen, a troubled teen who'd lost her mother a couple of years ago. In just over two years, she seemed to be spiraling downward. He'd had to get her out of L.A. and to a quieter place, a place where they could try that bonding thing again.

It wasn't happening this evening, though.

"Beer?" Jack asked him.

"Thanks, that'd be great."

"Where's your date?" he asked, serving up his draft.

Lief chuckled, knowing that Jack would be referring to Courtney, the only date he'd had in more than two years. "We had a slight difference of opinion and needed our space."

"That so?" He put the beer on a napkin. "Now what could a man in his forties possibly have in conflict with a skinny little fourteen-year-old girl?"

"Wardrobe choices. Television preferences. Internet sites. Homework. General appearance. Diet. And language, as in, the kind she uses on me when she's mad. And she's mad regularly."

"You check out that counselor I told you about?" Jack asked.

"She has an appointment for next week, but tell you the truth, I feel sorry for the guy. I kind of hate to put him through it. She's really got a mouth on her."

"I know Jerry Powell. He's tougher than he looks. I put my young friend Rick in counseling with him. Rick was twenty at the time, just back from Iraq one leg short, and my God, was he in a mean way. I didn't have much hope he was going to come out of it, but eventually he did. He gives a lot of credit to Jerry." Jack wiped the bar. "He gets a lot of angry, screwed-up kids. I guess he knows what to do." Jack leaned close. "This mostly about her mom passing?"

Lief gave a nod. "That and being fourteen in a new school, which brings all its own issues."

"I don't have a lot of experience with that. Rick was like a son to me and when he was that age he was the sweetest kid. Iraq had him pretty messed up for a while, but he's in a good place now, fake leg and all. Married, taking care of his grandmother, finishing college. Wants to be an architect, how about that?"

"Fine choice," Lief said. "I built movie sets in L.A. for years. Building suited me—I could think while I did something productive."

"No kidding? Bet that was interesting. I bet you met a lot of—"

Jack was cut off by the sudden appearance of Kelly Matlock coming into the bar. In fact, the entire bar, which was filled with men, became slowly quiet. When a beautiful blonde entered a bar full of forest-worn hunters, that was bound to happen.

"Wow," Lief said.

Kelly took off her jacket, hung it on the peg by the door and found her way to the only seat left at the bar. Next to Lief. Before he even realized what he was doing, he had risen while she sat.

"Well, now," Jack said. "I didn't expect to see you back so soon."

"I didn't expect it myself. How are you?"

"Excellent. Meet a new neighbor, Kelly. This is Lief Holbrook. Lief, meet Kelly Matlock, a chef from the Bay Area. She has a sister here."

Kelly put out her hand to Lief. "Pleasure."

"What can I get you, Kelly?"

"What are the chances you have a good, chilled vodka you could marry up with about four olives?"

"Ketel One work for you?"

"Perfect."

It was only then that Kelly looked around. "I've been here a couple of times and haven't ever seen it packed like this before," she said to Lief.

"Hunting season," he informed her. "I think you shook 'em up for a minute. They weren't expecting a beautiful woman to show up. So, visiting your sister?"

"Uh-huh. Did I understand Jack right—that you recently moved here?"

"That's right. About a month ago."

Jack returned and put a drink in front of Kelly. "Give that a try, Kelly. Tell me if it fills the bill."

She lifted the glass, took a tiny sip, let her eyes close briefly. Then she smiled. "You're brilliant," she told Jack.

He chuckled and reached below the counter, putting a bowl of nuts next to a bowl of fish crackers. "I love it when you flirt with me, Kelly." Then he was off down the bar to look after the mob.

"So," Lief began. "A chef?"

She took another sip. "Well, there's the problem. I'm still a chef, but I walked out on my restaurant with the head chef shouting at my back that I'd never work in San Francisco again. I thought I'd probably better stop here for a little courage before I break it to my sister that I'm unemployed and homeless."

Lief's eyebrows shot up. "I take it she's not expecting your visit to be…ah…extended?"

"She's not even expecting a visit. It was pretty rash, what I did. Have you ever been in a big restaurant kitchen?"

He shook his head. "Can't say that I have."

"It's brutal. You have to be fearless. I've always been a good cook, but it took me years to measure up to the backbone it required to scream back or dodge flying objects hurled by the chef in charge. And apparently it wasn't natural for me at all. I'm more of a cook than a street fighter."

He leaned an elbow on the bar and gave her his undivided attention. "And you know this because…?"

"Because I thought I was holding my own until I landed in the emergency room due to stress."

"You decided to resign?" he asked, stating the obvious.

She was very quiet; she sipped the Ketel One, then fished out an olive and munched on it.

"Nothing as tidy as that. I had a dear friend and mentor. I admit, we might've been getting too close, but he said he was separated from his wife, that a divorce was pending. Then the wife came to see me at work. Did I mention this mentor was a partner in the restaurant? Owns many restaurants? She told me her husband sent her to tell me to go away quietly. There was a scene in the kitchen—it took about five minutes for everyone to know what I'd been accused of." She paused for another sip. "Still," she added, "the worst of it was that when I called him to ask why the hell he'd send his wife to tell me to go away, he never responded." She turned her large blue eyes to Lief. "I kind of hoped the wife had been full of it. You know?"

Lief put his hand over hers and gave it a brief squeeze. "On top of everything, your heart was broken."

"I guess so," she admitted. "I should have known better. Now—how do I tell my sister that my boyfriend wasn't my boyfriend? That the career I've been killing myself for I was literally killing myself for? And that I quit without notice and will be her uninvited houseguest indefinitely?"

He couldn't help but chuckle. "You seem to have the story down. I'm sure she'll be very sympathetic."

"Probably. But also very surprised. Jillian is the flighty one. I'm the stable one."

"You know what, kid? You walked out on a bad situation. That sounds both intelligent and stable. Now you just need a little time to get on your feet."

"You know what they say about getting out of the kitchen if you can't stand the heat…" she said, shaking her head dismally. "I've become the cliché. What are you doing here anyway? In Virgin River?"

"Me?" he asked. "Just looking for a quieter place. And I like to fish and hunt. Made to order."

Suddenly Jack was in front of them. "How are you two doing?"

"You know what? I think we're doing great!" Kelly said. "This was just what I needed—a stiff drink and a little conversation. Amazing how much it helps."

"You good, then?" Jack asked.

"I'll have one more in a couple of minutes. And bring my friend Lief a beer on me. He's a good listener."

"Sure thing," Jack said. "Dinner?"

"Not for me, but I'll have some more nuts, thanks." When Jack had turned away, she faced Lief again. "Quieter than?"

"Los Angeles. My wife died a couple of years ago and my daughter is still having a hard time of it. She really needed a fresh start and a slower pace. Well, so did I."

Kelly looked stricken. "Oh, man, I'm so sorry. That really puts things into perspective for me. Here I am whining about my nonboyfriend and a mean chef…"

He laughed at her. "You weren't whining—sounds like a movie set. Lots of temper tantrums, scandal and dysfunction on the set."

"You're an actor?"

"Nope. I built sets for years and now I do some writing," he said. "I don't have to spend much time on-set, but when I do it's usually pretty nuts and I always think about how glad I am that I don't do it all the time."

Their new drinks arrived. "How'd you manage

working in that environment, if you don't mind me asking?"

"Cotton in the ears is very useful. I just wouldn't participate in the insanity. And hardly anyone forced the issue."

"How do you not need a full-time job?"

"Oh, I have a full-time job," he corrected. "I write screenplays. The producers and directors order them re-written and hire their own writers. Those writers have to endure the set—I'm usually just a consultant. I work alone, at home."

"I thought all scripts were written by teams of writers," she said.

"Not all scripts. Original screenplays are often written by a single writer."

"Wow. I wish I could figure out a way to be a 'consulting chef' rather than some lunatic's whipping post. Tell me what it's like to work alone. At home."

He took a breath. "The best word I can come up with is *comfortable*. I'm kind of introverted. But I can entertain myself very easily. All the things I like can be done alone. I fish—fly-fishing. I like to build—there's nothing to build right now but I'm chopping wood for the winter. I've been writing since junior high, but it took me many years to sell a script. I've never been good at those activities where everyone looks at you. I'd rather stay home. The best part of my life is fishing and being home." Then he grinned. "Of course my daughter hates fish, but she's fourteen—she hates air right now."

"Yikes. How is that working?" Kelly said.

"She's rebellious, snotty, antisocial, experimental and so irreverent." He laughed uncomfortably. "Underneath all that she's a teenage girl who misses her mom and is stuck with me. She's a beautiful girl with a high IQ and a confidence problem. I'm trying, but we're not getting better. Next week we'll meet with a counselor who specializes in troubled teenagers. I hope to God it works!"

"But you're drying!" she said.

Drying? Lief frowned. He looked at her glass—second drink, half gone. It was a strong drink, but still. She shouldn't be slurring. He wondered if it was his imagination.

"Are you slurring?" Couldn't hurt to be sure.

"'Course not," she said. But her eyelids started to drift lower. Then they snapped back open.

"How are you planning to get to your sister's place?" he asked.

"I frove. Drove. I have everything I own in the car 'cept my couch and recliner."

"Kelly," he said, leaning closer to her, speaking softly. "You know that stress you were talking about? You wouldn't be taking medication for that, would you?"

"Hm. Just a little something for the prood blessure and xiety. I'm not taking those sleeping pills, no way. If I fall asleep, I dream about the whole thing!"

"I guess that's good news," he said, gently moving her second extra-dry martini out of her reach.

"Hey!"

"I bet it said something on those pill bottles about

alcohol not being a good idea while taking that medication," he said. "You're a little loopy."

She straightened indignantly. "I leg your bardon."

He smiled before he laughed outright. "Drunk," he clarified.

"I certainly am snot."

He laughed again. Then he lifted his hand to beckon Jack. And as he did that, Kelly put her head down on the bar. Gonzo.

When Jack came back, he wore a perplexed look.

"It turns out Kelly's been taking medication and probably shouldn't have had a couple of power drinks," Lief said. "She's going to need a ride to her sister's."

Jack looked around. "Crap! The place is full!"

"I'll be glad to give her a lift, Jack. I should get home anyway to see if Courtney has burned the place to the ground yet. You might want to call her sister and let her know she's…ah…coming for a visit." He laughed again. "And that she's wasted."

"What's she taking?"

Lief shrugged. "Something for 'prood blessure' and 'xiety.'" Then he grinned. "I guess the girl's not used to taking much prescription stuff—never crossed her mind. Just tell her sister."

"What about her car?" Jack asked.

Lief shrugged. "Better parked here than on the road with her behind the wheel."

"Right," Jack said. Then Jack tapped her on the head. "Kelly?" he asked. "Kelly?"

"Hmm?"

"Um, Lief is going to drive you home. Okay?"

She lifted her head briefly. "Lief who?" Then she put her head down again.

"All right," Jack said. "Here's how to get there." He grabbed a notepad near the register and scribbled out directions. "I'll call Jillian and tell her you're coming."

Lief retrieved Kelly's jacket. He sat her up, and she roused briefly as he helped her put her arms in. "I'm going to give you a lift to Jillian's house, Kelly," he said. "I think you just got too...tired."

"Hmm. Thanks," she replied.

He grabbed her purse and put the strap over his arm, making her giggle. Meeting Jack's eyes, he said, "Put it on my tab. I'll see you soon."

"Drive carefully."

With a strong arm around her waist, he stood her up and walked her out of the bar, but outside on the porch, her legs became noodles and he lifted her into his arms to take her down the steps.

"Wow, I don't think anyone's ever carried me," she slurred. "Except maybe a paramedic—maybe he did." She patted his chest. "You're fun. I'm glad we met. What's your name again?"

"Lief," he said. "Lief Holbrook."

"Very nice," she said, laying her head on his chest.

He stood her up long enough to open the door to his truck. "I wish you'd try to help me get you into this truck, Kelly. It's high. If you pull, I'll push."

"Shertainly," she said, grabbing the inside.

Lief positioned her right foot on the running board,

pushed her butt upward and landed her in the seat. She made a loud *ooommmph* when she was inside. "Good," he said. "I shouldn't have any trouble getting you out."

Her head lolled against the seat all the way to Jillian's, and she blubbered in a drunken, semiconscious state—she loved Luca. They took her away in an ambulance, yet not one person came to check on her! She was too embarrassed by how foolish she'd been to call her sister and confess everything that had happened to her.

Oh, man, he thought. *A woman with almost as much baggage as me.*

Courtney thought that sometimes Lief just didn't get it.

She had all her beauty gear, for lack of a better word, spread out in her bathroom—mousse for the hair, eyeliner, lipstick. She was giving her short fingernails a once-over with the black polish.

Lief. She used to call him Dad. In fact, when he had married her mother and she was only eight, she had asked him if that would be all right—could she call him Dad? He'd said he would love that.

Of course that meant she had two of them, but since they were never in the same room at the same time, it wasn't a great challenge. And she saw even less of her real dad after Lief and her mom married. She thought her real dad, Stu Lord, was relieved, and she *knew* the stepwitch was. Stu had been the first to remarry after her parents divorced; she'd been two. She had her visits with him and her stepmom, Sherry, whom she *never* offered to call Mom. Her dad and stepmom had a couple of kids together, boys. Aaron was born when Courtney was four, Conner when she was seven. Her visits with them became fewer and fewer.

Courtney didn't mind that, her diminishing relationship with Stu. Stu and Sherry fought frequently, something that didn't happen with her mom and Lief. And the little boys were wild brats who screamed, threw things, pulled her hair and messed with her stuff. She was happy with her mom and Lief. Her mom and *dad*.

Then, right at the end of the school year of her sixth grade, her mom died. Just died! Something they didn't know she had exploded in her head when she was at work, and she went down, dead, never to come back. It hurt so bad, Courtney wanted to die with her.

Then there was a blur of shifting movements that she could barely remember, except that it always involved her suitcase, which seemed to stay packed. She went to live with Stu, where she didn't even have her own bedroom. She stayed in the guest room unless Sherry's mother visited and then she was shuttled to the toy room or family-room sofa. She visited Lief on at least a couple of weekends a month. Then, after six months of that, she went back to living with Lief and visiting Stu. Then after she cut and dyed her hair several colors, painted her fingernails black and wore black lipstick, Stu told Lief he could have her full-time, that she didn't have to visit anymore. He actually said it way worse than that, and she'd been relieved. She'd heard her stepmother call her "that weird little monster."

But Lief got *furious* that her father not only didn't want her full-time but didn't even want visits, so she got it—no one wanted her. Oh, Lief said he did, but he didn't. If he did, he would have been happy with her father for giving her back, but he was *not* happy. There was a huge fight; her two dads were yelling and got real close to hitting and she wished they'd just beat each other to death.

She didn't hear from her father again after that blowout. That had been months ago. The whole back-and-forth thing ending with Lief had started in seventh grade. And that was when she started calling him Lief.

She blew on her nails and checked them. They were dry. She applied the lipstick and gloss.

She had stopped growing then. She used to be a chubby little girl, and now she was a skinny short girl with a couple of bumps on her chest that were supposed to pass as boobs. Her Goth, biker-chick look meant no one would expect her to be all giggly.

She started looking up suicide clubs on the internet until Lief had caught her and taken her to a counselor who told her she was angry. *Duh.* She had to sit with that lame counselor every week, and on top of that, they did some stupid grief counseling with all grown-ups. She almost got back to liking Lief after he said he thought the counselor was lame, too, and that a grief group for adults was no place for her and refused to take her. She liked him for that.

They might still be in L.A. where she was born and had lived right up to ninth grade, if she hadn't gotten in some trouble, and she might not have gotten in trouble if her friends hadn't all disappeared on her. First it was because they couldn't stand her feeling sorry for herself, then she wasn't like them anymore with her black clothes and weird hair. So she found herself a few new friends who did things like get into their parents' medicine chests, score a little pot sometimes, lift money from their moms' purses and dads' wallets—for the pot, of course—and, about the only thing she found any fun at all, snuck out after the folks were asleep. They didn't really do anything; they hung out where they wouldn't get hassled, smoked some cigarettes sometimes. Bitched about the rules. Courtney wasn't into the pills and pot; she just experimented a little. She felt weird and bad enough; she didn't like not knowing how she was going to feel. She pretended, mostly. She had to. She couldn't stand the thought of being all alone again. If the good kids dumped her and the bad kids dumped her, who was left?

So Lief said, "This isn't working, this city. You find too much trouble and I'm sick of the noise and traffic. We're getting out of here. I'm going to find us something sane. I'd like if we could get back to at least being friends, like we used to be. And you could use a chance to start over. Maybe on the right side of the law?"

Now, Courtney had not wanted to move. Period.

Even though she'd lost her old friends and didn't like her new ones. There was something about boxing up her life and putting it on a truck, moving away from where she'd been with her mom that just freaked her out, even though she knew her mom wasn't coming back.

She liked the idea of getting back to being friends with Lief, though she didn't believe he meant that. She figured he meant getting back to her looking more like she used to. But the big problem was, this wasn't going to work—rather than getting back to one hair color, she was thinking about many piercings and a few tattoos…. How long before he just gave up? How long before he just turned her in, told the cops she wasn't his daughter anyway, go ahead and take her, find a place for her? Because she figured he was only doing this out of some promise he'd made to her mom. And she also figured that he'd get over it and have the locks changed or something. Every time he looked at her, he winced. He hated the multicolored hair, the jagged cut, the black clothes, and for some reason she couldn't really understand herself, they couldn't pass ten words without getting into it.

She looked in the mirror—her hair was wild and crazy, her eyes dark and scary. Perfect as far as she was concerned.

So. They'd had another argument. This one was about homework. She told him it was done; he said, "Let me see it." She said, "No." He said, "You're getting a D in both math and English and you have a high IQ—I have to see the homework." She told him he'd have to trust her and he'd laughed, said she'd have to earn that. She said she'd tear it up before she'd turn it over. Yadda, yadda, yadda. Finally, struggling with his temper, he decided to drive around for a while, maybe go to one of the coast towns and walk around, cool off, and when he got back in a couple of hours, she'd better be ready to share the homework.

Ha! Fat chance, she thought.

When he said a couple of hours, he meant three or four. She knew his drill—he'd give her plenty of time to actually do her homework and himself plenty of time to feel like he could tolerate her again. He left at five-thirty. She was good till nine.

She hadn't made any real friends, but a couple of guys who looked a lot like her had picked up on her willingness to take a few chances, if only to have some company. Once Lief was gone, she picked up the phone and called B.A., which was short for either Bruce Arnold or Bad Ass. He was a junior who should be a senior, seventeen.

"Hey, my dad went out," she said. She called him Lief to his face but around school he was "her dad," just because she didn't want to explain anything. "Wanna come over for a couple of hours?"

"What for?"

"Hang out?"

"I could…"

"Could you bring beer? Because he doesn't keep any here."

"I could bring a few. My old man would never miss it. How do I get there?"

She gave him some directions and it took him about twenty minutes. When he got to the house, he looked around at the rich interior, whistled and said, "Hot damn!"

Three

While Lief drove Kelly to the big Victorian in which her sister lived, Kelly was semi-passed out. But she mumbled and muttered the whole way.

He had certainly understood everything she said right up until she put her head down on the bar. Sounded like she'd had a fling with a guy she thought was available but who turned out to be very married. Oh, such an ordinary tale. Men told that story all the time. Why men stayed married to women they wanted to cheat on, Lief had no idea. Up until he'd met Lana, he'd never been in a serious relationship; he always had a woman around, was playing the field, having a little fun, but hadn't been engaged or married. When he met her he had instantly known two things—she was the one, and he'd never want another one. In fact, here he was, widowed a little over two years, and he hadn't been tempted even once. Of course, he had Courtney. Hard to think about anything but getting through another day.

But this lovely Kelly had gotten his attention the

second she'd walked into the bar. He'd felt a little zing just looking at her. She was pretty, very fresh and lush. And nothing like Lana, which came as a relief. He wasn't sure he could ever feel the slightest response to any woman after losing Lana. Lana had been small, dark-haired with dark eyes. Kelly was blonde, blue-eyed, had a round, full figure, and his first thought had been what it would feel like to get his hands on her, to hold her body up against his. That soft, rich, luxurious body. She didn't have one of those Hollywood bodies—too thin with fake perky boobs. She had a real woman's body—something to hold on to. And that mouth—full pink lips. The second he'd seen her lips, he had licked his.

Then he'd recovered his sanity and had just listened to her for a while. Sounded as if she'd gotten screwed, literally and figuratively.

The front light was on and there were two people standing on the porch waiting, no doubt in response to Jack's call. That would be Colin and Jillian, the sister and her boyfriend. He got out of the truck, and Jillian was right there. Lief recognized her once he saw her. In fact, that's when he realized he'd seen both the sisters at Jack's last summer when he'd been checking on the progress of his house purchase.

"What happened?" she asked him.

"Well, I think this probably took your sister by complete surprise," he said. "She mentioned she'd been to the doctor for something or other, and when her speech started to slur before she finished her second drink, I asked her if she'd been given some prescription medication and she said she had. So—I don't think she realized..."

"Doctor?" Jillian asked. "Medication? She's sick?"

"I don't think so, no," Lief said. "Listen, I don't want to say too much right now. For all I know it was the drink talking, I could've gotten the details all wrong or something. Let her tell you why she's up here unannounced, okay?"

"Colin?" Jillian said.

But Colin was already opening the passenger door, unbuckling Kelly and lifting her out. Lief felt a momentary pang; he'd like to be the one holding her.

"I'll carry her up to the bedroom, Jilly," Colin said. "You grab her purse and anything else that goes with her."

"There's just the purse," Lief said, reaching into the truck for it. "Her car is locked up at the bar."

"Should I call the doctor?" Jillian asked him.

Lief shrugged. "She's breathing fine. She was talking all the way out here. Maybe you could look through her purse, see if there are pills or anything that, mixed with a couple of martinis, might knock her for a loop. You could call a pharmacy and ask about the effects if you find anything. I didn't think to do that..."

"Martinis?" Jill asked. "Really? Martinis?"

"Oh, yeah, she was very specific. A good, quality, chilled vodka married to four big green olives."

"Wow. She doesn't do that often."

"She said you weren't expecting her and she had a lot to explain."

"I'd really like to know."

"I'm sure you will know—first thing in the morning."

"Can I, ah, offer you a cup of coffee or anything?"

"Thanks, that's nice of you. I need to get home. I'll come by sometime tomorrow…just to see if she's doing all right. And if *you're* doing all right. Her car is full of her stuff." He grinned. "Kind of looked like she's planning to stay awhile."

"That's okay," Jill said. "That's good. But—"

"I imagine her keys are in her purse."

"Thanks. Gee, I wish there was some way I could repay the favor…"

"No big deal. Jack would've brought her home, I'm sure. But the bar was full of customers, so I offered." He looked around from where he stood beside his truck. He whistled. "Looks like an interesting place."

She smiled at him. "It's shaping into a real commercial organic farm. When we get things under control, I'll have you out for a tour. You can grab the last of our crop—harvest is wrapping up. We're concentrating on melons and berries now."

"No kidding?" he asked with a smile. "How come I didn't know about this place?"

"I've only been here since last spring. I've been farming a small plot through summer, just to see what I can grow. Now we're getting more farming space prepared for spring. Maybe I'll show you around when you come back tomorrow." Pausing for a minute as if in thought, she said, "I hope Kelly is okay…"

"Go see for yourself. Call Doc Michaels if you're worried. I'll leave you guys to it."

"Thanks again," she said, and while he got back in the truck, she hightailed it up the porch stairs and into the house.

Lief glanced at the dashboard clock as he turned to watch the road as he backed out. Eight o'clock. It seemed much later. He hoped he'd given Courtney enough time to calm down and get her homework done.

He worried whether he'd made the right decision, bringing her here, a place that made a one-horse town look like a metropolis. A strange little Goth kid like Courtney didn't look as out of place in a big city.

Rural Idaho had been the other option for them, where his parents still owned the family farm, though they were retired. He had two brothers and a sister there, all older than he was, married with families, all living not too far from the farm. But truthfully, he'd been afraid to do that. Courtney was so crazy sometimes, he didn't want to expose his family, his nieces and nephews, to her antics. Okay, to be honest, he didn't want them to see how dismally he was failing her.

His sister had said, "Lief, don't put yourself through this! Pack her up, take her to her father, let him figure it out."

He couldn't do that. Poor Court. He'd seen the pain in her eyes each time she wandered from the home she'd had with her mother to the unwelcome space she had with her father. God, it ripped him up all over again each time.

When he pulled up the long drive to his house he saw that all the lights were on, a beat-up old Jeep sat in front of the house, and before he even turned off the truck engine he could hear the throbbing of acid rock.

Part of him hoped, almost against hope, he'd find Courtney sitting at the kitchen table with a rosy-cheeked, normal-looking teenage girl, the two of them doing homework together despite the fact that the music was deafening.

He entered the kitchen from the garage. There was a bottle on the breakfast bar that separated the great room from the kitchen—Corona, half full. He looked into the great room and saw a tall teenage boy in ratty jeans loading DVDs from Lief's entertainment center into his backpack. No Courtney. The kid was stuffing the disks into the backpack so frantically it almost looked like a smash-and-grab, but instinctively Lief knew better.

He walked into the large room, picked up the remote from a sofa table and killed the music. The kid jumped up, his lanky hair swinging back from his face. Right at that exact moment, Courtney appeared in the entrance from the hall leading to the bedrooms and bathrooms, holding her own Corona.

"Lief!" she said.

The boy bolted, headed for the front door.

"B.A.! Bruce!" she yelled after him.

Lief merely stood there, observing the panic, the flight, the beer, the backpack that was abandoned. The front door opening and slamming closed was the only sound. When it was completely quiet, Courtney was the first to speak.

"Well, I suppose I'm grounded again."

"What's the point, Court? I don't think you've been off restriction for a day in the past year." He walked to the backpack and crouched, opening it. "You can give this back to your friend tomorrow at school. If he even attends school." He reached inside and began to pull out the movie DVDs, stacking them on the floor. "Without the movies, of course."

"I didn't know he was doing that," she said. "I just went to the bathroom."

"How well do you know him?" Lief asked. Christ, the kid had managed to get about thirty discs in his backpack.

"I just know him from school, that's all. We were just going to listen to music."

"And drink beer." He left the backpack and stood to face her.

"I bet you drank beer when you were a kid," she said with a lift of her chin.

"At fourteen? Not hardly." He'd had farm chores; he'd played football, even though he'd been small for his age then and had gotten the stuffing beaten out of him. "Jesus, Courtney. How far are you going to push me?"

"I *said* I didn't know he was doing that!"

"Maybe you should think about getting some more trustworthy friends," he suggested.

"Don't you get it?" she said, stepping toward him. "Nobody *likes* me!"

He was quiet for a long moment. Then he took another couple of steps toward her. He reached out and took the beer. "Will they like you better if you let them steal from us?"

"I didn't," she said, and there was a slight hiccup in her voice. "I just went to the bathroom."

"How much has your friend had to drink?" Lief asked.

"Why?"

"Because he's driving. Because he took off out of here like a bat out of hell and while I'd really like to tan his hide, I don't want him to get hurt."

She shrugged. "He just got here a little while ago. He brought two beers, that's all."

"Okay," he said. He went to the kitchen and poured out both beers. He went back to the great room. "I'm going to my room to read for a while before bed. I'm going to set the house alarm. I'm really not up to chasing you down in the middle of the night, Courtney. I'll see you in the morning. Luckily, you shouldn't have a hangover."

To his back she said, "I'm not going to sneak out."

He looked over his shoulder at her. "Good," he said. Then he went to his room.

Sometimes Lief didn't know if he was more pissed or hurt by Courtney. He gave her everything he had. Why couldn't she throw him a bone now and then? Just some small gesture like please or thank-you or even homework. It didn't have to be good homework, even though he knew she was extremely intelligent. Just finished.

How long could she nurture the pain on the inside that made her so vile on the outside?

The house fell quiet again. Lief reclined on his lonely king-size bed, book in his lap. The vision of Courtney, all of fourteen but looking more like twelve, sneering at him over her beer kept obscuring the pages. He was going to have to get with that counselor, see if there was help for them. He was not optimistic—if he couldn't find good therapy in Los Angeles, what were the chances he'd find it here?

In the morning, the first thing he did was head down the hall toward Courtney's bedroom to be sure she was there. Fortunately, he didn't have to go all the way to her room; he heard the shower in her bathroom. As he passed through the great room, he noticed the DVDs were put away. Put away or maybe stuffed back into the backpack for the little felon in question. He turned off the house alarm, made the coffee, headed for his own shower. She should be ready for school on time today; it didn't take her long to mess up her multicolored hair.

When he got back to the kitchen, her homework and a note were on the table.

I made a copy of my homework for you to look at, but I'm taking the bus today so I left. Will you pick me up after school? Please.

Bone.

* * *

The very first rays of sunlight streaming into the window stirred Kelly from sleep. She sat up in bed and took stock of her surroundings—Jillian's guest room. And there beside her in the bed, sleeping facedown, Jillian.

"Hey," Kelly said, giving her a jostle.

Jill turned her head and peered at her through tangled hair. "Ugh. You're up."

"Last thing I remember, I was chatting it up with some cute guy at the bar. Over a killer martini."

Jill pushed her hair out of her eyes. "It didn't kill you. But it tried to kill me."

"Huh?"

Struggling to a sitting position, Jill faced Kelly. "Do you realize what you did?"

Kelly let her eyes briefly close. "Gave myself a very large headache?"

"I went through your purse. You were taking both blood pressure medicine and antidepressants or something like that. Both bottles say alcohol could intensify the effects."

"I can see that now."

"I had to count the pills left to make sure you hadn't OD'd. But I sat up and watched over you until you started to snore at about three in the morning. And boy, can you snore! I don't think I've slept for ten whole minutes."

"Oh, man," Kelly said, rubbing her temples. "Who knew?"

"You know, if you'd had a little glass of wine,

you might've gotten kind of tipsy. But a martini? Overkill."

"I needed a shot of courage before dropping in on you and spoiling your hot new romance with Colin. And about those pills—I started the blood pressure stuff as directed, but the antianxiety pills were as needed. But I was feeling pretty anxious on the way up here, so I popped one. And I was still feeling pretty anxious a few hours later, so I had another one for good measure."

"You'll be happy to know you weren't at all anxious by the time you got here."

"Whew. Kind of scary to think I'd drive like that!"

"You didn't. Your car is at the bar. The cute guy you were talking to brought you out here. Colin had to carry you to bed."

"Oh, please tell me you're making that up!"

"Not making it up. Now, what has you so anxious?"

"A lot has been going on for the last week. Can we have coffee? And aspirin? And I'll tell you all about it. I might've really screwed up my life."

Lief made phone contact with the counselor Jack had recommended and had an appointment for himself, after which he could go to Valley High School and pick up Courtney. On the way to Grace Valley, he decided to swing by Jillian's big house to check on Kelly. He didn't have to look far; he found her sitting by herself on the back porch, her feet drawn up and a throw wrapped around her shoulders.

He was grinning as he got out of his truck and approached her. "Well, you look none the worse for wear."

"Oh, God," she moaned. "I guess it was too much to hope I'd never see you again."

"Aw, I'm crushed," he said. "I thought we bonded."

"That's one of the reasons I was hoping…"

"I'm glad you came through it. I wanted to check on you. You look fine."

"Well, the bad news is, I don't remember your name. The good news is, I do remember mine. That means I haven't killed off too many brain cells."

He chuckled and took the first step up the porch to lean against the post. "They grow back," he said. "Takes a while, though. You could be dumb as shit for a couple of weeks."

She laughed in spite of herself. "I can live up to that."

"How do you feel?"

"Dumb as shit," she said. "See, I had this prescription for stuff that was supposed to make me less 'anxious.' I didn't think it was working fast enough, so I took a second. Then I took a martini…."

"Almost two martinis, actually."

"And you are?"

"Lief Holbrook. And you're Kelly. And I gather you have no experience with drugs like that."

"I have been addicted to food and love," she said dismally.

"Ah, yes, the mentor-slash-lover," he remembered.

"Really, did I tell you all that?"

"Enough so that I can honestly say I don't need any more details. Sounds like you got screwed by a guy who told you he was available when he wasn't. Legally, anyway, per the wife."

"Oh, my God, I did tell you everything!"

In a flash of deep sympathy, Lief said, "That must have hurt you so much, Kelly. I'm really sorry."

He saw the liquid begin to gather in her large blue eyes. He found it interesting that one so fair could have such thick, long, black lashes. "Yes. Well. Stupid me," she said. "You'd almost have to believe I killed those brain cells months ago."

"It'll pass. Really."

She wiped impatiently at her eyes. "I know. So. Do you have experience with these drugs?" she asked boldly.

"I took antidepressants for a short time and had a similar experience. Had a couple of beers one night and slept like a dead person. I woke up terrified that the house could have burned down without me knowing. A little depression was probably safer."

She remembered suddenly. "That's right, you lost your wife."

"A little over two years ago. And yes, I took something for a while, not knowing how much it was really affecting me because I felt pretty much the same—devastated and pathetic. I haven't taken anything since."

"You recovered?"

"From being devastated and pathetic? God, I hope so.

From depression? Probably. From missing her? Not yet. But I'm told that comes with time and gets easier."

"I'm sorry," she said.

"Thank you. You said that last night."

"Must have come before my magnificent exit. Listen, can I offer you some tea?"

"Thanks, but I have an appointment to get to. But I'd really like to have a look at this place—the house, the grounds. Your sister said she'd give me a tour, treat me to the last of her crop…"

Kelly finally stood, pulling the wrap around her. "Jilly Farms, as she calls it. Organic fruits and vegetables. She's out there now, working. Colin is upstairs in the sunroom, painting. He's an artist, among other things. The house was renovated before she bought it— it's enormous and very interesting. If you'd like to come back when you don't have an appointment, she'd love to take you around the gardens and house and I…" She cleared her throat. "When my headache goes away, I'd be happy to cook for you. It's what I do—cook."

"That would be nice," he said, smiling. "I'll give you a few days, then call."

"And I'll tell Jill that I made us a date."

As Lief was backing out of the drive, Kelly watched and ran a hand through her mussed hair. *Must my life continue to be one big practical joke?* If some hot guy was going to stop by to see if she was all right, why couldn't she have at least pulled a comb through her wild hair? Or put on *clothes?*

Apparently she wasn't too emotionally upset to notice his kind of thick, floppy, Robert Redford hair, square jaw and amused brown eyes that crinkled a little bit at the corners. He was one of those blond guys who tanned well. She'd noticed that, too. She especially liked his forearms. His long-sleeved denim shirt had been rolled up a bit, and the golden hair on his muscled forearms had glistened in the sunshine.

There was something else about him. She couldn't put her finger on it. He was dressed like all the other Virgin River guys, but he had a way of making a pair of jeans and boots look classy. Maybe it was the way he spoke—well-educated and precise. He even sounded like a professor when he swore.

She smiled. Widowed, huh? she thought. Could be he was almost ready to get on with life. She shook her head and chuckled to herself. Maybe if they ran into each other a third time she could humiliate herself in some new way, just in case he needed convincing that she was a total flake.

But he was pretty hot.

The counselor's simple Grace Valley house that Lief pulled up to didn't exactly encourage him; he'd visited far flashier digs for therapists without getting a whole lot of help. Then there was the counselor himself—a very, very tall, skinny…no, make that *boney,* scarecrow with shaggy, almost white-blond hair and large ears. And the biggest feet Lief had ever seen. He hoped to God

Courtney didn't just flat out make fun of him. Right to his face.

"Mr. Holbrook, hello," the man said cheerily, extending a hand in greeting. "I'm Jerry Powell. How are you today?"

"Fine," he said, shaking the hand. "I mean, not fine. I've never figured out what you should say to a counselor on your first visit. That you're fine or that you need help desperately?"

Jerry laughed. "Come on into the office, Mr. Holbrook, and tell me how I can help."

When they were seated—Jerry behind the desk and Lief facing it—Lief just launched in. "Well, my wife died a couple of years ago and my stepdaughter's not handling it well. Her biological father and stepmother didn't embrace her, didn't pull her into their family, and she's depressed and—"

Jerry held up his hand, indicating he should stop. "Okay, hold on a sec, I apologize, I should have led this discussion. I realize you're here on behalf of your stepdaughter and that the two of you have issues. Let me just tell you a couple of things before we get deeper into the issues.

"First of all, part of my function in this county is that I'm retained by the school district for court-ordered counseling of young adults. What that means is, I usually only know what they've done to warrant that penalty without getting many details about their personal lives, about what might've motivated them acting out. Sometimes I know there's been abuse in the family, death or divorce, that sort of thing, but there's no one to tell me how they're feeling but them. And I have to let the adolescent try to explain what pushed them into the behavior that caused all the trouble. It's amazing how well it seems to be working. So—to that end—give me the basic facts, address incidents or behaviors if you think it's pertinent. And then tell me about *you*. About *your* feelings, not hers. You and I will talk. Then Courtney will give me her feelings."

"I bet she won't," he said.

"I'm relentless," he said, and then smiled. "Besides, adolescents really can't identify too many feelings. They're not being stubborn. It's an acquired skill. They're working on growing up. It's one of those things they have to develop."

"Okay, then. My wife died," he said, starting over. "A little over two years ago. At first my stepdaughter... I think of her as a daughter... Courtney seemed to grieve painfully for a while, which was quickly followed by weird, antisocial behavior. She's kind of Goth now with the kind of friends that lie and steal and lure her out after hours. I just caught her last night with an older guy in the house stealing my DVDs while she was in the bathroom. They were drinking beer. She's fourteen but looks nine."

"Nine?"

"Not nine, maybe, but so small. She's so little to act so old. One of the first things you're going to notice about Courtney is that she's extremely bright. High IQ. She was always in accelerated programs at school, but now she's close to failing. She's intellectually advanced and emotionally..." Lief lifted one shoulder in a half shrug. "Immature? I don't know... Wounded?"

"How does this make you feel, Mr. Holbrook?"

"Call me Lief, please. It makes me feel like an idiot. A failure. Like I'm going to lose her to some disaster like drugs or grand theft auto or suicide."

"Do you think suicide is an issue? I'll take that information from you gladly—I should know."

"It's hard to say," he answered with a shrug. "I found some websites that she'd looked at that deal with suicide and I almost lost it—I asked her if she was thinking about suicide. She said, 'Everyone *thinks* about it, but I'm not going to do it.' How do you know if something like that's curiosity or an imminent danger?"

"We watch," he said. "I'll be certain to direct our dialogue to give me more information."

"The girl barely eats. I don't think she's anorexic—she eats enough, I think. But she's gotten so thin and she's never hungry. I'm a farm boy—that bothers me more than you can imagine. Some people think I know inside stuff about her age group, about troubled teens, because I wrote a couple of screenplays about young people in crisis, but I wasn't writing about *them*—I was writing about *me!* And my crisis was a long, long time ago and had to do with a dead horse, not a dead mother."

Jerry sat up straighter. "What movies?" he asked.

"*Deerstalker. Moonwalker.* A couple of other things..."

"My God, you're *that* Lief Holbrook.... You won an Oscar and an Emmy." He almost burst with excitement. "Yes, I can see how there'd be preconceived notions. Those were brilliant scripts. I have both of those movies."

Lief looked down briefly. "Thank you," he said.

Jerry leaned toward him. "And tell me, Lief. Your wife died and your stepdaughter is giving you fits. Besides frustration with her behavior and appearance, how are you getting along? How do you feel?"

Lief let his eyes bore right into that silly-looking counselor's pale blue eyes. "Lonely. Sometimes pretty miserable. Like a complete failure where Courtney is concerned. And terrified of never getting her back."

"I understand completely. Let's set up your appointments now, then we'll have another forty minutes or so to chat before you have to go."

"*Our* appointments?"

"I'll do what I can for Courtney, of course. It's really my specialty even if it's not yours. But brother—you could use a friend who understands right now, too. If it's not too bold, I think you should give me a try. I actually studied this stuff."

"You any good?" Lief asked.

"I am," he said, smiling almost shyly.

Four

Courtney didn't see Bad Ass Hopper until almost last period at school. She'd carried his backpack around all day long, anticipating the moment. She was prepared to lug it around for the next day or week or month if he didn't show up at school.

By the look on his face when she cornered him at his locker, he actually thought about running. "Don't bother," she said. "Here's your backpack. My dad took out the DVDs you were going to rip off from us. Never come around me or my house again." She turned to go, then turned back. "You should be called S.A. instead of B.A. For Stupid Ass." She looked him over contemptuously. "You ought to be ashamed of yourself. You're lucky I could talk him out of calling the cops. Infant."

She was halfway down the hall before he found his voice, his nervous voice. "Yeah? Well, better than a devil-worshiping *elf!*"

It only made her smile; he certainly lacked imagination.

Her last class of the day was psychology, of all things. She thought the teacher looked at her funny, like she was someone who could certainly use a little psych. It happened Courtney found the class interesting, but she never let on.

She took her seat at the rear left, as far away from others as possible. This time Amber Hawkins chose the seat next to her. Damn those classroom tables that sat two.

"Hi Courtney," she said almost shyly.

"Hi."

"I heard you give it to B.A."

"Lucky you."

Amber giggled. "You're a real booger, aren't you?"

"Booger?!"

Amber giggled again.

Courtney knew that Amber wasn't one of the real popular girls, but she fit in here far better than Courtney did. She was a farm girl or something. She wasn't a cheerleader or on a dance squad, dressed plain and kind of out of style, didn't wear makeup, didn't seem to lunge after the boys as the popular girls did.

"We're in algebra together," Amber informed her.

"We are?" Courtney knew they were, but she decided to play it as though she'd never noticed.

"I was wondering—do you get it? I mean, *get* it? Algebra? Because I'm lost. Worse than lost. I think I'm dead."

Courtney sighed. "Really, it's not that hard."

"Are you getting good grades?" she asked.

"Well… No. But not because I don't get it. I admit, I haven't been keeping up with assignments. And if you tell my dad that, I'm going to suck all the blood out of your neck!"

Stupid Amber just giggled. "Well, okay, then, I'll have to not tell him. So, do you think you could maybe help me sometime?"

"How am I gonna do that?"

"Um, you could ride the bus home with me. My dad would drive you home after we study."

Courtney turned in her chair to look at Amber. "Listen, Amber, you live on a farm or something, right?"

Amber looked a little startled. "Are you allergic to animals? Because I could go to your house. Or we could stay here and use the library and my dad could pick me up and drive you home. He'd do that for me to have a fighting chance in math."

"Why's it so important to him?"

She shrugged. "We have a family business, the farm and vineyard. And construction and other things. I have older brothers, all wizz-guys. An engineer, an accountant, an MBA."

"That must be one helluva farm."

"It's just a farm," Amber said.

"Look, chick, I'd scare your parents to death—"

Amber giggled yet again.

"Stop that!" Courtney demanded harshly.

Amber stopped. In fact, she got a little pale. "Sorry," she said softly.

"I meant stop laughing, I was being serious. I don't think I'd fit in around your place. You know?"

She put her hand over her mouth this time to restrain herself. "It's okay, Courtney. It's just all that Hollywood stuff. They wouldn't take it seriously. But whew, they're sure taking my D in math seriously! I gotta do something!"

"Did you ask the teacher?"

Amber nodded gravely. "He doesn't explain it any better in private than he does in class."

Then Courtney laughed.

"Ladies?" the psych teacher asked. "Is there something you'd like the rest of the class to know?"

Courtney stood to her full four-foot-eleven height. "Yes, Mr. Culmer. You're going to need to hire a consultant to help with the, ah, tie selection. I think Mrs. Culmer is slipping—she really blew it on that one."

The class fell apart with laughter. They were hysterical; Mr. Culmer was getting redder by the minute. When the class finally quieted and Courtney was again in her seat, the teacher said, "And this coming from a fourteen-year-old with pink-and-purple hair. Thank you very much."

"My pleasure," she said, grinning largely.

Courtney had been on plenty of farms; Lief's parents lived on a farm, the farm he grew up on, even if it wasn't a working farm anymore. He also had uncles and cousins with farms—in Idaho it was mostly potatoes. She hadn't thought too much about missing visits to those farms until she was bouncing along on a yellow bus with Amber to go home with her to do homework. She was *excited*. She didn't let it show, of course.

She thought it was kind of funny that when they used to visit the Holbrook farms in Idaho, Courtney had never worried about whether she could fit in, but in Virgin River she stood out like a sore thumb. When her mom was alive, she didn't have pink-and-purple hair, black fingernails and odd, black retro clothing, either.

Courtney and Amber had planned to do homework together when they got to Amber's house, then Courtney would stay for dinner and they might either do some more homework or play video games or whatever until Lief came to pick up Courtney and take her home. Amber's dad had offered to drive her home, but Lief had insisted. He wanted to meet Amber's parents, probably to make sure they weren't satanists or serial killers.

So—Amber's parents were much older than Courtney had expected. They were grandparents. She should have anticipated this since Amber's older, married brothers were all college graduates who worked in the "family business." And for older people, they were very weird—they didn't even flinch when they took in her appearance.

First was Amber's mother, who greeted them in a warm, good-smelling kitchen. She was wearing loose jeans tucked into her rubber boots, and her gray hair was kind of all over the place. "How do you do?" Amber's mother said. "I'm Sinette Hawkins. It's so nice of you to help Amber with math. I guess Hawk and me, we're just too far past all that new math. And her brothers are busy helping their own kids."

"I don't mind," Courtney said.

"Now are you sure your father doesn't want to join us for dinner?" Sinette asked. "Because there's always more than we can eat. I do that on purpose—someone is bound to stop by and Hawk likes a hot lunch in the middle of the day, so I keep plenty of leftovers."

Ah, that would explain Amber leaning toward the chubby side, Courtney thought. "No. He said he has something to do."

And right then a kid in a wheelchair zoomed into the kitchen. Amber introduced him as her nephew, Rory. He was only eight, wore thick glasses, and maneuvered that chair around like it was a Corvette. "I'm ready for my spelling words," Rory announced. "Amber, you wanna do my spelling words?"

"I can't, Rory. I have to do my homework with Courtney. She came all the way out here to help me with my math."

"How long does it take to do spelling words?" Courtney asked.

"Maybe fifteen minutes," Amber answered with a shrug. "He'll get 'em all right."

"Then let's do 'em," Courtney said, barely recognizing herself. But he's in a wheelchair, she thought. And even *that* doesn't give you slack from homework?

During homework, Courtney found out that Rory had muscular dystrophy. When she asked if he'd get out of that wheelchair pretty soon, Amber said, "There's no cure. Yet." Courtney was afraid to ask any more questions. After homework, they went out to the barn where they kept one cow and two horses. There were also chickens and a couple of goats and a few dogs, one of whom seemed to move a little slow. "She's pretty much ready to whelp," Amber said. "The family's got a bet going—want to get in on it? Her last litter she dropped seven pups."

Courtney bet nine.

Hawk, Amber's dad, was a skinny old farmer. They caught up with him while he was hosing off his tractor out by the family's big vegetable garden. It was hard to tell if his name was the shortened version of his last name or due to his hawkish nose. He was a little hunched but strong, like maybe he'd been working real hard for a lot of years. Yet when he met Courtney, he turned out to be a little silly.

"I been looking forward to this," he said, putting out his calloused hand to her. "Been dyin' to see the hairdo!"

"Dad!" Amber scolded, clearly mortified.

"What? I been dyin' to. Must take commitment, eh?"

Courtney laughed. "Sort of."

"Courtney," Amber said pleadingly. "He swore he wouldn't make fun."

"I didn't make fun," her father protested. "I can't help wondering what it feels like. Can I touch it?"

"It's just hair," Courtney said, leaning her head toward him.

"So it is. I just have to ask—what did your dad have to say when he first laid eyes on it?"

"It totally freaked him out," she said almost proudly.

And Hawk smiled knowingly. "Knew there had to be a good reason."

When Lief saw that window of opportunity—Courtney making a homework date with a girlfriend from school—he was ready to get back to that Victorian on the premise of a tour and some free garden stock. It had only been a couple of days, but Courtney didn't provide many such opportunities. He realized he'd never thought ahead enough to ask Kelly for a phone number.

The tour and veggies were an excuse, though he did find the property curious and interesting. But really, it was the brokenhearted blonde with the delicious mouth who drew him. And bless her little soul, Lief was almost glad she was overcoming lost love. That would buy him some time. Although he just couldn't stop thinking about her, he had so many complications in his life to sort out. First of all, it wasn't likely Courtney's behavior was going to improve if Lief introduced a new woman into their already tenuous relationship. And any woman getting involved with them would probably be horrified by Courtney's sass if not her style. Add to that, it had been years since he'd been attracted to a woman other than his wife and didn't even know where to start. He used to be good with women; it never took much effort to hook up. He really hoped it was like riding a bike...

Yeah, it would probably involve years of therapy for himself and Courtney before he would even get up the courage to chance a kiss.

But when he thought of Kelly, he thought of someone whose beauty and warmth enveloped him, someone he longed to hold, to sink into, to possess. There was a softness and allure to her that made him feel as though he had no will of his own. The second she'd walked into Jack's he'd felt it, and to his surprise, he'd kept feeling it long after she was out of sight.

But it surpassed sweet comfort—he also thought of sex. *Urgent* sex. She was the sexiest thing he'd seen in a long time. He had a feeling he could be completely reborn in her arms.

He drove out to the house, parked in the front and rang the bell. She came to the door looking as if she'd just had a wrestling match with the Pillsbury Doughboy—tendrils of her hair escaping a scarf that tied it back, something floury on her cheek, her apron stained pink here and there. She was drying her hands on a towel. "Lief!" she said. "You're about the last person I expected to see!"

He nodded. "That's because I said I would call. But—I got away without a number. If you'll give me one, I'll leave now, drive to the bar in town, call you and drive right back. So it doesn't look like I'm imposing on—" He sniffed. "What *is* that wonderful smell?"

She smiled at him and he realized at once that it was really too easy to bewitch a chef—just smell her cooking and she was as good as captured.

"I've been baking. The rhubarb crop is in and apparently I'm the only person in a hundred square miles who can make a good rhubarb pie. And then there's rhubarb jam." She shrugged. "It was going to go bad if I didn't."

He almost swooned from the aromas. "Thank God you came to town," he said.

"Come in," she invited with a laugh. "I'm just cleaning up the kitchen. I'll see if Jill has time to take you for a tour of the house and grounds. Then, if you're very good, I'll give you a slice of pie."

"Are you sure? Because I really meant to call in advance and ask you to pick a time…"

"I'm picking a time," she said, pulling on his hand. "Come in. I'm still busy in the kitchen and kind of desperate for my shower, but maybe Jill is free. Let's see."

He followed her into the house and noted there was no furniture until he got to the kitchen. There, as promised, was a mess. But resting on the kitchen table in the large breakfast nook were ten pies. And there were now other smells. His head tilted back and his nose began to work the room.

She noticed. "I'm roasting a leg of lamb for dinner. Can you stay?"

"Oh, I'm sure I'm imposing…"

"On a chef?" She laughed. "I'm more likely to be insulted if you decline."

He grinned at her. Maybe that old saying about the fastest way to a man's heart was through his stomach was true, because suddenly he wanted her even more. *Wanted!* He really thought he was far past that kind of fierce yearning. He had found himself amazed even to be intrigued. This desire was just awesome, and he relished it. "I'll stay. My daughter is doing homework with a friend and having dinner there tonight."

"That's right," she said. "There's a daughter. I apologize. I'd forgotten. I'll have both of you next time."

He just laughed; they'd have to revisit that idea. "Courtney is actually my stepdaughter, though she uses my last name. It's complicated. I'll explain later. But what are you going to do with all those pies?"

"I don't know. I could use a bigger freezer, but only the most essential equipment is in the house at the moment. I guess I'll spread 'em around. A few for Preacher, that's for sure—he told me he's been trying to make a decent rhubarb pie for years. I can't believe how much stuff Jill has that's running out of time— tomorrow I have to get a good start on blackberries. She's had friends and neighbors out here picking for a good month and there's still such a big crop left, someone has to do something with it. Blackberry preserves, jam, pie filling…. I came up here to surf the Net for a job, and I'm working my tail off. Let me go out to the garden and ask her if she has time to scoot you around in her garden mobile…"

"Garden mobile?"

"It's how she gets between her gardens. Have a seat— I'll be a minute."

As Kelly hurried out the back door, Lief didn't go

far. He pulled out one of the stools at the work island and just looked around. For some reason, all the messy pots and bowls around the large kitchen made him feel at peace. Ever since growing up on a farm with a lot of siblings and hands, a busy, messy kitchen full of good smells always made him feel safe and protected. And the sight of ten pies cooling on the table was familiar as well—his mother always baked en masse, sharing with family, friends, neighbors, anyone.

Kelly was back quickly. "Jill has just been kicking around the pumpkins, squash and melons. She's right outside. While you have your tour, I'm going to clean up my mess."

He stood. "If you wait, I'll help. I had good training. I'm a good kitchen cleaner."

"Maybe you'll get your chance another time. Go on— she's waiting for you."

Even though Lief was more interested in the chef than the landscape, he really got into his tour. Jill drove him around acres of land that was partially prepared for organic farming. A winter crop had been started; she was drying seeds from her own fruits and vegetables for the next season's crop, and she'd started building retaining walls to use like steppes to level the slope of the hill to maximize her planting space in the spring.

The fall harvest of pumpkins, melons and squash was amazing—pumpkins that could indeed make Cinderella's carriage.

"I'm saving the really big ones from Kelly so the town kids have a crack at them. She has a pumpkin soup she can't wait to get to and so I'm pushing the smaller ones at her. And these huge zucchini and winter squash—it's more experimental than anything. Come on, let's go see what Colin's painting. This morning he was working on a herd of elephants. He's just back from shooting the Serengeti—lots of beautiful big game."

The sunroom on the second floor of the house stretched the length of the building across the roof of the back porch. That was where Colin liked to paint because the light was good. The paintings—ranging from wilderness art to big African game—were astonishing. Also in that sunroom were a sectional, entertainment center and large flat-screen TV—their living room, or a reasonable facsimile.

Lief was fascinated by the creativity in this house. Jillian stretched her imagination in the garden, Colin painted incredible animals from all over the globe, and Kelly was cooking. Today it was pies, but tomorrow it could be dishes that might only be found in a five-star restaurant in San Francisco.

"Come on, Lief," Colin said. "Let's get a beer and sit on the back porch. Jilly has to shower off the garden and Kelly is working on making me the shape of Santa Claus. We're on our own."

"I feel like I should help somehow," Lief said. "I dropped by unexpectedly and now I'm even going to be fed and entertained. Maybe I could hose off the gardening equipment or wash the pots."

Colin just laughed at him. "What I've learned is— these girls are going to do exactly what suits them and the best thing for you to do is stay out of the way." When they got to the kitchen, Colin opened the refrigerator and surveyed the contents. "We have 'near beer' and high-test. What's your pleasure?"

"The real deal, by all means," Lief said. "How did you stumble into this nirvana?"

Sitting on the back porch in perfect October weather, Lief heard about how Colin came to Virgin River after being retired from the army, a place to recover after a helicopter crash while Jillian had escaped a corporate job in Silicon Valley. They found each other by accident, but in a town of roughly six hundred, they were bound to meet. It was the falling-in-love part that was extraordinary. "I'm not a young guy," Colin said. "I don't think Jilly would be offended to hear me say I've met a few women—quite a few. I lived a transient, military life and wasn't ever tempted to settle down. But Jilly? She makes me want to grow my roots *deep*."

"Sounds serious," Lief observed.

"Oh, I'm serious about Jilly. But we're winging it for right now—just one day at a time. What about you? How did you end up in a place like this?"

He retold the story—wife died, daughter having a hard time of it, needing a smaller, friendlier town than L.A., trying to get past the rough patch of losing a wife and mother, fresh start. The question about what he'd done in L.A. didn't come until later, when they were all sitting down to dinner together. "I'm a writer," he said.

"As in newspaper?" Kelly asked.

Right then he suspected he was completely safe from any kind of notoriety. "No, as in script writer."

"Seriously?" Jillian asked. "Like TV or something?"

"Something like that. Movies, actually," he said.

"How interesting," Kelly said. "I haven't seen a movie in years. Well, I sometimes see them after the Academy Awards, when they finally make the cable networks. I've been held hostage in kitchens since I was eighteen."

"And I was taken prisoner by a software manufacturer," Jill said.

"I've been either in Afghanistan or the hospital. You don't write war movies, do you? I only go for war movies."

Lief smiled. "Nah. Mostly just family stuff. Kind of 'coming of age' stuff." He was completely safe. Even if they'd heard of the films, they would never have heard of him, which was absolutely perfect. "This is the best lamb I've ever tasted. And these potatoes—fantastic. I grew up on a potato farm in Idaho and I've never experienced anything like this."

"Thanks," she said. "I was missing one or two things, but I think it all worked out."

"Look out, Lief," Colin warned. "She's a little hard on the waistband."

"You could take it easy," she suggested. "You don't have to stuff yourself."

"Then stop making everything so good!" Colin argued.

Although Kelly was prepared to clean up her kitchen

and Lief offered to help, they were pushed away by Jill and Colin. They took cups of hot coffee out to the back porch and enjoyed a cold fall evening. The sky was clear and peppered with a million stars; there was no wind, but the temperature had dropped significantly.

For a long time they sat in silence, enjoying the clean air, clear sky and hot mugs in their hands. Finally it was Lief who said, "This is a wonderful, artistic house—the growing, painting, creating in the kitchen…"

"And beautiful," Kelly confirmed.

"Will you stay awhile?"

She shrugged before she said, "Jill and Colin are kind of new together. They've only been a couple since summer. I don't want to cramp their style, if you get my drift."

"You think they need privacy," he said.

"All new couples need privacy."

"I don't know about Jill, but Colin seems to enjoy having you in the kitchen."

"Don't get me wrong, no one is making me feel like I should move on. But I'm thirty-three—and I don't want to live with my sister for the rest of my life. I need a little time to get over—" She stopped to think. Get over *La Touche?* San Francisco? Luca? Her disastrous treadmill? "I think a brief vacation is in order. Then I'd better get on with things."

"Well… I hope it isn't too brief," he said. "I wouldn't mind a chance to get to know you better."

She chuckled. "That almost sounded like a flirt. From a Disney kind of guy…?"

He turned in his chair to look at her. "Is that how I seem?"

"Isn't it what you said? Movies for families? Disney comes to mind..."

He smiled just slightly. "And you?" he asked. "Betty Crocker?"

"Ack! Please!" she said. But then she laughed. "All right, all right. I shouldn't make rash judgments. I'll be here for at least a couple of weeks, and that's if finding my next position is *very* easy."

"After eating your dinner tonight, not to mention the pie, I'm sure you're going to find the next gig pretty quick." He took a sip of his coffee, then glanced at his watch. "I should go. I have to pick up Courtney before she wears out her welcome. It's her first visit to her friend's house."

"You act like you can't trust her at all," Kelly observed.

"I can't. Like I said, she's had a real struggle since her mom died." He stood. "But we'll get through this, one way or another. A normal girlfriend from an average family could go a long way to helping that effort."

Kelly stood also. "Is this her first *normal* friend?"

"Her name is Amber. I talked to her folks to be sure the after-school and dinner invitation was cool with them. They're farmers with three grown and married sons and grandchildren. I got the impression Amber is the caboose—an afterthought, maybe. Courtney describes her as kind of dorky but nice. A couple of nights ago I left her alone for two hours and went home to find her with a seventeen-year-old guy who brought beer and was liberating the DVDs from my entertainment center while Courtney was in the bathroom." He smiled just slightly. "Dorky Amber sounds like a dream come true."

"Lord above!"

"Yeah, one thing after another," he lamented. "But imagine losing your mother at only eleven years old."

"I lost my parents pretty young," Kelly said. "I understand that it can be hard. But I have to admit, I know almost nothing about kids. Especially teenagers."

"Have you thought about having a family?" he asked.

She shrugged. "Not really. I always thought the subject might come up if I ever met the right guy."

"You thought you had," he reminded her.

"Uh-huh—and he was fifty years old with five grown children. The thought that I wouldn't have children never even bothered me. Being a mother was never a driving urge." Then she smiled. "I wanted a restaurant."

He smiled back. "They probably don't talk back as much."

"Oh, you don't know restaurants!"

"It was really nice of you to invite me to stay, even though I dropped in without notice. I enjoyed myself. And the food..." He rolled his eyes skyward. "I like to cook, but I'd be embarrassed in front of you."

"We'll get you over that. Take a pie to dorky Amber's house as a thank-you. Maybe we can get Courtney invited back, free you up for an encore meal."

"I'll take you up on that. I admit, I need all the help I can get."

Lief and Kelly passed through the kitchen. When they gathered up a pie for Amber's parents, Lief scored one for himself, as well. He said good-night to Jill and Colin, and they each carried a pie out the front door. Lief opened the passenger door and put the pies on the floor of the truck, suggesting that as the safest place. Then he closed the door to face her. She put out her hand to say good-night.

He took the hand, pulled and brought her into his embrace. Turning with her in his arms, he pressed her up against the closed door of the truck and, for just one blissful moment, held her there. "God," he said, feeling everything he thought he might feel if he could hold her body against his. Plush, erotic, sweet. He put a finger under her chin to lift it, then kissed her—just a brief kiss. Her eyes were round and large, watching his. So he went for it, covering her mouth in a powerful kiss, a penetrating kiss. He urged her lips open; ah, she was delicious. And when he felt her arms come around him to keep him close, the arms of this brokenhearted woman, he tasted victory, as well. His desire escalated and suffused his entire being.

He moved his lips just a fraction of an inch from hers. "You taste even better than the pie."

"Wow," she said. "Nothing Disney about you."

He plunged his fingers into her silky blond hair, tilting her head back so her mouth was slightly open and ready. He took that mouth once more, amazed by how natural it felt. When he pulled away, he said, "That was the point I hoped to make. Is tomorrow too soon to see you again?"

She shook her head, her eyes still round.

"Good." He gave her another short kiss.

"I'm working on blackberries," she said a little breathlessly.

He smiled at her. "I'll see you sometime tomorrow. No 1950s Betty Crocker about you."

She grinned at him. "Toldja."

Courtney's dinner experience at the Hawkinses was very different from those she had at home with Lief. Amber's older brother, Rory's dad, came to dinner with another of his kids because his wife was working. It was a pretty full and loud table, and the food was more country than she got at home—pork chops, mashed potatoes with dark gravy and greens. She never got gravy at home—Lief used a minimum of fats in his cooking.

Courtney was seated next to Hawk, and he was in her business the whole time. While she was putting the gravy on her mashed potatoes, he leaned over, pointed and said, "You missed a spot." When she passed on the greens he said, "You're gonna want to try those."

"Because they're vegetables?" she asked.

"Naw. You can get your vitamins from ice cream for all I care. Because they're good. Nothing in the world like Sinette's greens." He put a small dollop on her plate. "First off, she grows 'em. Then, she makes 'em with bacon grease and garlic. Have one tiny taste, then if you pass on 'em, you can have more potatoes."

That made her lift her eyebrows. It wasn't like *If you don't eat your vegetables, no dessert*. The greens were delicious.

"There," he said. "Know what I'm talking about, don't I?"

After dinner and dessert, Amber and Courtney finished up their homework from other classes. It was the first time Courtney had all her homework done, and done well, since school had started the end of August.

Then Lief came, bearing gifts. "A friend of mine made ten rhubarb pies today and a couple came my way. This is for you," he said, putting it in Sinette's hands. "She—my friend—said to try it and if your rhubarb pie is better, she'll need a recipe exchange."

Sinette laughed. "Well, she better be at the top of her game because my recipe came from my grand-mother!"

So Lief asked Amber's parents how homework had gone when what Courtney believed he meant was, *Was Courtney bad? Did Courtney make trouble?*

"I think they're all caught up and Amber said it helped. She's had a time with that algebra!"

In the car on the way home, Courtney said, "So, who is this *friend?*"

"Huh?" Lief asked.

"This *friend* who made ten pies?"

"Oh," he said. "Her name is Kelly and she's a chef from the Bay Area. She's visiting her sister and invited me to dinner." He looked over at her and grinned. "Since my usual date was busy, I accepted and got a pie out of the deal."

"Oh. And so are you *dating* now?"

"Not yet," he said. "Do you think life could be that kind?"

"You're saying you *want* to date?"

"Why don't you ask me what you really want to ask me, Courtney. Stop beating around the bush."

"If you're so smart, what do I *want* to ask you?"

He sighed. "No, I am not over your mother—I miss Lana every day. And yes, I would like to have another adult relationship in my lifetime—I'm lonely. And no, no one will ever be more important than your mother. Or, for that matter, than you. I promise you I won't be less of a father if I ever get lucky enough to actually have a girlfriend at some point."

She thought about that for a moment. She wasn't sure how he did that—answered every question she wasn't sure how to ask. So she said, "Like I *care*."

Five

Kelly had only been in her sister's house for a short time, but things began to change for her in small but meaningful ways almost immediately. It all began with a cooking show. She hooked up her very small, portable kitchen TV on the counter so she could see it while she cooked. Of course the very first program she viewed was *Luciano Brazzi's Dining In*. While she peeled and cut up apples to can some applesauce, Luca was preparing his famous eggplant rollatini. She watched his handsome face, his playful and engaging manner as he dipped the eggplant slices in beaten egg, then seasoned bread crumbs, then Parmesan… He joked with his pretty kitchen helper; his hands smooth and confident; his white teeth gleaming against his tanned skin, his robust laugh so seductive. He was at ease, comfortable, at peace, self-assured. Clearly he was not suffering from a broken heart.

She began to cry, and then, before the rollatini went in the oven, she was sobbing. He was perfectly *fine!* The man did not have a trouble in the world. He wasn't lonely or depressed or suffering with the misery of longing. If there was anything to get over, he'd gotten over it.

He opened one of those famous jars with his face on it, Brazzi Spaghetti Sauce, warmed it and poured it over the whole magnificent meal and that was it. "You bastard," she screamed right to his televised face. "You led me on, made promises to show me opportunities and sent your *wife* to deal with me! As if I were a common tramp you had bored of." She sniffed, blew her nose and said, "I am so done!"

To which the TV responded, "And that is my eggplant rollatini! Brava! And *ciao* my *bellas!*"

"*Ciao,* dickwad," she said, turning off the TV.

Then things improved daily, if not hourly. No pressure; no crazy kitchen to go back to, and the relief in this was magnificent. And though three of them shared the house, everyone went their own way. Jill spent almost all her time either outside or at her computer in her office while Colin was either prowling around the mountains with his camera or painting upstairs in the sunroom. It was the first time Kelly could remember feeling freedom like this. Even on past visits or vacations she'd constantly been thinking about getting back to the grind and was usually worried about some work-related issue.

Almost all meals and certainly all dinners were prepared by Kelly and she thrived on her small but special audience. Jill's farm assistant, Denny, often joined them for lunch and sometimes for dinner. He was a handsome young bachelor of twenty-five, perpetually cheerful and funny. "I thought I'd stumbled on the perfect job in Jilly Farms, and that was before you showed up, Kelly," he said. "Now I have the perfect job and restaurant! I don't think I've ever eaten this well in my life! Kelly, you're not only a genius but a gorgeous genius."

And Kelly looked at the square, dimpled jaw, bright eyes, hard-muscled physique on his six-foot frame and said, "Oh, Denny, I wish I'd met you ten years ago!"

"Well, I'd have been fifteen, but that's no big deal," he said with a sly grin. "I've always liked older women."

Older woman? She wasn't that much older! She glowered at him and said, "You wanna eat, smarty pants?"

Rather than short nights or sleep that came on the heels of exhaustion, she slept a good, peaceful eight hours or more. Her head was clear; she didn't face daily conflict.

She'd only been at Jillian's for a week when Jill said, "When the movers empty your flat of household goods, have everything brought here. Take the whole third floor—it'll give you space for your sofa, favorite chair, TV, desk—it's more spacious than your flat was. You'll have as much privacy as you want and if you want to be around people, you know where we are."

"I wasn't planning a long stay—"

"Listen, you could live in this house for a year without even bumping into anyone, if that's what you want. But let me tell you what I want," Jill said. "I want you to give yourself enough of a break to be sure your health is good, your emotions level and positive and your poor heart mended. The first thing to do—let Dr. Michaels give you a quick checkup to be sure your new blood pressure medicine is doing its job. My guess is that once you've had some time away from that nuthouse of a restaurant, you won't even need it anymore."

Kelly had spent most of her adult life avoiding doctors, and she hadn't had a single symptom or incident since moving into Jill's house. But it made sense to see the local doctor.

As for her positive emotional state and poor broken heart? She was working on it. Things were coming into perspective—all her fantasies about life with Luca were a mistake and she should have known better.

Getting herself kissed by a sexy guy didn't hurt. Whatever it was with Lief—not quite a romance but something more than simple friendship—it made her feel better about herself. When he was near, she just couldn't stop looking at him—that thick, burnished blond hair, expressive brows, warm brown eyes all combined to make him so handsome. But that body and what he did to a pair of jeans just knocked her out.

Lief dropped by daily. Determined not to be a drain on the household, he took it upon himself to chop wood, getting Jillian started on a big pile that would get her through winter. He'd show up in the morning and split logs for a while before sitting at the work island while Kelly was cooking. Problem was, it was pretty hard for her to focus on her project of the day while he was hefting that ax out by the storage shed. The beautiful strain on his shoulders, back and arms could send her right into an erotic trance.

And he caught her staring out the kitchen window every time. He would flash her that wide, white grin before getting back to work.

He never mentioned it, though. Once his log-splitting was done for the day, he was content to sit in the kitchen and talk.

"Tell me how one goes about writing a movie," Kelly said.

"Just about the same way one creates a recipe," he said. "You experiment with taste, I experiment with words and feelings and settings. I have an image in my head that I try to get on the page. The script is like an architectural drawing with details and directions to build a movie."

"How many have you actually sold?" she asked.

He shrugged. "Half a dozen. The selling isn't the important part—it's the filming and releasing. Lots of original scripts are optioned, which is kind of like 're-served' for a period of time. Then when there's principal photography, when they begin to actually shoot the movie, they're officially sold. But they still have a long way to go before a viewing public might see them."

"But when do you write them? Late at night?"

"I haven't been doing that much writing lately—I've been setting up a home, spying on Courtney, fishing, chopping wood, thinking and trying to get things under control. Like things were once upon a time."

"I take that to mean, when Courtney's mother was alive."

He nodded. "Lana worked in wardrobe for a production company. She was a single, working mom when I met her and she was getting along very well. We were married four years when she died, suddenly. Aneurism. She was at work. We were in shock, me and Court, but I love writing and was trying to work my way through the grief when I realized Courtney's life was going to hell. She was being shuffled between her dad and his second family and me, not sure where she belonged anymore. Her appearance and behavior changed—I think it was gradual but I felt like I looked up one day and here was this Goth creature with felonious tendencies."

"And you decided to come here?"

"Not fast enough," he said. "I got advice from everyone I knew—friends and family. The names of counselors, grief groups, child-raising experts from Tough Love to Dr. Spock. I floundered and Courtney got in trouble. This was a pretty desperate move to help her. Us. To help us."

She leaned on the work island and asked, "Who helped *you?*"

"Oh, I managed. I had a support group through a Unitarian church and a couple of good friends who hung in there with me long after I'm sure I'd become a huge, depressing downer."

She smiled at him. "In spite of the harsh realities of what you've been through, you're not a downer now."

"Thanks, Kelly. I'm ready for the next phase of my

life. I just have lots of things to work out before that's my only priority."

Sometimes they walked around the property, of which there was plenty. Lief and Kelly were kicking around the pumpkin patch in back of the house when he asked her, "What really happened in the restaurant to make you run away to Virgin River?"

She took a breath. "There's a long answer and a short answer to that one. The long answer involves years of education, culinary training and apprenticeships in several different countries, including the U.S., with the single primary goal of rising to the position of chef de cuisine or head chef in a major restaurant and then being a partner in a very well known, five-star restaurant. Every institute I studied in or kitchen I worked in was crazy. The competition was always brutal, the personal relationships were complex and often destructive and dysfunctional…"

"Hollywood can be like that," he said.

She stopped walking. "Yeah. I bet. We should compare notes…"

"Your notes first, Kelly," he urged. "Go on."

"Hm. It takes a certain kind of person to make it in that life—a person with nerves of steel, confidence that's immune to constant criticism, single-minded goals, a profound determination and belief that you will ultimately not only survive but win the war—and it is a war. On top of that you'd better have a very strong support team to watch your back. Of course at the same time it's a jealous, competitive business and no one trusts anyone.

Everyone is trying to rise to the top. I didn't realize it was taking its toll until I crashed on the job—passed out and had to be taken to the hospital. Scared me to death." She stopped walking through the beautiful big orange pumpkins and said, "I'm a great chef."

"I know," he said with a smile. "I'm a witness."

"I'm so organized, it would scare you. I have good instincts about the use of food. And, I truly and honestly believe I could run a big kitchen without all that insanity. In fact, if I had the chance and could hire the manager, I could run the whole house without craziness!"

"I believe you."

"But I bet I'm kidding myself if I think I'm going to get the chance. My biggest chance on the horizon was Luca. One of the first things I loved about him was that he was not insane. When he came to the kitchen, the whole place fell into order. No one dared raise a voice or argue with him. He was more than a mentor, he was a role model. He promised me a shot at leading one of his five-star restaurants. And you know what happened there."

"That might not be the only route to your success, Kelly," he said.

"Maybe not. But right now the economy is down, big fancy restaurants are struggling. When I find my next job, it's not going to be as classy as *La Touche*."

"I've actually eaten there, you know," he told her.

"Not really!"

"Really. Might've been before your time."

"Do you remember what you thought of it?"

"I thought it was arrogant and *nouveau*. Making people who have had reservations for weeks or months wait two hours for a table? Stupid arbitrary move—trying to make the establishment rather than the fare appear high-end. The waitstaff was good but the management should get people to their tables. A really good restaurant relies on their food. As I recall, the food was good, but I'd never go back."

"That's what I think, exactly. I bet you hardly remember the meal because you were pissed at the treatment!"

"So in a word, what would you say was the main issue?"

"No quality of life," she said. "After over fourteen years of hard work, I wasn't getting any closer to my goal, didn't have friends, didn't have a lover, didn't get to create my best work in the kitchen. What did I have besides high blood pressure? Jillian at least has giant pumpkins. I walked out. I usually plan my life *years* in advance—but I just walked out."

He smiled at her. "I think you're very smart. Now," he said, looking around, "what are we doing here?"

"I'm going to pick some acorn squash. I have a squash bisque that will kill you, it's so good. I also have a tomato bisque that's heaven on earth. I like to serve it with a gourmet grilled cheese—something with roasted red peppers."

"Sounds perfect. Courtney has a homework date at Amber's house on Thursday night," he said, pulling her against him.

"Why do I feel like I'm cutting class to make out?"

He laughed at her. "Because you are! If I can just get my daughter on track, I'll have more freedom to move around in. But I'll take what I can get—and for now I'm so grateful for that homework date, I'm breaking out in a sweat."

Their next unofficial date was to the river on a beautiful October afternoon. He had all his fishing gear with him, but instead he spread a blanket and they sat together near the river's edge, talking. He kissed her and said, "I'm counting on you to tell me when this is no longer a rebound. It's probably too soon for you to get involved with a man."

"I don't know that there is a rebound situation," she explained. "If there is, it's probably all in my head. I can see now that I nurtured a lot of fantasies about Luca— his importance in the food world is pretty sexy and overwhelming to someone like me. He's a handsome, influential man. I think his power attracted me. And then there was his attempted seduction."

Lief lifted a brow, tilted his head and asked, "*Attempted* seduction?"

"Oh, I was totally hooked. I adored him. But I must have been out of my mind. He's not only one of the most successful and important chefs in the world, he has a huge family. If all my fantasies had come true and I'd ended up as his second wife, they would have tortured me. As it is, I couldn't even get a message to him through his assistants. Can you imagine what it would have been like?"

He smiled and ran a finger over her shoulder, down her arm and laced his fingers into hers. "You were in love with him, Kelly. You don't just rule it out."

"I don't know, Lief. I might've been in love with the *idea* of him. We have so much in common—starting with our professions. In my fantasies, I saw myself working with him, inspiring him even as he took me to the next level."

Lief was quiet for a moment. "I have one question. How long did it last?"

"What part? The contact between chefs? The friendship? His mentoring? His attention and flirtation?"

"I was actually thinking of the sex…"

She looked at him in complete shock. Then she laughed. "There was no sex! I never slept with him!"

"Then why did his wife come to see you?"

Kelly flopped on her back and looked up at the sky. "That's the part that had me confused for a while— but it became irrelevant. Five-star restaurants make up a small town, and in my world not only was Luciano Brazzi the king, his wife was the queen. Not only did she believe I was having an affair with him, within five minutes of her leaking it, everyone I worked with believed it. Everyone I might *ever* work with believed it within twenty-four hours." She looked at Lief. "He told me he adored me, that he thought he was falling in love with me, that he wanted to end his sham of a marriage and pursue a serious thing with me. I told him to repeat all that when he was a single man. He talked a lot about it, I lapped up every word, but it didn't happen." She gave Lief a sheepish smile. "I did get kissed," she said. "It was awesome."

Lief was completely stunned. Based on what she had said, he had envisioned a long, steamy, satisfying affair. Something that would be hard to get over.

"A *kiss?*"

She nodded. "Like a couple of thunderheads coming together. It had me very excited about the potential."

Lief thought about this for a moment. Then he leaned over her and put his lips against hers and asked, "Better than this?"

"Oh, far better," she said with a smile.

He tried again, and this time he tongued open her lips. He loved the wet velvet of her mouth. And her special taste was a kind of earthy ambrosia that he was already addicted to. There hadn't been that many kisses between them—it had been less than two weeks since that fateful night he'd had to drive her home. But God above, he wanted to live inside her mouth. "Better than that?" he asked.

"Slightly better," she said.

"Forget him," he said, covering her mouth in a demanding kiss that plunged into her. Ah! Her arms came around him, and her tongue joined the play, dueling with his. Their mouths were fused, open, hot and wet, and he slid his large body over her smaller, soft, sweet body. He loved the lushness of her, the fullness of her hips and breasts. She made him hard, that's what.

He pushed against her. With a knee placed in a strategic position, he parted her legs a bit and pushed deeper. Her pleased moan was music to his ears, and, though it was early stages yet, he took a chance, slipping a hand under her sweater and over her breast. He could feel her nipple harden under the bra, beneath his hand, and he desperately wanted it in his mouth.

"Better than this?" he asked, his voice hoarse and a little breathless.

"Not so much," she said, out of breath herself.

"We're gonna have to move on this one of these days," he announced. "I've been wanting you since the minute I met you."

"I think there's something you should know…"

"Hm? What's that?" he asked, placing small kisses around her face and neck.

"I haven't had many relationships," she said.

"Hey, I've only had one in the last seven years and none in the last two," he told her. "Not a handicap, trust me."

"Thing is, I haven't had much… I mean, I was real busy with food. There were a few short flings, that's about it. And I haven't had much…"

He became more alert. "I know eventually you're going to finish that sentence," he said.

"Sex," she said. "Not much sex."

"That's okay, honey. In fact, that's sweet."

"And as far as really good sex? Rock-your-world sex? Satisfying sex? Basically…" She let that sentence drift off. But he waited. He lifted one brow. She took a breath. "Basically, none."

He was quiet a moment. "As in... None?" he asked. When she nodded, he asked, "How about sweet or comfortable or compatible sex?"

"Not really. I had a few short things. With guys I met in the business, you know. They were over quickly. And each one left me wondering why I bothered."

"Gotcha," he said. He brushed the hair back from her temple. "Listen, if you ever decide to change career fields, maybe give seminars to women on how to really set up a challenge for a guy, I think you're on to something here..."

"I wouldn't blame you at all if you decided this really wasn't worth your time," she said.

He was still positioned over her. He smiled into her eyes. Then he went for that delicious mouth again, teased her, demanded of her, forced her lips open and then waited for her tongue to start the play before he went deeper, harder. He kissed her with his whole body, and she felt it, pushing back against him. When she was breathing hard, gasping a little, he pulled back a bit. "No such luck, honey. You're not going to ask yourself why you bothered this time. Trust me."

"Kiss me some more," she demanded. "This is pretty good. At least when you apply yourself."

Oh, this is going to be good, Courtney thought when she walked into the counselor's waiting room. The button-down collar of the guy's plaid, short-sleeved shirt couldn't have been tighter on his long, skinny neck. He looked a little like a heron.

"Courtney, hello!" he said cheerily. "I'm Jerry."

"Hi," she said, deadpan.

"Come in the office." He stepped aside and let her enter ahead of him. She took the chair facing the desk, and he went behind the desk. "Something in your manner tells me you've done this sort of thing before."

"Ya think?" she asked, lifting a thin, black eyebrow.

"Assuming that's the case, what do you think we should talk about?"

She leaned back in the chair. "I guess you probably want to talk about the fact that my mother is dead."

He didn't register even the slightest shock. He tilted his head and said, "I would've started with how you like it around here. Must be quite a change for you."

"Quite," she echoed. She knew she had several choices—she could make this a challenge, make it easy, make it interesting or make it horrible. "It's a little more rural than I'm used to." She decided on interesting.

"Are you getting to know people yet? Making friends?" he asked.

"I have one friend, but she's sort of someone who needs me to help her with homework, so once she gets it she might not be my friend anymore."

"There's a troubling thought," he said. "Don't you suppose she could have found someone she *liked* to help her rather than someone she would just *use?*"

She considered shifting to horrible. Except that he

seemed to speak her language, oddly enough. "I think she probably likes me. In her way."

"And do you like her?" he asked. "In your way?"

She shrugged. "I guess."

"Let's start there. What do you like about her?"

Courtney narrowed her eyes. "Her lameness does not totally offend me."

Jerry smiled indulgently. "What else?"

She decided to take pity on him since he was truly an inferior nerd. "I kind of like hanging around her house, her farm. Her family is kind of nice. Her dad is funny. Old and pretty broken down, but silly. When I stay for dinner I get good, fatty, greasy stuff instead of all that health-food shit my dad makes."

"Right there is a massive recommendation," Jerry said. "I'm afraid I'm falling down in the health-food-shit department."

"No kidding? And she has a little nephew in a wheel-chair. Her older brother's kid."

"Oh?"

"Muscular dystrophy. He's eight. He might have some times he's less sick than others, but he's not going to get better. He's going to get worse until he dies. Not very many people make it to adulthood if they get it as a kid."

"Did your friend explain all this to you?"

"No," she said, shaking her head. "I looked it up on the internet. Because of what she said, I pinned him down to DMD—Duchenne muscular dystrophy. She said there was no cure and he wasn't getting better and he's already in a wheelchair. He's really kind of cute with his glasses sliding off his nose—looks like that little kid in *Jerry Maguire*. And he's scary smart—he's eight and doing seventh grade spelling and math. And he's funny. His parents let him zone out on video games to keep his reflexes exercised, but there's nothing they can do about the muscles in his back or legs."

"You like him. You like the whole family," Jerry observed.

She gave something like a nod. But then she said, "Makes you wonder if there's any God, seeing a kid like that get something like that."

Jerry leaned forward. "Courtney, you joined the geniuses of the centuries in wondering that very thing. Unfairness and injustice are two things that really threaten blind faith."

"Why are you talking to me like I'm an adult?" She made a face.

He looked surprised. "Did I say something you didn't understand?"

"No," she relented. "Yeah, I like the family. I like the animals, even if there aren't that many. My dad grew up on a potato farm and we used to go there. We haven't been there in a while."

"What animals?" Jerry asked.

"There's a golden retriever mix who's about to have puppies and you can feel them move around inside her—I bet there's gonna be nine. I mean, it's a real bet—I even put a dollar in the jar. There are chickens, goats, one cow and two horses. A million cats, like at my dad's Idaho farm. They keep the mice down."

Jerry smiled at her. "If you like hanging out at farms, you're going to make plenty of friends around here. Lots of farm kids around here."

"Yeah, well. I have exactly one friend so far."

"But do you trust her? Like her? Is she a good person?" Jerry asked.

"She is good. Kind of lame and dorky, but she wouldn't know how to be a bad person."

"I'm going to tell you something that might be a little hard for you to buy into right now, but a couple of good, trustworthy, loyal friends—it's a lot. In junior high and high school, kids collect friends in such big numbers it sometimes seems ridiculous to think you could get by on just a couple of good ones. But really, one good friend rather than a dozen you're not too sure of—no contest."

She was quiet for a minute. "I had a lot of friends before my mom died."

Jerry was respectfully quiet for a minute also. "I'm very sorry for your loss, Courtney. The death of a close loved one can often change the landscape of everything else in your life."

"Is this where we segue into talking about my dead mother?"

He smiled at her, but it was a comforting smile. "Segue. Movie talk. You'll probably have to explain that term around here. I thought we'd keep this short today, our first day together, and sneak up on the more difficult subjects over time. You okay with that?"

"Yeah," she said. "I think I'm already tired. I don't know why—it's not like I had to walk here."

"It's okay. I think we're off to a decent start. You didn't even make fun of my wardrobe or haircut. I don't always get off that easy."

"I decided not to hurt your feelings, in case you're—you know—sensitive."

"Thank you. Very sporting of you. Want to come back after school on Monday?"

She straightened. "How long do I have to do this?"

"I don't know," he said with a shrug. "I assume we'll both know when we've had enough."

She scooted to the edge of her chair. "Do we have to do this until my hair is all one color, my fingernails painted pink and my clothes pastel?"

He grinned hugely. "Courtney, look at me. What are the odds I'm going to take pokes at anyone's style?"

"Do *you* have any good friends?"

"Yes. A few quality friends, actually."

She snorted. "*That's* promising! I'll come Monday, but let's not go overboard."

"Deal. Now, I want to give you some ground rules. Mine, not yours. I'm also talking to your dad now and then, but I'm not talking to him about you. Oh—he can talk about you if he wants to, but I'm not going to be asking him about you. And you can talk about him, but I'm not going to ask you about him—not unless there's some compelling reason to ask something. Like if you tell me he beat you up, I'd probably ask about that. But—and here's the most important thing—I'm never going to tell you what he said or tell him what you said. We have a confidentiality agreement. You don't have to worry. You can safely air all your complaints or concerns here."

"So you expect me to believe that if I call him a low-life, blood-sucking, parasite son of a bitch, you won't rat me out?"

He smiled at her. "Exactly."

One of the things that Lief had discussed with Jerry in counseling was where Lief had found reassurance, confidence and self-esteem as a kid. It didn't matter where or how you grew up, these were things all kids needed. Lief told Jerry it had come to him in two places—his writing and his animals. On the farm he'd had a horse and a dog he called his own.

Since Courtney had never showed any interest in writing, Lief found himself at the Jensen Veterinary Clinic and Stable. Before he even got around to looking for someone to talk to, he saw a man in the round pen, working out a colt. He leaned on the rail and just watched for a while.

A young Native American man in the pen moved slowly around a young Arabian—a very spirited young Arabian. The horse pulled on the lead, reared, pawed at the dirt and the man remained focused on the colt's eyes, his lips moving as he talked softly to the horse. At length the colt calmed and allowed himself to be led in a circle inside the pen. Eventually he lowered his head slightly and allowed the trainer to stroke his neck. The trainer spoke to the colt, and it appeared as if the colt nodded, though that was crazy.

It wasn't until the trainer was leading the horse out of the pen that he noticed Lief. He lifted a hand and said, "Hello. I'll meet you in the barn."

By the time Lief went inside, the horse was secured for grooming and the man was approaching him, hand outstretched. "How do you do, I'm Clay Tahoma."

"Lief Holbrook," he said, taking the hand. "I watched you with the colt for quite a while."

Clay just shook his head. "When I'm working with a horse, I don't seem to notice anyone or anything else."

"I have a fourteen-year-old daughter. If you can gentle her the way you did the colt, I'll put you in my will."

Clay laughed. "I know a lot more about horses than young girls, my friend. Does she ride?"

"I tried to put her on a horse a couple of times, but she shied. When I offered her riding lessons back in L.A., she wasn't interested. I thought we might try again. Can you recommend someone? I'll be honest with you— sometimes she's a handful."

"My wife and Annie Jensen teach some riding," Clay said. "They're very good instructors. And, my wife, Lilly, tells tales of her teenage years that make me go very pale. Add to that, we'd be grateful for a daughter one day—are we insane? But there you have it—if anyone can understand and handle a difficult teenage girl, it would probably be Lilly. Would you like to bring your daughter around sometime? Let her meet the horses and talk to the instructors?"

"Is it convenient after school one day? Provided she's interested. I learned not to force her into anything. It isn't worth the struggle. She can be so angry sometimes."

Clay smiled. "There is an old Navajo saying—I heard it all the time growing up. 'You cannot wake a person who is pretending to be asleep.' She could be using anger to cover more vulnerable needs."

"Any other old Navajo sayings around the house you grew up in?"

"Yes," he said, with a grin. "Do as I say, or else. And many variations on that."

Six

Kelly's small shipment of household goods from her San Francisco flat arrived at the end of her second week in Virgin River. Together, she and Jill sorted through the boxes—the personal items went up to the third floor, the kitchen items stayed in the kitchen. It took less than an afternoon to set up Kelly's bedroom and arrange the loft into a sitting room complete with desk, sofa and chair, table and TV.

"This looks very comfortable," Jill said. "Colin and I will be sure to knock on the wall if either of us is coming upstairs for any reason. The open staircase doesn't give you too much privacy, but at least the door to your bedroom closes."

"This is *too* comfortable," Kelly said. "If you put me in the cellar, it might motivate me to look for work."

Jill flopped down on Kelly's couch. "I'd be happy if you never left."

"No offense, cupcake, but I don't want to live with my little sister forever."

"I can understand that. Really, I can. But I felt a lot of pressure to make some kind of decision about what I was going to do next when I got up here, and to keep my hands busy while I was thinking, I ended up plowing the back forty and growing everything I could imagine. Now it's what I'm going to do next. Can't you justify a few months, at least?"

"But I'm not even thinking about what I want to do next, Jill," Kelly said. "All I can think about is what I *don't* want to do next. I could be emailing people I know in the business to let them know I'm available, but every time one comes to mind I remember working with them was a real challenge. I should post my resume on several different chef's employment websites, but I'm afraid all that will turn up is one more crazy, stressful kitchen. I need something different. And I have no idea what that might be."

Jillian just smiled at her.

"What?" Kelly said.

"Some new kitchen appliances are arriving in a couple of days. When I closed on the house, Paul ordered me some custom appliances to fit the kitchen because the stuff that's in there now is all temporary. I'm getting a double Sub-Zero refrigerator/freezer, six-burner Wolf range, two dishwashers, trash compactor. It's going to be so beautiful..."

Kelly sat up straight. "Seriously?"

"It had nothing to do with you coming," she said, shaking her head. "Even though I didn't think I'd use most of that stuff, I thought the kitchen should be properly finished. Next year, if planting goes well, I'm going to furnish the living room, dining room and sitting room and have a decorator come out to talk about window coverings and area rugs."

"You little seductress," Kelly said.

"So just relax awhile. Do whatever it is you do to unwind. Enjoy the attentions of that man who keeps coming around…"

"During school hours," Kelly added with a laugh. "I never actually had an affair with Luca, but I sure feel like I'm having one with Lief."

"So how is he in…you know…bed?"

Kelly leaned close as if imparting a secret. She looked right and left before she whispered, "I don't know."

"Crap," Jill said, disappointed. "Well, why are you sneaking around?"

"I'm not. *He* is. I thought he should just tell his daughter we're dating and include her sometimes and he said I didn't know what I was suggesting. He said Courtney can complain about a million dollars. But he also said she seems to be having some happier days—she has a friend that Lief feels pretty good about, a counselor she doesn't seem to mind talking to and he's trying to convince her to go to a local stable where she can get some riding lessons. She's thinking about it. She might, if only to have more in common with her new friend, who has a couple of horses. I have no idea what all that means."

"Do you know *anything* about teenagers?" Jill asked.

"I was one once." Kelly said. "That's it."

* * *

What Kelly liked to do to relax, to think, was cook and bake. She had squash, blackberries and apples coming out her ears. There was also a healthy amount of late tomatoes, heirloom peppers and beans. It wasn't really enough in the tomato department to keep her too busy, but she reminded herself that California was the tomato world and she could go to the farmers' market. She got online and found out when it was held and made a note to herself.

She borrowed Jill's truck and made a run to Eureka to buy some larger pots and cases of canning jars. One nice thing about these small, country towns—they carried those quaint, old-fashioned country canning jars that would be hard to find in San Francisco.

Over just one weekend she produced jars of applesauce, sliced apples for pie filling, more blackberry preserves and pie filling, freezer bags full of her grandmother's Italian sauce and acorn squash bisque. And what she had was enough product to open a booth at the farmers' market.

"I'm going to have to spread this around," she told Jillian. "Seems like a waste of money, doesn't it?"

Jill shook her head. "Didn't cost anything but the jars. I was growing just to see what I could grow, giving most of it away. I only got my commercial licenses a couple of months ago. I have no idea what kind of licenses and permits you need to sell processed food."

"I do. It's a lot of inspections and paperwork. Some of the certificates I already had to have to work as a chef in this state, but your kitchen isn't approved, although it can be."

"Well, we can put up some shelves in the cellar…"

"You should really have Paul Haggerty get someone out here to put a wine cellar down there—it's perfect. I'm trying to fill up the pantry. You'll have plenty of stuff after I leave."

"Spread your goods around town, Kelly. Take a bunch of it to Preacher. He'll serve some and put some up in the bar. Take a couple of cases to Connie at the Corner Store—she'll either sell it or hand it out. I mean, it's safe, right?"

"I'm a *chef!*"

"And Nana didn't kill us with her stuff," Jill added. "Wow, look at this kitchen and pantry. How did you do all this?"

"Well—while Lief's daughter is off school on weekends, he's busy hovering over her so I couldn't see him. I just kept going." She smiled as she looked around at the many jars. "It was really fun. I can get into a one-woman kitchen."

When Monday, a school day, rolled around, Lief wanted to spend time with her. But Kelly had things to do. She had boxed up many of her prepared canned and deli items, labeled them and put a calculated shelf life on them. The canned applesauce, apple pie filling, blackberries and Italian sauce were good for a year, but the tomato bisque and squash bisque contained butter and cream, which gave them a very short shelf life—five days if refrigerated.

Lief, still working his way into her good graces, was more than happy to load his truck, cover the boxes and drive her into town. "If you're giving some to Preacher to sample and serve, I'll be glad to buy you lunch and a beer. How does that sound?"

"Like you're seducing me," she said.

"No, I'm serving your needs, after which I hope to seduce you!"

"I have to admit, I like the way you think," she said.

So they went first to the bar. It was before the lunch hour when Jack and Preacher would have a little time on their hands.

Kelly lined up her jars on the counter for the proprietors. "All of these were made from organic Jilly Farms produce. I'm saving some in her pantry because next week I'm going to hit the farmers' market, buy some local end-of-season vegetables and make batches from other growers' stock. I'm willing to bet that my sister's produce has better flavor, but who knows? Maybe it's all about the cook and not the ingredients. We'll see."

They lined up spoons and small bowls. Lief was allowed to participate in the tasting. It was like a wine, beer or coffee tasting—flat crackers between samples, new spoons for each. "And I'd like to heat this bisque," Kelly said. "Permission to use the kitchen?"

"Granted!" Preacher said.

The reviews were raves all around, and of course

Preacher wanted to know how much she could sell him, what recipes she would share with him, whether she'd provide more.

"You can have this supply if you're willing to serve it—I'd like to know what your diners think. I don't share my great-grandmother's recipes, but I have lots of recipes I can share with you. I'm going to make my nana's pumpkin soup, roasted pumpkin seeds, pumpkin pie, pumpkin bread and pumpkin muffins for the Halloween open house."

Preacher's cheeks got rosier as she listed these items until she finally finished and he said, "Whoa! I have to give you something for this, Kelly."

"How about a couple of sandwiches," Lief suggested.

"Just sandwiches? And a slice of my chocolate velvet cake?"

"Perfect," Kelly said. "And I'd like the jars back, if you don't mind. I'll reuse them after sterilizing."

"It's turkey pastrami today," he said. "And if you play your cards right, a little tomato bisque."

"Lay it on me," Lief said.

"We'll eat slow so we can hang out awhile and maybe pick up some reactions from your lunch crowd."

And that was what happened, with a twist Kelly didn't realize was unusual for the bar until Jack explained it to her. Preacher usually served up one item per meal, per day and there was no fanfare. He could be talked out of leftovers by the right person, but there wasn't anything as fussy as a menu. He stayed mostly in the kitchen, brought out finished meals as they were ready, kept to himself and was not usually talkative.

However, on this special day, he was literally meeting every diner, explaining the presence of a guest chef and her special bisques—referring to her as a chef rather than a cook—and offering a free sample of either squash or tomato bisque. His samples were hearty servings, typical of Preacher; the lunch crowd raved and shook her hand in welcome. This gave her a chance to invite everyone she met to the pumpkin patch for a pumpkin picking and more of her goodies.

Then a couple entered, sat up at the bar, and when the woman looked around, Kelly's breath caught. Muriel St. Claire, Oscar-nominated actress. Celebrities had visited *La Touche* many times—this was hardly Kelly's first sighting. But it was astonishing to see her *here*. And the shocks just kept coming. Muriel locked eyes with Lief and said, "Oh, my God, as I live and breathe!"

"Muriel!" Lief said in surprise. And the two of them met in the middle of the bar and embraced like old friends.

"What are you doing here?" he asked her.

"I *live* here," she answered, laughing. "And you?"

"I bought a house here—I wanted to get Courtney out of L.A. And maybe have a quieter life."

"It doesn't always stay quiet," she warned him. "We have our wild times in the mountains! Meet my guy. Walt, come here!" she called.

Kelly watched as a handsome guy in his sixties joined them; Lief shook his hand and Kelly heard

Muriel introduce Lief as "The Wunderkind"—an Oscar-winning screenwriter for a movie she was in, one in which she'd been nominated for supporting actress. "How old were you when that happened, Lief? About twelve?"

"Thirty-five, Muriel," he answered with a laugh. "Come meet a friend of mine." He turned toward her, and Kelly, still in a state of shock over many revelations, stood up. "Kelly, meet Muriel and Walt. Muriel is an old friend."

And you, she thought, *are an Oscar-winning writer? Not just a writer, but a famous writer?* But she said, "Pleasure." She put out her hand.

"I'll write him a recommendation," Muriel said. "This one is a gem. If he weren't young enough to be my son, I'd chase him myself."

"I'm not young enough to be your son," Lief said. "In fact, in the years I've known you, you've dated men younger than I am!"

"Sh," Muriel said. "I don't want Walt to know too much about my shady past."

"Too late for that," Walt said. "Nice to meet you both."

"Join us," Lief invited. "I want to hear everything you've been doing."

Kelly was mesmerized by Muriel's update about films she'd done since Lief's, both nominated but not winners, and her attempt at retirement near where she grew up—a place she could keep her horses, do some riding and get in some duck hunting with her Labs. Kelly heard about Walt's army career and family. And then, thank God for Walt—he asked about Lief's work. Kelly had realized she knew terribly little about it because of her assumptions and his downplaying of his importance in his field.

"I've been writing or attempting to write since junior high and finally settled on screenwriting, moved to L.A., got work building sets while I took some courses at UCLA and wrote a little."

"And wrote a blockbuster called *Deerslayer* that took six academy awards," Muriel said.

Deerslayer? Kelly thought. She'd heard of it; never seen it. But the movie, at less than ten years old, was already a classic.

"I don't think I know that film," Walt said. "Chances are the army didn't ship us that one in country…"

"It's a brilliant retelling of The Prodigal Son or James Fenimore Cooper's *Deerslayer,* or both," Muriel explained. "A teenage boy is angry with his parents because they have to put down his horse, runs away from the farm, gets caught up with a militant group of anti-government isolationists who are at odds with the Feds and has to be rescued by the family who won't stop believing in him. The boy is caught in the middle. Everyone is in danger. It's the most touching film!"

"A little coming of age, family kind of thing?" Kelly heard herself say to Lief. She had so much to learn about him. No one seemed to notice her awe.

"Lief, I've asked Sam to come for a visit, do a little riding and hunting, and he's threatened to accept. I'm going to call him and tell him you're here—that might get him to commit."

"Tell him I have room for him if he can't take much more of you," Lief said jokingly.

"Sam?" Kelly asked.

"Sam Shepard," Muriel said. "He was in the film with me, my counterpart. He's a brilliant writer himself and kind of mentored Lief."

Lief covered Muriel's hand briefly. "He was harder on me than my father, and I still like him. But I'm not showing him any work! I've become sensitive. He's brutal."

For an hour or so Kelly just listened while Muriel and Lief reminisced. She didn't recognize most of the names of their mutual friends and colleagues, but then occasionally one would drift into the conversation that anyone would know. Jack Nicholson. Meryl. Diane Keaton.

But there was a lot of non-Hollywood talk. Lief caught them up on his family in Idaho. Muriel squeezed his hand and asked how Courtney was doing, and Lief said, "Okay, but just okay. Getting used to the idea that she's stuck with me hasn't been easy on her."

"She's lucky, that's what," Muriel said.

"I don't know about that, poor kid…" Lief replied.

I told the man everything in the world about me, knowing so little about him. I was hoping we'd have a meaningful relationship because I've been hungry for that without remembering that this is a real man with a deep and complicated life.

She'd asked a few questions, but accepted his

superficial answers happily. *Because I was more concerned about protecting myself without even considering how vulnerable he might be.*

While they talked and laughed, while Muriel and Walt raved about her bisques and asked where they could get more, Kelly kept stowed inside that there was so much she wanted Lief to tell her. No one noticed that she was quieter than usual because Lief and Muriel were having a reunion. And then when lunch was finished and it was time to carry on with their plans, they all hugged and promised to get together very soon, at the pumpkin patch open house for sure.

The next stop was Connie and Ron's Corner Store right across the street, where she found Connie thrilled to be able to stock some of Kelly's offerings. "Since it's not on my inventory, I'm sure I can't afford it," Connie said.

"No problem. It's all yours if you'll just display some of this stuff and ask for some feedback. That would be so helpful. I know the women around here are fantastic cooks—I'd love to know how I measure up."

"I have to give you something if it sells," Connie insisted.

"A donation to finance new jars would be helpful," Kelly said. "And when the soups get close to their expiration date, either enjoy them or give them to Preacher. They're all natural, no preservatives, and won't last long. Maybe you have hunters or fishermen looking for something to warm up."

"Maybe," Connie agreed. "We'll see how it goes!"

When they were back in Lief's truck, he took her hand. "I want to show you where I live," he said. "Can you take a detour by my house on the way home?"

She turned to him and said, "Oh, Lief, we have so much to talk about."

He lifted his eyebrows and looked a little surprised. "Like?"

"Like this life of yours that I haven't really known about."

"I kind of liked that you didn't know the public part," he said. "You know—that exploited part—the conjecture on who's seeing who, who's divorcing, who's the next Oscar bet. But of my real life? I'll tell you anything you want to know."

"Then let's go see where you live. And have the conversation we should have had a couple of weeks ago."

Lief's house was utterly beautiful. Now that Kelly knew a little more about his background, this came as no surprise; he must certainly have a good income. It was new, spacious with high, open-beam ceilings, was tastefully decorated and, the real selling point for her, had a wonderful, big kitchen.

After a brief tour, they sat at the kitchen table with coffee. She asked him how he grew up.

"A fairly poor farm kid who read James Fenimore Cooper?"

"We were pretty well-educated farm kids," he said with a smile. "The schools were good. And my folks were strict. That little Amber who Courtney is hanging with these days? Her folks remind me of mine in some ways. They're pretty simple people, who know the value of an A."

"Why did you want to be a writer?"

"I don't know. I liked to do a lot of things, but when I had my nose in a book or when I was scribbling out a completely made-up story, I'd get a little lost. If no one could find me, I'd be up in the hayloft with a book or a notebook. I'd go to a different place in my mind. Maybe my real life just wasn't interesting enough for me. My older brothers thought I was a complete geek and never shut up about it. I also played football, did farm chores, rode my horse, hunted, fished… But I wrote when I was alone because it felt good. I thought I was going to write novels, but eventually movies got my attention and I decided I liked film. I think it's all the dialogue. I like to listen to the way people talk to each other. What made you want to be a chef?"

"Nana," she said. "Jillian was five and I was six when our family was in a bad car accident. My dad was killed and my mother was disabled and confined to a wheel-chair for the rest of her life. My great-grandmother took us in. Now, we *were* poor—sometimes desper-ately poor. Nana knew how to make it—she gardened, canned, could turn beef rough as old shoe leather into something you could cut with a spoon, she cooked like a genius… She also ironed and did laundry for neigh-bors, anything that would keep the wolf from the door. She was our mother's caregiver, but we all helped with everything—we were a team. All that, along with Social

Security, not only got us by, she managed to save a little for emergencies. Jill loved the garden, hated the kitchen. I loved the kitchen."

"Hate the garden?" he asked.

"I like the selection of food. At *La Touche* we had vendors we ordered from, but I liked to go to the dock to select the fish, go to specialty markets for some of our produce, go straight to the butcher for meat. I don't have much interest in growing it, just using it. I can alter the outcome of everything with the pinch of one spice, the addition of one herb."

"You have a gifted palate."

"Sensitive palate. I know because I test it against the palates of other tasters. I listen. I experiment. What was once survival is now art."

He smiled as though he knew.

"Oh, boy," she said. "Tell me about *Deerslayer.* I think there's some history there…maybe survival to art…"

"It might be me spinning gold out of straw," he said. "Country kids rarely have it easy. I resented that until I was at least thirty—that nothing was ever given to me. Everything came so damn hard. I hated that the only way I could play football was if I used my older brothers' gear—I was the third one to use the helmet, pads, even the nut-cup. Do you have any idea how beat-up that stuff was? My dad said, 'Guess you'll have to play real good then since your gear ain't so fancy.' I was kind of scrawny and asked for a weight set Christmas after Christmas, birthday after birthday. And one year my dad said, 'Lief, got you a weight set—follow me.' He had just gotten a hay and firewood delivery—he told me to stack it all in the barn. Before dinner."

She laughed at him; she imagined he must be gifted because listening to him tell a story was wonderful!

"I wrote about those things in my classes at UCLA. I was working as a builder, writing at night, taking classes on film, writing and production. I wrote about putting down a dog when she had a run-in with a piece of farm equipment and lay whimpering..."

"Aw," Kelly said. "Did you take her to the vet?"

He shook his head. "We didn't have time or money for vets unless the family livelihood depended on that animal, and my dog was suffering. I had to do it. And then there was my horse—he'd been my horse since I was about eight and I was sixteen when he tore a tendon and went lame. My dad tried a lot of home remedies, even called the vet for that one, but we didn't do expensive surgery on leisure animals. It was a major indulgence to have that gelding in the first place. But he did splurge and have the vet put him down. I ran away, I was so pissed. But once I got cold, lost and hungry, I headed home. My dad found me when I was about halfway home. He'd come looking for me. And my dad said something like, 'Look, Lief, I'm sorry life is hard. I wish to God it wasn't.'"

"*Deerslayer?*" she asked.

He reached for her hands. "It started as a short story, like the football gear, the dog, the weight set. I was taking a class from a writer who told me my writing was good but quaint. He asked me if I wanted to tell quaint, down-home Americana stories, because if I did, that was all right. Someone might even film it. Or I could ratchet it up, try to capture some experience and emotion that would take that kid's experience to the next level. I experimented—I tried having him snatched by aliens... I liked that one," he added, grinning. "Then I had him accidentally kill his brother... I think I was pissed off at one of my brothers at the time. Finally I came up with an idea that I thought might work—an innocent but dangerous involvement in a militant anti-government group that rescues the runaway, then flips him against his roots, then puts him in the middle and uses him against the Feds. And he has a family who wants him back—a family on no one's side—not the isolationists' or the Feds'. Just the kid's." He shrugged. "I guess it worked."

Her mouth hung open. "How did you come up with this idea?" she asked.

He leaned toward her. "Local color and imagination. Kelly, where do you think Ruby Ridge is?"

"So what are you doing these days instead of writing?"

"Lately I've been watching someone cook," he said with a smile. Then he grew more serious. "And I've been focused on Courtney... And thinking. Sometimes the hardest work I do doesn't look like writing. You know, there were so many times I wished Courtney could experience some of the challenges I had but not quite as hard. I wouldn't want her to have to put down a pet—that's just awful. But maybe if she didn't have the best of everything, maybe that would help her in ways I can't help her. But I *never* wanted her to suffer like she has since she lost her mom."

"I'd like to hear more about Courtney's mom," Kelly said.

But the phone rang and Lief stood to answer it. "Maybe later," he said.

"Lief!" Courtney said in an almost desperate whisper. "I have to go home with Amber! I have to!"

"What's wrong, Courtney?" he asked, frowning.

"Amber called home a while ago. The puppies came! They're *here*! I *have* to go home with her! We'll ride the bus!"

He chuckled. "I thought something was wrong."

"Can you pick me up later? Like around nine?"

"Eight," he said.

"Eight-thirty! I'll do my homework! Please!"

"I'll be there."

He turned to look at Kelly. "It happens Courtney is going to be busy tonight."

Lief might've been hoping for a close encounter with Kelly, but he wasn't entirely disappointed with what he got. She was cooking for Jill, Colin, Shelby and Luke, so she was more than happy to include Lief. And luckily for Lief, Shelby and Luke had a baby in tow, making it their preference to keep earlier hours. By eight Lief was on his way to the Hawkins farm.

Sinette let him in the front door. "Gelda and family

have taken up residence in the mudroom, Lief," she said. "Right behind the kitchen."

"What have you done to me, Sinette?" he teased.

"If Hawk doesn't get that dog fixed, I might be fixin' him! Nine this time. And I swear to God, I think they're half wolf!"

"Gelda's not the best planner, I guess," he said. "Maybe some old wolf snuck up on her."

"I doubt he had to sneak," Sinette said, walking away from him toward the kitchen.

There was the sound of hushed voices coming from inside the mudroom, the whisperings of children. He stood in the frame of the door and saw that Amber, Courtney and even Rory were sitting on the floor, cuddling brand-new puppies. Rory's wheelchair was pushed off to one side. They all looked up at him at the same time.

Courtney held a little blond pup close to her chin. "This one is mine," she said vehemently. "His name is Spike."

"Spike?" Lief said, trying not to laugh.

"He'll grow into it," she said confidently, gently putting him back in the box. "Seriously, he's mine."

"We'll talk about it," Lief said. "We're gonna have to get going, Court. Did you get that homework done?"

"Pretty much," she said.

Courtney lifted the puppy from Rory's hands to return it to Gelda's brood. Then Lief watched in wonder as Courtney stood and gently pulled Rory upright. Rory hung on around Courtney's neck while she maneuvered him into his wheelchair, propped his feet on the bottom and ruffled his hair. He was almost as big as she was. Or, Courtney was almost as small as Rory.

He felt his eyes sting. That was his girl—kind and loving. Generous. Sometimes he missed her so much.

"Ready?" he asked.

"Let me get my stuff out of Amber's room. Be right back."

Lief wandered back toward the living room where he found Hawk and Rory's dad playing a little cribbage by the front window.

Without looking up from his game, Hawk said, "Your daughter won the bet on how many pups."

"Is that so? What did she win?"

Hawk looked up briefly, a lopsided smile on his face. "The pups."

Lief laughed. "You're a real pal."

Then Courtney was beside him, jacket donned and backpack slung over one shoulder. "'Kay," she said.

"'Night, Peacock," Hawk said, still concentrating on his game.

"'Night, Hawk. Thanks for dinner."

"Always a pleasure, Peacock. You take care."

Seven

Jillian and her assistant Denny were tilling a half-acre plot on the west side of the Victorian, getting it ready to mulch to prepare for a spring planting. Jillian was handling the gas-powered tiller while begloved Denny was behind her, removing large rocks from her wake. Even in the chilly October morning, they were both sweating.

When she got to the end of a row and turned, she noticed Colin was standing at the garden edge. He'd taken quite a hike from the house to get here, so thinking it must be important, she went to him.

"I thought you were painting," she said.

"I am. I was. Listen, something strange is going on in the house. Kelly's loft is above the sunroom and there are sounds. At first I thought she was singing in the shower or something. But then I thought maybe she was crying."

Jill lifted an eyebrow. "Are you sure Lief isn't in the

house? Maybe they're doing something that sounds like singing or crying..."

Colin was shaking his head. "Nope. I even looked around outside for a car or truck. Should I just stay busy for a while and ignore it?"

"She said she had something to do this morning, but she didn't say what... I just assumed she'd be busy in the kitchen."

"Whatever it was, I think it made her cry. A lot."

"Well, maybe I better check on her, make sure nothing is seriously wrong. Maybe they had an argument or something."

"I was hoping you'd do that."

"Why? Are you worried?"

"Not so much that, but I was hoping you'd drive me back to the house in the garden mobile. I'll stay on the porch until you investigate."

Jillian was actually surprised that, by the time she was climbing to the third floor, there were still sounds of sniffles and whimpers. It made her a little scared; Kelly was not known for crying. Halfway up the staircase she stopped and knocked on the wall. "Kell?" she asked.

"Hmm?" Kelly responded, then she blew her nose.

"Can I come up?"

"Uh-huh," she said with a loud sniff.

She found Kelly sitting on her sofa, box of tissues by her side, a bunch of wadded-up tissues on her little side table.

"Honey!" Jill said. "What in the world is the matter?"

"The movie," she said, pointing a tissue-filled hand toward the TV screen. "The one Lief wrote and won an Oscar for! Oh, my God, it's so *sad!*"

Jillian kind of slumped onto the couch beside her. "Lief won an Oscar?"

"Uh-huh. I just found out yesterday. I didn't even have time to tell you about it—the kitchen was full of people last night, including Lief." She gave her nose another blow. "It was really something. We took all my stuff to the bar to give to Preacher and who do you suppose we ran into but an old friend of Lief's—Muriel St. Claire, the actress. She was in the movie and she lives here now! And she said she's invited their other old friend to visit—Sam Shepard. Lief is famous."

Jillian shrugged. "I've never heard of him…"

"Well, you've heard of Muriel and Sam, I trust!"

"Oh, yeah. But I barely know who famous actors are, much less writers. In fact, I can barely name two directors."

"Me, either. Oh, Jill, this movie is just amazing! He's brilliant."

"And did they talk about movies and famous people the whole time?"

"Just a little. Mostly they talked about dogs, duck hunting, fly-fishing and what's so perfect about Virgin River—basically that it's woodsy and rugged. Would you have taken Muriel St. Claire for a hunter?" She shook her head. "Shew."

"What's the movie about?"

"I don't know how to explain it. A sixteen-year-old boy runs away, gets caught up in the middle of an FBI and ATF raid, gets rescued by his family… It's kind of like *Old Yeller* meets *Witness*."

"There's a dog and the Amish in it?"

"A horse. And no Amish either, but a bunch of good-hearted, hardworking country farmers with a lot of courage and faith and family commitment. You and Colin can watch it if you want—I begged a copy from Lief so I could see what he was talking about."

"And do you see?"

A big tear rolled down her cheek. "I see we have absolutely *nothing* in common! He's a brilliant writer who knows a bunch of brilliant movie stars and I barely read! I haven't been to a movie in so long, I can't remember the last one."

"Didn't seem like that was required," Jill said.

"I could see why Luca was attracted to me and vice versa—it's all that kitchen and food stuff. I can't imagine what Lief would see in me—I don't know anything about what he does."

Jill smiled. "But you've figured out he does it very well."

"So?"

"What do Colin and I have in common? I grow vegetables and he paints. But I love watching him paint. I'm so impressed by his art. And I catch him looking out the sunroom window all the time, or sitting on the back porch waiting for me to come in. I think you should tell

Lief the truth—that you're amazed and impressed and even a little intimidated."

"He did say he likes to cook but wouldn't be brave enough to cook for me..."

"There you go!"

Kelly gave her nose a final blow. "I have to go see Lief. Then I'm going to the farmers' market. I'll be home in time to throw something in front of you for dinner."

Lief wasn't expecting anyone, and certainly not Kelly. It had been exactly one day since he'd shown her where he lived. A phone call, maybe. But when he opened the front door, there she stood on his porch.

"You didn't tell me it was so *sad!*" she said. She looked him up and down. He was barefoot and bare-chested, his hair damp, a towel looped around his neck. And oh! What a hunk! She should have expected that mat of blond hair, the broad shoulders. But those muscles? Much more defined than she'd expected. "Uh-oh. Did I get you out of the shower?"

He pulled the door wider. "I was out. What are you doing here?"

"I watched your movie this morning. It was so sad, I had to talk to you! Every thing or person I really got attached to dies in that movie! And that was based on your own childhood...?"

"Well, very loosely," he said.

"You killed off your father!?" she said with a sniff.

"Not actually my father, but the father in the script. Sam Shepard. Come in, Kelly."

"I'm on my way to the farmers' market, but I have to know about this." She allowed herself to be pulled inside. What she wanted was for him to take off his pants so she could fill her eyes with the rest of him. But what she said was, "Do you want to find a shirt?" And then she fanned her face with her hand.

He grinned at her. "Sure," he said. "Give me a second."

She didn't move from just inside the door. When he came back, she said, "What did your family think of that movie?"

"Well, my mother called it pap, except the part where the mother is played by Muriel St. Claire and the father by Sam Shepard. But she didn't like being widowed so young. My dad, on the other hand, thought it was awesome. He said he hopes he goes out in a hail of bullets like Sam did rather than eighty-five years old and face-down in a potato patch." Then he smiled.

"That movie almost killed me," she said. "I sobbed for an hour!"

"You liked it," he accused.

"I don't know. It's going to be a long damn time before I watch another one of your movies! I'm going to need a better briefing before I do." She sighed. "I think I might have PTSD."

He chuckled. "It was hard to write, too."

"Did you cry while you wrote it?"

"I got a little choked up, but when I started feeling it, I thought I'd hit a home run. That's what I was looking for. Will you please come inside?"

She just stood there. "Was it that hard to be you, when you were sixteen?"

"I think it's hard for everyone to be sixteen." He pulled her into his arms. "You know what? When I feel you against me, I get a little drunk." His hands were running up and down her back, his chin balanced on top of her head. He inhaled the pure scent of her hair. "You feel so damn good. You smell like heaven."

"We have nothing in common. Nothing."

"I think we have a lot in common. I like to hold you like this, you like being held like this. You like to cook, I like to eat. The movie business, who cares? You don't have to watch 'em. You and my mother can sit on the porch and snap beans or something while I watch with my dad, who hopes to go down in a hail of bullets."

"I don't think I'm going to get over it very soon. I'm emotionally damaged."

"We'll make out awhile and you'll feel better."

"You know, Lief—I think we're making a big mistake here. We shouldn't get involved—this isn't going anywhere. I have to get a job, and there's no job here. You have to get your family life in order and write more devastating, Oscar-winning scripts that blow my mind. I don't know anything about teenagers and you have one and you're keeping me a secret from her." She shook her head. "This is all a big mistake."

"What if it's not?" he asked. "What if it's perfect?"

"Are you looking for a mother for your daughter? Because I can assure you, I'm not it. And I don't even know her!"

"Until I met you, I wasn't looking for anything at all. Since meeting you, I'm kind of looking for a girlfriend." He smiled at her. "That's all. Poor Court—I'm the only mother she's going to get, I think. But, I'm going to bring Courtney and Amber to your Halloween party. That should bring you out of the closet."

"It's not a party, it's a kind of a picnic. A pumpkin pick."

"Everyone's excited about it. I think the town sees it as a party. And I'm bringing the girls."

"What do you think the odds are Courtney will find me even tolerable?" she asked him.

"Odds are fantastic," he said. "She wants a puppy from Amber's dog's litter. She picked him out and named him. She's going to like everything about me for at least a few weeks. I'm going to take full advantage of it! Now, come on," he said, leading her farther into the house until they got to the great room. He sat on the couch and pulled her down on his lap. "Let's make out until you have to go to the farmers' market."

She let her fingertips run through the reddish-gold hair at his temples, very sorry she'd suggested the shirt. "I shouldn't stay another minute. I think you're taking advantage of my vulnerability."

"I hope to eventually take advantage of everything you have," he said. He pulled her down until they were reclining on the couch. Then he started kissing her, which he had lately become even better at. Then he began to sneak his hand under her shirt. "I have an idea," he said between kissing. "Let's let these out for a little while."

"Are we making love now?"

"Not yet," he said. And his hand found the front clasp to her bra, popping it open. First his hands and then his mouth found her naked breasts, and she not only moaned in pleasure but arched toward him. "See? Yet another thing we have in common—I love your breasts and you love that I love them."

"I thought we should talk about your movie and the implications…" she said, but she said it with her eyes closed.

"We can talk about that later. Right now I want to talk about your perfect nipples and how right they feel in my mouth…"

There was one fatal flaw in Kelly's notion to inform Lief there was no reason for them to get any closer than they were, and that was that when he kissed her and touched her, everything inside her went soft and sloppy and she wanted to take her clothes off. She hadn't gotten completely naked so far, but if he kept doing that kissing-touching thing, with the tongue and lips, it was just around the corner. After all, she hadn't been properly loved yet. And he kept promising she wasn't going to find it a waste of time. She ached for more of him.

Kelly felt a little flush, and her lips were tingling as she drove to the farmers' market in Eureka. In fact, other parts of her body were still tingly, too. He certainly was

getting good at that make-out thing. And while she was
supposed to be thinking about what she was going to
pick up at the market, instead she was thinking about
how close to him it made her feel to have cried over his
movie and then have recovered from it in his arms.

She was still surprised she'd had the willpower to
leave his house, and he'd had the willpower to let her
go.

But she needed stock. Or she couldn't cook.

It being past mid-October, the farmers' market wasn't
as crowded as she supposed it was in August when all
the produce was in, but she was surprised by what she
did find. She grabbed a wagon and started shopping.
Given the moderate weather, there were late peaches,
pears, plums and lots of lemons and limes. She was
pretty stocked up with large boxes of the fall fruits,
something that would keep her very busy with jelly and
preserves, when she was sidetracked by a woman offering samples.

Kelly stopped at the booth. "Hi," the woman said.
She lifted a plate. It was covered with crackers topped
with cream cheese and a green jelly. "My pepper jelly.
Help yourself."

Kelly took a small bite, her tasting technique. It immediately sparked on her taste buds. "Mmm! Wonderful!" she said before taking a second bite.

The woman smiled. She was about Kelly's height,
blonde and maybe early fifties. She had a lovely, welcoming smile and warm brown eyes. "Thanks. I'm
proud of it."

"It's really fantastic." Kelly lifted one of the jars. It had a nice little label, probably put together by the local print shop. *Laura's Pepper Jelly*. She helped herself to another cracker. "How long have you been doing this?" Kelly asked.

"A couple of years. I just come out twice a week. And I put some jelly at the co-op."

"Ah. Health-food co-op?"

"Right."

"What's in this?" Kelly asked.

"Green peppers, jalapeños, sugar, honey, apple cider vinegar—pretty simple, really. After I made my first batch, people started trying to buy it from me, so my husband made me some labels and told me I should sell it. Why not, huh?"

"Is it pretty complicated, selling processed food at the farmers' market?"

"Well, there are permits required—Health Department inspection, that sort of thing. Everyone seems to be trying to get that done before the market opens in the spring, so there's always a wait. This time of year it should be easy. Then the next problem is getting space."

Kelly put out her hand. "I'm Kelly."

"Laura," she said, then laughed. She held up the jar. "Obviously I'm Laura. Laura Osika."

"I was hoping to get some late organic tomatoes," Kelly said.

"Well, the co-op will have lots of organic vegetables, some local and some shipped in. But there's this stand out on Rt. 199 that's open till about five o'clock. It's run by a commercial farmer who's growing year round— all organic. Some of the best stuff I've tasted. And I'm a vegetarian. And I'm a damn good cook."

Kelly grinned at her. "Are you, now?" Then she dug around in her big shoulder bag and produced a business card. "I'm a chef and I like your jelly. Give me five. No, give me ten. And then give me a call sometime—I'd love to talk more about selling here or at the co-op. Seems like I have nothing to do but cook."

"Are you kidding? You're a chef? And you want ten of my jelly?"

Kelly chuckled. "I was formerly sous chef at a five-star restaurant in San Francisco called *La Touche*—look for it on Google it sometime. It's famous. I quit—the stress was too much. I'm going to have to find a new job, but for now I'm visiting my sister in Virgin River and canning everything I can pick, buy or steal." Kelly shrugged. "It's what I do to relax."

"Yeah, me, too."

"Oops," Kelly said, grabbing that business card back. "I forgot—I have a new cell phone." She dug around for a pen and scribbled a new number on the back of the card, handing it to her. "Cell reception in the mountains is spotty, but you can leave a message and I'll get back."

Laura was in enough shock that she hadn't bagged those ten jars of jelly. "Have you studied all over the place?"

"Culinary institutes in Paris, Italy, Spain, U.S.A. And

worked with some amazing chefs. But it takes nerves of steel—very competitive and demanding. I'd give anything to have a small restaurant that I could run *my* way."

"Why can't you?" she asked.

Kelly laughed. "Well, only because I'm not rich."

"Damn, Kelly, you shouldn't let a little thing like that stop you!"

"Why aren't you mass-producing Laura's Pepper Jelly?" Kelly asked with a lift of her brow.

Laura leaned close. "Are you kidding? I don't want to! This is a little gold mine! Best kept secret in the west— the flea markets, farmers markets and co-ops. I work three days a week for enough stock to sell for two days and I almost always sell out and my profit is a hundred percent."

Kelly looked at the jar—priced at $2.50. "It cost you $1.25 to produce this?"

Laura nodded and said, "That includes the cost of the jar, transportation, permits, memberships, licenses and booth."

Kelly nodded. "Bring it up to $2.99." Then she winked. "Better still, $3.99. You're giving it away!"

"That's what my husband says. I'll give you a call this week," Laura said, bagging up ten jars and taking twenty-five in cash from Kelly. "I think we have information to trade."

"You bet! Now I'm off to check out the co-op and that vegetable stand." She put out her hand. "Nice meeting you!"

* * *

Lief drove Courtney to the Jensen Veterinary Clinic and Stable even though she said she wasn't all that interested. "That's fine," he said as they drove. "I'd just like you to look around, meet a couple of the instructors and horses, see if it sparks any interest for you."

"But *why?*" she moaned.

"Lots of reasons, Court. Your friend Amber has animals and you seem to like being around her house—if you're going to do any riding with her, I'd prefer it if you had some lessons first. And—I talked to one of the instructors. She said nothing helps build confidence in a teenage girl like riding, like being able to control a large animal. She, Lilly Tahoma, said that's why she's teaching—when she was a young girl, it was probably the most important thing she did to help her learn responsibility, trust and commitment."

"You think riding horses is going to get me to do my homework on time?"

"No," Lief said. "I think being allowed to hang out at Amber's is going to get your homework done."

She sighed heavily. "Amber's is okay, but I don't think we're going riding. One of their horses is old and the other one is sometimes a problem. I like the dogs, though. And we're agreed, I'm getting that dog. Right?"

"I'm just about there," Lief said. "You do understand that having a dog around our house is going to be a lot different than having dogs at the Hawkins farm."

"Different *how?*" she asked.

"Well, on the farm, you tend to let 'em run loose and the big dogs train and look after the pups. They stay with the pack most of the time. There can't be any running loose outside our house—he'd get lost in a second. A lost pup ends up being dinner for some bobcat or eagle. He'll have to be watched and trained."

"Trained to do what?" Courtney asked.

Ah, Lief thought. She's never had a pet. How had he and Lana completely overlooked the importance of that? Because they were always working and traveling; pets hadn't fit into their lifestyle. "To pee on the grass," Lief said. "And to not eat the house. Puppies chew everything."

"Do you know how to train a dog to do those things?"

"It's been a while, but I think we'll manage. You don't realize it yet, how busy that puppy is going to keep you."

"Then I don't think there will be a lot of time left over for things like riding…"

"You don't have to make a decision about riding," he reminded her. "Just have a look around, talk to the trainers."

"Since we're in the truck headed there, I don't see much choice," she said.

"Good. You're catching on."

"Waste of time," she muttered.

How, Lief asked himself, *do I stay sane?* "Keep an open mind…"

When they arrived at the stable, Lief was glad to see

Annie Jensen, the vet's wife, had a couple of teenage girls on horses in the round pen. She was standing in the center of the pen shouting and pointing while the girls practiced their dressage training. There were some cones in the pen, and the girls maneuvered their mounts around them. Their backs were straight, chins up, hands gently lifting the reins. Lief was relieved to see the girls were wearing jeans and not anything as fancy as jodhpurs. There was a truck and trailer parked outside the pen, the back open and ramp down. The girls looked too young to have driven the truck, but maybe a parent brought them and their horses and was in the barn or vet's office. "Hang out here for a while, Courtney. I'm going to see if I can find Clay or Lilly."

"Sure," she said, leaning on the fence.

And as he walked away he was thinking, *Oh, man, I hope this wasn't a huge mistake.*

While Courtney watched the two girls riding in the pen she had to admit to herself it looked kind of fun, but these were older girls. Fifteen or sixteen. And she was not only just fourteen, but maybe the smallest fourteen-year-old girl in her class. There was no way she was ever getting up on one of those huge animals. She thought she might fit under its chin.

"Hi. Are you Courtney?"

Courtney turned to the voice. Coming toward her was a very small woman, maybe only a few inches taller than Courtney. She was a woman, though. Her body was full and curved while Courtney's was still straight and flat.

And she was beautiful—dark hair, tan Native American skin and the most unusual bright blue eyes. She pulled off a heavy glove and stretched out her hand. "I'm Lilly Tahoma. Your dad said he was going to bring you by today."

"Where is he?" Courtney said, looking around.

"He must be in the office. Come with me a minute—I want to show you something." And with that, Lilly turned and walked away, expecting Courtney to follow.

She was a little reluctant. But surely these people knew what they were doing and wouldn't let her be stomped to death by one of those huge beasts.

Lilly was way ahead of her, opening the door to a pen. She pulled on a dark horse's halter, leading her out of the stall. Courtney kept a safe distance.

"I'd like you to meet Blue, Courtney. Her full name is Blue Rhapsody, but I call her Blue." Lilly was stroking her nose and cheek, kissing her long muzzle. "I found her, if you can believe that. I was driving and saw her rolling around on the ground, sick. I called Doc Jensen and Clay and they took care of her, but she'd been abandoned. I was able to adopt her."

Courtney stood back about six feet in case the horse reared and began to stomp her.

"You can come a little closer. Blue might be the gentlest, most trustworthy horse in the stable. She's the one we always choose for a new rider."

Courtney took a few more steps. She looked over her shoulder to see Lief in the barn door, leaning against the frame, watching, his arms crossed over his chest. She hadn't once mentioned to him that the very idea of getting up on one of those big animals terrified her.

"She's completely docile, Courtney. Especially in the barn, with me—it's a controlled environment. Nothing here to spook her."

"How old were you when you learned to ride?" Courtney asked.

"I'm not even real sure. Very, very small. I grew up on the Hopi reservation and my grandfather put me on a neighbor's horse. We didn't have horses, but the neighbors did and they taught me to ride. Then we moved and I wasn't on a horse for years—till I was in my twenties."

"Well," Courtney said, keeping her voice down, "I've been around a horse or two, but I've never been on one."

"Are you a little uncomfortable around them?" Lilly asked.

"I would say, a lot."

"I see that as a real plus," Lilly said. "Tell you why— you're likely to pay close attention to safety, more so than some of these hotshots I teach who think they're unbreakable. And you won't have any bad habits to un- learn. You'll get it right from the start. But the most im- portant thing—when you develop your equestrian skills, you're going to feel like a goddess!" Then she laughed. "Come a little closer. Here. Touch her neck, right here. And her jaw—here. Give her a stroke. Ah.... Blue, you are the queen of the stable, aren't you?"

Courtney reached out a tentative hand. When she stroked the horse's neck, Blue nickered softly, moving her head toward her a bit. Courtney pulled back her hand, and Lilly chuckled. "Did that surprise you, Courtney? She likes you, that's all. That was a sweet, affectionate sound, like a kitten's purr. Here," she said, pulling a few carrots out of her back pocket. "Would you like to give her a carrot?"

"No. You go ahead."

"All right, watch this. I'm going to hold it way back here and stick the skinny end in and let go the second she takes it. If I were giving her a sugar lump or something small, I'd lay it in my hand and hold it out flat— we don't want to be involved with those big teeth!" The horse took the carrot and worked it around in her mouth. "Go ahead, Courtney. It'll help you bond with her a little."

"Listen…" Courtney began.

"It's okay, Courtney. You can trust me. I'd never let anything happen to you with my horse."

When Blue was done with the first carrot, Courtney fed her the second. And of course Blue took it happily and chewed it right up. But Courtney wasn't that impressed. She was still afraid of this huge horse.

But she was beautiful. She gave Lilly a nudge with her muzzle and Lilly said, "Aw, you're welcome." Then she gave Courtney a nudge, and it almost knocked her back a foot, more out of surprise than anything. Lilly laughed. "That was a thank-you, by the way."

"Yeah. Sure."

"My suggestion is that you spend a couple of hours with me in the stable. You can help me brush her, feed her, maybe turn her out. Talk to her, get to know her before we put a saddle on her for you. The next step would be you in the saddle and I'll have her on a lead. You'll be amazed how fast you get comfortable. Once you like it in the saddle, we'll advance slowly, always at your pace."

"I just don't see why it's such a big deal," Courtney said.

"Well, maybe it won't work out for you. But if it does, it can make a girl feel so powerful to be able to handle a thousand-pound animal with the slightest press of a thigh or flick of a wrist. Plus, we love getting a group of girls together out on a trail ride. Our older kids sometimes have group trail rides—boys and girls. It's a fun, healthy sport that promotes the kind treatment of animals and fair competition. It's all good," Lilly said. Then she smiled.

"I just don't…"

Courtney's voice trailed off at the sound of horse hooves pounding toward the barn. The back doors were open to the trail that led between fenced pastures and seemed to stretch all the way into the hills, and down that trail blazed a beautiful chestnut-colored horse with a blond mane and tail. And upon this horse, a beautiful boy. Man, for sure. He was lowered in the saddle while the horse charged at what appeared lightning speed.

Then the man rose upright and pulled back on the reins to slow the horse. The horse pranced a bit, turning sideways, then fell into a nice trot right into the stable doors. And the strong athletic young man leaped off, hanging on to the reins. He was also Native American, his cheekbones high, his skin beautifully tan, a long black braid down his back and his teeth so shockingly white that when he smiled Courtney almost wet her pants.

She knew her eyes were wide and hoped she wasn't drooling.

"My stepson, Gabe," Lilly said. "Gabe, meet Courtney. She's considering trying out riding—a brand-new adventure for her."

"Cool," he said. Then he looked at Lilly. "I'd get this horse a jockey and trainer, no kidding. He's unbelievable." Then he turned and led the horse away.

Courtney whirled away from Lilly and Blue and walked over to where Lief waited by the front barn doors. "I'm going to need boots," she said.

Eight

When Kelly pulled Jill's truck up to the Victorian's back porch, she saw her sister sitting in one of the chairs, all dirty and sweaty from a day in the gardens, tipping back a bottle of water. Kelly gave her a wave and began unloading from the back. She had boxes of fruit from the farmers' market, bags of tomatoes, onions and peppers from the roadside stand, several different jars of all-natural salsa, relish, sauces and jellies from the co-op, supplies from the grocery.

Jillian picked through one of the bags Kelly dropped on the porch beside her. She pulled out a jar of sweet relish. "Interesting shopping trip," she remarked.

"You have some late peppers coming in, don't you?" Kelly asked.

"Yep. Some very pretty, dark red, cherry sweet peppers like Nana used to grow. Yellow sweet Cubanelle, some miniature yellow bells, and pimiento that's just so sweet and nice you'll want to eat them like apples."

"Any jalapeños?"

Jill shrugged. "Not so many hot peppers, but a few. Why?"

"I thought I'd do some preserves, jellies and some of Nana's relish. With the peaches, how about some chutney?"

"Wonderful," Jill agreed.

"With the way I've taken over your kitchen, I hope you and Colin don't wake up one morning with the itch to chase each other around naked all day."

Jillian laughed. "Denny and the UPS guy should get a big kick out of that, not to mention all the other people who feel comfortable just dropping by, like Colin's brother and sister-in-law."

"I might have found a job. Sort of."

"Here?" Jill said loudly, hopefully, sitting straighter in her chair. "Here?"

"Maybe."

"What kind of job?" Jill asked excitedly. Kelly dug around in one of her bags and produced a jar of Laura's Pepper Jelly. Jillian took it from her and studied it. "She gave you a job?"

Kelly shook her head. "I bought some of her jelly at the farmers' market. She makes it in her home kitchen and sells it at the market. It's her specialty and it's wonderful. And I got to thinking—I love working in a one-woman kitchen, I have tons of wonderful recipes that were Nana's, and there are lots of places besides the farmers' market that might be interested in my goods."

"Can you just *do* that? Just make it and sell it?"

"Permits are necessary, but remember—I helped run

a very large restaurant kitchen. I know the ropes—I just have to find out what the county requirements are."

"Oh, my God! You could stay!" Jill nearly shouted.

"Okay, don't get too excited—I've been looking for something to do to justify my existence while I think about what to do next and this might be it. I'm not talking about anything permanent, but something to help me pay the rent."

"Kelly, you will never pay rent here. You're my *sister!*"

"Yeah, well, I appreciate the sentiment as much as your love and loyalty, but I really hate feeling like the poor relation. I want to pay rent—it's important to me. You must understand that."

"Maybe later," Jill said. "You have to let me give this to you for at least a little while. You'd do this for me if I needed you to. Concentrate on this project for now—we'll talk rent later. I'll start harvesting peppers for you tomorrow." Then she leaned close. "Think you can actually make money doing this?"

"Laura said it's her best kept secret—she almost always sells out and her profits are at least one hundred percent. The only problem I see is volume. I'm not sure how much I can produce or how much I can sell. The farmers' market is due to close the end of November so I'll have to find other retailers, like small groceries, delis, co-ops and places like that." She shrugged. "It's going to be an experiment."

"Man, it would be wonderful if you could stay!" She took off her straw hat and ruffled her dark hair. Then she suddenly stilled. "I have a feeling Lief wouldn't mind either!"

"Please, I've only known him a couple of weeks," Kelly said. But her ivory complexion betrayed her, and she warmed with blush.

Jillian grinned. "Hah! Look at you! You like him."

"Well, I have to like him! He hangs around all the time. I even watched his movie. But that doesn't mean he has anything to do with relishes and chutneys—that's just a way for me to keep from going back into some crazy kitchen full of insane egos. But let me tell you, that's a big thing—not making that mistake again."

Jill leaned back in her chair. "But I have to ask you— what about Luca? Is your heart still hurting?"

Kelly's eyes sparkled. "Lief has a way of driving Luca far from my memory. In fact, I find myself wondering what I was using for a brain when I thought I'd let myself fall in love with someone like Luca. All that was ever going to do was make my crazy life even crazier."

"Well, that's quite a change…"

"Is it reasonable to say that I love my work as a chef but hated my life in that dysfunctional chef's world?"

"I think you're going to be okay in this kitchen, Kell. No one around to get in your chutney."

One week before Halloween, with the help of Denny and Colin, the grounds at the Victorian had been transformed. There were bales of hay, scarecrows, construction paper bats flying in the trees. Colin had borrowed a ladder from his brother and hung a witch on a broom high in an oak tree that was resplendent with the colored leaves of autumn. He had also carved a half dozen of the odd-shaped pumpkins for the front porch, saving the big, perfect round ones for the town kids. His artist's hand had created the most fantastic jack-o'-lanterns. There were also tall, thick candles of orange and black, lanterns and baskets of fall leaves and flowers. Orange, rust-colored, dark red and yellow mums lined the walk. Denny and Jillian had borrowed an old-fashioned hay wagon from the Bristol's farm, picked a bunch of pumpkins and loaded it up.

Kelly set up her refreshment table outside, right at the base of the back porch. She had a big pot of pumpkin bisque, muffins, pumpkin pie and pumpkin bread. Right inside the kitchen there was more of everything. There were plenty of paper plates and small cups for the bisque. Jack and Preacher brought their portable barbecues and big tubs of beer and soda as they did for every town gathering. They put up a table of buns, condiments, chips, cups, plates and napkins along with a big glass jar for donations. They were very civic-minded but had a business to run and families to support.

Noon was the opening hour on a bright and sunny late-October day, and cars were pulling up the drive and honking their horns at 11:45 a.m. Kelly, who had staked out her goody stand and was ready for business, yelled into the house. "They're starting to arrive!"

Within a minute, Jillian jumped through the back door onto the porch. "Heh! Heh, heh, heh, heh, heh!" she cackled.

Kelly looked at her in shock. And then she burst into laughter.

Jill wore a black, long-sleeved shirt, a short black skirt that stuck out like a bell, red-and-white striped stockings, ankle boots and a witch's hat. Her hair was done in braids that sprung out away from her head, thanks to pipe cleaners woven in. She carried an old-fashioned broom, and when she smiled she revealed blacking on one of her front teeth.

Right behind her came Colin, dressed as a modern hunk. As in no costume at all. He crossed his arms over his chest, looked Jill up and down and chuckled, his eyes sparkling. It was very clear that she could thrill and surprise him. No matter what personality Jillian presented, he obviously thought she was adorable.

"You didn't mention you were coming in costume today," Kelly said.

"I wanted it to be a surprise!"

Jack and Preacher had their coals hot but were holding off on the dogs and burgers until they had customers. "Best-looking witch I've seen all day!" Jack yelled.

She bowed toward them. "Wait till you see my partner."

Denny walked out of the house behind her—the perfect scarecrow. He wore bib overalls over a plaid flannel shirt, a straw hat, and someone—probably Jillian—had put red lips on his handsome mouth and two round spots of rouge on his cheeks. He even had straw sticking out of his sleeves and pantlegs. Kelly beamed. "You are magnificent," she said. And no sooner were the words out of her mouth than people started coming around to the back of the house from the front drive. Whole families arrived with kids racing to the pumpkin patch.

"I hope this isn't the shortest party in history. We're going to run out of pumpkins in no time," Jill said. "We've only got about a hundred." And with that, she took off for the west end of the garden at a trot, cackling the whole way.

There was no way Kelly could have prepared herself for the way the town took over the afternoon. The party had barely started when three men who she would later learn were Buck Anderson and two of his sons came around the corner of the house leading ponies that they'd transported for rides for children. Dr. Michaels brought a big tub, and right behind him was his wife, Abby, with a big bag of apples for dunking and a set of twins scampering to keep up. Someone brought a mini-trampoline, obviously from their own backyard, and before she knew it the property was full of people. She was handing out muffins, slices of pie, cups of bisque and pumpkin bread like mad, so grateful she had a large backup supply in the kitchen.

All over the property there were clumps of friends and neighbors visiting, laughing, holding plates of burgers or dogs or muffins from Kelly's supply. Kids were quickly picking out pumpkins from the patch, running them out to the truck or car so they could come back to the party.

It was still very early in the afternoon when a ghoul came around the corner carrying a large tray covered with caramel apples. Behind the ghoul was a man carrying a second tray, this one covered with red candied apples.

"Laura!" Kelly said when they got closer. Her new friend from the farmers' market arrived with goodies. "What is this?"

"I never go to a party empty-handed. Caramel with chopped walnuts, candied apples with chopped cranberry—for your friends."

"You're wonderful! But you're not selling jelly today?"

"I like lots of different things. And I *love* Halloween!"

"I think all these people do," Kelly said, looking around and noting that while most people wore their jeans and boots, many were costumed. And bless the nice Virgin River folks who made it a party by bringing games and ponies. Balls and catcher's mitts appeared, lawn chairs came from the backs of pickups, little circles of friends settled in for an enjoyable afternoon. Preacher and Jack flipped and turned their burgers and dogs, served up soft drinks or beer, and joked with old friends. They seemed like simple, unpretentious, regular folks who liked each other and knew how to enjoy a fall afternoon together. What a concept.

Since coming here Kelly had learned what she didn't want out of life. All the fame and money she'd always thought would be the reward for hanging in there and winning the competition for the head chef slot meant nothing, not when you couldn't sleep at night and had to have an EKG to make sure you weren't dying.

But then when she stood behind her refreshment table for a couple of hours and witnessed the easy camaraderie, relaxed pace and happiness of these people, it filled her with possibilities.

She would like to live in a place like this for the rest of her life.

It was after two before she spied Lief and the girls. Kelly instantly recalled seeing Courtney when she'd visited Virgin River last summer—she was unforgettable with her multicolored hair. In fact, if Kelly hadn't known better, she'd think the girl had dressed up for Halloween. But the one thing that really affected her was how thin Courtney was. Kelly wanted to feed her.

Kelly had always been very ambivalent about having children; it was never a deep need within her. She always assumed that if she one day married a man who wanted children, she might be talked into one, but only if it didn't pull her out of the kitchen for too long. She didn't think she had any maternal instincts at all. And yet as she looked at Courtney, she felt the oddest urge to embrace her, to get her a decent haircut so she'd look like other girls her age, to plump her up so she appeared healthier.

The young teen with her, Amber, was rosy-cheeked and a bit fleshier. They *were* an odd couple, Kelly thought. What makes a teenager go to such extremes as Courtney had? Was it for attention? If so, how much more attention could Lief give her? And if Lief and Kelly actually did end up in a relationship, how in the world would she handle someone like Courtney?

"I'd better start tasting," Lief said to her as he looked away from the girls and approached. "I can't imagine all this is possible with a couple of average-sized pumpkins!"

"You're going to be very impressed. Let's start here," she said, ladling some of the thick cream soup into a paper cup and garnishing it with a parsley sprig. "You know how long a pumpkin stays fresh? Forever, that's how long. My great-grandmother used to leave a couple on the vine as long as possible, at least until there was a danger of frost damage. Then she'd put them in the cool, dark cellar..."

"Let me guess. This isn't pie filling out of a can?"

"I beg your pardon. I rarely *ever* open a can! I steamed and pureed."

He smiled, swirled it to study the texture, then took a little sip. His eyes grew round. "This is amazing!"

"That soup is not pumpkin pie in a bowl, sir," she said.

"It is not," he agreed, finishing his small cup. "Kelly, you have such a gift."

"I do, don't I?" When he pitched the paper cup in the large trash can beside her table, she said, "Now the pie. I don't very often try to improve on my grandmother's recipes, but I did have a pumpkin pie I liked better than hers. That sort of thing rarely happened," she said, wedging him out a very thin slice.

"Come on," he complained.

"Lots of people here today, Mr. Holbrook," she said, giving him the slice.

He took a bite with the plastic fork. Again he made an ecstatic sound, and his eyes rolled back in his head. "That's no ordinary pumpkin pie!"

"It's more of a pumpkin cheesecake."

"Please, please, please marry me!"

She laughed. "We'll have to get permission from your little goblin," Kelly said.

"We better hurry while she's still sucking up for a puppy," he said between bites.

"I want to stuff her with muffins," Kelly said.

"Rest easy," Lief said. "Her mother was very slight. I think Courtney is going to be a late bloomer, height-wise."

"Is she a picky eater?"

"Pretty much," he said, biting into a muffin and then moaning in ecstasy. After he swallowed, he said, "Fourteen. Picky everything."

And just then the teens were beside Lief. "Courtney and Amber, this is my friend Kelly."

"So, you're the girlfriend," Courtney said.

Kelly lifted one blond brow along with one corner of her mouth. "Not really. I haven't accepted that position yet, and who knows, I might not."

"Aw," Lief said under his breath.

"Here, have a muffin," she said, holding a plate out to the girls.

"What's in 'em?" Courtney asked.

"What do you like?"

"Pork chops, potatoes and gravy."

"What a coincidence!" Kelly said. "You're going to love them!"

"I think I'll pass," she said, hands going behind her back.

Amber plucked one right off the plate and took an immediate bite. "Mmm," she said. "Very good. Thank you."

"You're so welcome. Want to try some pie?" Kelly asked Amber.

"Yes, please." And to the pie, Amber also said, "Mmm."

"I'm getting a hot dog," Courtney said, turning from them to patronize Preacher's barbecue instead.

Kelly had the brief thought that if Courtney decided to dunk for apples, she might hold her head under water. Just for a while. Then she cringed to think she could match the kid for meanness.

Amber finished her pie and pitched the paper plate in the trash. "Thank you," she said. "Nice meeting you."

"And nice meeting you, Amber," Kelly said. And when they were both out of earshot, Kelly turned to Lief. "That went well."

He just laughed and shook his head.

"Was that Courtney finding me tolerable?"

He chuckled some more.

"What are you grinning about? That was borderline rude!"

"I'm sorry," he said. "Nothing can put me in a bad

mood today. Courtney is spending the night at Amber's so she can bond with her puppy. She'll probably sleep on the mudroom floor next to the litter box, but I don't care. I'm going to take them out to the farm, drop them off and come back here. And stay very, very late. Like a grown-up."

"Oh," she said with a smile and tilt of her head. "I see."

Kelly had thought they'd surely run out of pumpkins, but there were even a few left behind. Many of the families who came had their own pumpkin patches, but didn't want to miss a party. Everyone took away their stuff, from barbecues to ponies, as the sun was setting. Kelly cleaned up her kitchen with Lief's help, Jillian changed out of her kinky witch's garb, Denny changed clothes and headed out for a date, and Colin made sure all the trash was in the back of Preacher's truck to be taken to the Dumpster in town. Keeping garbage away from the bears was a matter of importance.

When the fall weather had started to cool and the leaves had begun to change, Colin had bought a small portable fire pit with a dome-shaped screen top. It wasn't exactly big enough to keep people warm, but the ambiance was nice. He set it up for Lief and Kelly, but, pleading exhaustion, he and Jillian headed for the second floor. "If you want to stay outside, light the Duraflame I put in there. I'm shot. I'm going in," Colin said.

"Going to bed?" Kelly asked.

"I'm probably going to the sunroom to put on the TV where I'll fall asleep in fifteen minutes…"

"And then I can wake him and steer him to bed," Jill said.

"I like the idea of a fire," Kelly said. "Lief?"

"Let's do it," he said, setting the Duraflame alite.

They brought a couple of chairs off the porch into the yard, placed them very close to each other and snuggled up in front of the fire.

And talked.

The conversation began with Kelly saying, "I'm kind of alarmed by how awful I was with your daughter. Not *to* her, *with* her. I have no idea how to communicate with a fourteen-year-old."

"Don't overthink it—she was rude. She's often rude, and while there might be a million logical reasons, she pisses me off all the time. You didn't do anything wrong."

"But how do you deal with it?"

"Many ways. Sometimes I get angry. Sometimes I'm very logical and enforce the consequences. Today, while we were in the car, I merely mentioned to her that I noticed and it didn't make me feel very good. And God bless Amber, who piped up and said, 'Really, Court, you could be nicer.' I also have her talking to that counselor, taking riding lessons, spending time at the Hawkins farm where, apparently, she's charming, and—believe it or not—we're actually making progress."

"Oh?"

"Seriously. She's brought her grades up a little. A

puppy and riding lessons depend on it. Plus, in helping Amber with her math, they've been working on homework together. It might be hard for you to imagine, but Courtney is very intelligent. Up until her mother died, she was always in accelerated programs. And every day wasn't Halloween."

"I think I get everything but the riding lessons," Kelly said.

"Well, I had a horse…."

"Yes, I know. It led to your father, Sam, going down in a hail of bullets…"

He chuckled. "Yes, I lost my horse to an injury, everything else in the *Deerslayer* story was pure fiction. But riding can be so good for a kid. I tried to convince Court to just check it out, just see if it could appeal to her, with the secret hope that it might give her something that would take her from grief and anger to confidence and responsibility. But, as it turned out, my idea didn't sway her at all. However, the instructor's stepson, about eighteen years old with broad shoulders and a braid down his back to his waist, appeared at the stable and Courtney decided she'd give riding a shot."

Kelly laughed. "So under it all, a normal girl."

Lief put his arm around her shoulders. "That's what I'm hoping."

"I bet you were hoping I'd know exactly what to say to a surly fourteen-year-old with hair in several colors…" Kelly said.

"Well, I don't, that's for sure," he admitted.

"I hope you're not too disappointed…"

He grabbed her chin in his thumb and finger, turned her face up and looked into her eyes. "Nothing about you disappoints me, Kelly. I wasn't attracted to your mothering skills."

"Lucky for you. I don't have any."

"That's not what I'm after. I'm not looking for someone to take care of Courtney for me—I'm going to do the best I can with that. In fact, I wasn't after anything. You took me by surprise. I saw you and something started to happen to me..."

"Yeah, and I started to pass out on the bar and needed help getting home..."

He smiled at her. "I've been off the market a long time, so it was unexpected, but the minute I saw you I needed to kiss you. When Colin lifted you out of the truck to carry you upstairs, I wanted that to be me. You turn me on like mad. And I know I have a lot more on my plate than you ever bargained for, but try to remember it's *my* plate, not yours. Now, I don't get many nights off and I don't want to spend this one grousing about my teenager." He took a breath. "Come home with me."

She was shocked. "But what about...your *teenager!*"

"She can't drive. The Hawkinses wouldn't leave her on the doorstep if she needed to come home—they'd call me. I'd go get her. Go write a note to Jill. Come home with me."

"Seriously? Because I'm not sure I'm ready for that. Quite yet."

"I was sure the minute I met you."

Oh, she wanted to. She knew what it was like to be off the market, too—it had been a couple of years that she'd been unable to see anyone but Luca in her vision. And she felt the pull with Lief. Like him, she'd felt it almost immediately. It would feel so good to slip into his bed, feel his arms around her, experience him. She had the craziest idea that with him she wouldn't feel she'd just wasted her time… But…

"I'm sorry, Lief. That's not going to happen tonight…" She took a breath. "And believe me, I *am* sorry…"

He kissed her brow. "Just not ready yet?"

She shook her head.

"I think I could get you ready…" he said, kissing the corner of her mouth, her neck, her ear.

"I'm not really old-fashioned, either. And I'm not going to kid you—you're very tempting. But my life is a little unsettled now. And yours isn't exactly—"

He tightened his arms around her. "I know. It's cumbersome. It is what it is. I'm not going to apologize."

"Then you'll understand this," she said. "Before I find myself in love with you, I'd better make sure I'm up to it."

"Perfectly understandable. Maybe I should have waited, too."

"Waited?" she asked.

"To fall in love."

Nine

Kelly was up long before the sun, burrowed into the kitchen, chopping, dicing, cooking, boiling jars. Thinking.

Jillian was an early riser, and by the time she came into the kitchen, there were already two dozen filled canning jars lined up on the counter and another large pot simmering with a new batch. Jillian looked in the pot. "Nana's peach chutney?" she asked.

"And spicy peach and tomato," Kelly said.

"Good lord, what time were you up?"

"I'm not even sure. At least three hours ago." She gave her pot a hearty stir.

"Did Lief leave right after Colin and I turned in last night?" Jill asked.

"No. He stayed late. We pulled a second Duraflame out of the shed."

"And you've been awake for hours? What's up with that?"

Kelly looked at her sister and shook her head. "I didn't

sleep well at all." She banged the spoon on the side of the pot, laid it in the spoon rest and leaned against the counter. "I always saw myself as a good planner. Real sensible and logical and not overly emotional."

"Pragmatic, I would say," Jill agreed. "But sensitive. You're very sensitive, Kelly. What's the matter? Did he hurt your feelings?"

She shook her head again. "He told me he loves me."

"Get out!" Jillian said. "Love? Really, love?"

"What a fool, huh?" Kelly asked, wiping her hands on a towel. "He must be crazy."

"Well... I wouldn't call him a fool. I'd just call him quick and to the point. And obviously someone who doesn't need a lot of time to know what he wants..."

"Honestly, my ridiculous romantic situations lately make your romantic foibles look like kid's stuff."

Jillian perched up on one of the stools at the workstation. "I've given all that up since I met Colin. He is my last impulsive act." Then she smiled sentimentally.

Kelly took the chair opposite her sister. "Do you have any idea how long it's been since I had a real boyfriend? I mean, a reasonably available, totally single, relatively normal boyfriend? Over two years and that was a brief one. Since then I've fallen in love with a married man with five grown kids and the wife from hell and a single father with one of the most...*interesting* teenage daughters I've ever met."

"At least you didn't sleep with the married man..."

"I haven't slept with the single father, either! And

trust me, I'm not feeling any more calm because of that decision!"

Jillian smiled. "Love talk didn't lead to sex talk?"

"No," Kelly said, clearly disappointed. "I couldn't let that happen. I don't think I'd better get any closer to him right now. He has a complicated life. Issues with his daughter."

Jillian grinned. "I met her. She liked my costume."

Kelly lifted a brow. "Did she ask you to black out a tooth for her?"

"Hey, I liked her." Jill laughed. "She's a smart aleck."

"Well, clearly you're no threat to her. She wasn't all that nice to me."

"Oh, that'll probably pass. When she gets used to you."

"Jill, yesterday was pivotal for me in some ways. While we were hosting the town I fell in love with Virgin River. A person just won't grind their molars flat in a place like this—there are too many good souls around to shore you up, lend a hand, make you laugh, make you feel like an important part of something. And here's a perfect man, too—gorgeous, sexy, sincere, strong and *ready*. But I'm not equipped to take on a teenage girl who lives to press the edges of the envelope. And no one takes on Lief without taking on the daughter. She wasn't dressed up for Halloween, you realize. That's her look!"

Jill laughed. "What about the dad?"

Kelly thought for a moment. "I adore him," she said after a moment. "He's everything a woman could want in a man. And for as much as I think his daughter is too much baggage for me, I admire him so much for refusing to make her less than a priority. He's completely devoted to her. And not out of some weird obligation—he really understands what she might be going through since losing her mother." And then she went back to stirring her pot again.

"He sounds pretty perfect."

"Yeah. Everything that makes me love him also makes me keep him at arm's length. I'm just not ready."

"And you're trying to cook your way out of it?" Jill asked.

Kelly shrugged. "That's what I do. Cook my way through the problems."

"And what are you going to do with this stuff?"

"While I'm waiting for permits and licenses, I'll keep giving it away as free samples, see if I can get anyone interested. Then when I'm legal, I'll know where to take my stock."

"Excellent idea!" Jill agreed. "Have you thought about selling on the internet?"

"I have absolutely no idea what that involves!"

"Let's look into it," Jill suggested. "Might be a good idea. If not, we move on."

"We?" Kelly asked.

Jill put her elbows on the work island and leaned toward Kelly. "I love that you're living here. I love having you use this beautiful new kitchen. I love that you can use what I can grow. We'll make a great team. The longer I can keep this little love fest going, the better I like it."

* * *

Just a few days after that conversation, Colin came into the kitchen while Kelly was up to her elbows in Nana's sweet relish. It hadn't taken her long to have a thousand jars of canned gourmet specialties stacked up and out of the way in the unfurnished dining room.

"This is just amazing," Colin said. "You're like a factory."

Kelly shrugged off the compliment. "I'm pretty efficient. And it doesn't hurt to have a nice big six-burner gas stove. While the relish simmers, I chop and mix. While the relish cools, I simmer a new batch. I probably produce over a hundred jars a day."

"Have you heard from the health department yet?"

"Yes," she said, smiling. "With the economy struggling, restaurants closing and growing in the off-season, they're not busy. I'm going to have an inspector any day now. And this kitchen is going to get an A-plus."

"And you," he said.

"I'd better. I already have my state food handler's certificate."

"I have something for you to look at." He put his sketch pad on the work island. "If I'm overstepping or none of this appeals, you won't offend me by just saying so. I was fooling around, that's all."

She flipped through the pictures with captions. "What is this?" she asked.

"Possible labels for your canned delicacies. I know—you didn't ask me to do this and I got involved on my own. But Kelly, you could use something besides a

Magic Marker. Seriously. And if you have a something in mind, just say so. I can have labels printed for you in no time."

She glanced through the pictures, from baskets of vegetables to images of her face, logos, slogans—they were fantastic. There was one that really caught her eye. On the top it said "From Jilly Farms." Right under that it said, "Spicy Peach & Tomato Chutney." On the right side was a picture of Kelly, on the left a picture of Jillian. On the bottom—"All Natural, All Organic, All Delicious."

"Where did you get the idea for this?" she asked.

"Well, Jilly trademarked Jilly Farms as well as the slogan, and the other night she said she wished she could just keep growing for your cooking—it's so much more appealing to her than shipping her produce to restaurants and delis. It gave me this idea. You might be getting some of your fruits and vegetables from other stores and farms at the moment, but it occurred to me that this was possible.... I thought maybe Jilly could one day be your supplier. Have you been out to the greenhouses lately? Because she's got a good winter crop going out there, thanks to irrigation, lights and warmers."

She stared at the label, lifted her eyes to Colin's, looked at the label again. "Colin, I love this," she said in an almost reverent whisper. Then, looking at him again, she said, "You would never get rid of me this way."

He grinned. "Pretty soon you'll have to accept the fact that no one wants to get rid of you. And I'm not exactly suffering, having you here. Besides, she has Denny to run the farm and I'm almost ready for another trip. This time I'd like Jilly to come along."

"You mean that?"

"Why not? Of course I mean it. And I can tell, you like it here."

She grinned right back at him. "God knows I love this kitchen."

By a week after Halloween, Courtney was astride a horse. Blue. She'd already learned to feed her, brush her, walk her around the pen and then the pasture. She wasn't quite brave enough to clean out her hooves or groom her tail, but she was beginning to not only trust her, but love her. And she would never admit to *anyone*—not Lief or Lilly—but being in the saddle made her feel *huge!* She'd grown so tired of feeling puny and childlike.

Gabe Tahoma had only to say, "Good job, Courtney! You're getting the hang of it!" to make her feel like Miss America.

Just a couple of weeks into November brought a slight change in her appearance. Lief had taken her to buy boots and jeans. She then needed shirts, down vests, gloves and a new jacket. He threw in a hat for good measure. Courtney gave up the black nail polish and total noir leggings, ankle boots, skirts and tight tops. She found she liked wearing jeans and boots to school. Not many of the girls dressed in that cowgirl way. They were a little less country and more into fashions they saw on internet fashion sites. Courtney found their more middle class–trendy couture far less intimidating than that Rodeo Drive stuff she'd been up against in L.A, which was a comfort.

And she was letting the color fade and grow out of her hair.

"Ach! I hate my hair!" she complained to Lief as he drove her to school one morning.

"Really?" he asked, apparently completely confused. "What in the world could you possibly hate about it?"

"It doesn't know what color it is! Letting color grow out is worse than anything! It's torture!"

"I see," he said. "Anything I can do to help with that?"

"Yes! I need a haircut! Is there anyone within a thousand miles who could give me a decent haircut?"

"Undoubtedly," he said tiredly. "I'll ask around."

Next thing she knew, she was sitting in Annie Jensen's shop in Fortuna with Annie herself caving in to not only a cut but a color that might wend her back to where she started before the pitch-black and hot pink began. She blew Courtney's hair dry into a nice, sleek, smooth and more grown-up style.

"I'm sure that's not exactly what you're after, Courtney," Annie said. "But I'm willing to keep trying."

"It's kinda…nice," Courtney said, running a hand over her hair.

"I hope it's okay…"

A couple of days later when she was at her lesson, Gabe said, "Whoa, Courtney, that's a new look for you. The hair. You're getting almost hot."

Her hand went to her hair and she blushed.

"Now, don't flirt with me," he said, laughing. "I have a girlfriend."

"I know that," she said. But of course she hadn't known about the girlfriend. What she did know was that she had an impossible crush on him, and she absolutely knew he would never *really* notice her.

But he liked the way she looked. That made her feel beyond good.

There were a few things that, slowly but surely, she began to admit to Jerry Powell. Not because he was any good as a counselor or therapist, but because she was pretty sure he was even more capable of keeping her secrets than Amber was. So when he said, "Are you building some muscle there, Courtney? Or is it just the different clothes that make it look that way?" she didn't snark back.

"I might be," she said carefully. "I can't really tell, except my muscles are *all* sore! All of them. Even my toe muscles are sore. And when I complained, Lilly said it was kind of amazing how many muscles you could use riding. Then she flexed her thigh and told me to punch it—it was like a rock! She said that right now I was likely building muscle, but one day I'd probably use riding to keep my weight down and my body toned."

"Does it feel good?" Jerry asked.

"To build muscle? No—it hurts!"

"No," he laughed. "Riding. Is riding fun?"

"Well…the riding part, sort of. A lot of it isn't such fun…"

"Like?"

"Like it's going to take me four more inches taller and twenty pounds heavier before I can get that saddle on by myself. But meanwhile, if Lilly is busy doing something else, sometimes Gabe helps. And watching Gabe put on a saddle…" She rolled her eyes heavenward.

"I take it Gabe is handsome?"

"They *named* handsome after Gabe!"

Jerry chuckled. "Are we thinking about naming boy-friend after him, as well?" he asked.

"I wish. He's eighteen, in college and has a girlfriend. But," she added, blushing slightly, "he said I was kind of cute."

Jerry lifted a brow. "Is that a fact? Did that feel good to hear?"

"Now what do you think?" she asked him. "Of course, even though it doesn't really mean anything…"

"It could mean he thinks you're kind of cute…"

"Yeah, in a little girl way. We went on a short trail ride, a bunch of beginners. Lilly, Annie and Gabe took us, except all the other beginners were little girls like in fifth and sixth grade, and I'm in high school but *look* like I'm in sixth grade!"

"Well, what did your mom look like? Was she a small woman?"

"Sort of. Not too small, but she was thin. Not skinny—just thin. But she looked like a woman!"

"Are you worried about that?" he asked her. "About looking like a woman?"

"I'd settle for looking like a freshman!"

"You know that you're not the only teenager who

comes here for counseling, right?" Jerry asked her. "You know that's my specialty, right?"

"Right," she said.

"Well, I don't think I'd be breaking any particular confidence if I told you that almost every teenager I know is unhappy with some aspect of their appearance, and also that between the ages of eleven and nineteen, sizes, shapes and other specifics vary widely. One year I had a sixth-grade client with five o'clock shadow and a sophomore client who could've been mistaken for a sixth grader. Almost to the last one, they lament that they just can't 'be like everyone else.' And none of them is like everyone else. There doesn't seem to be an *everyone else*."

"Well, from where I'm sitting, there are lots of everyone elses! And why do you use words like *lament* with me?"

He smiled patiently. "Because you know what it means."

"Are you sure?"

"Yes," he said. "Absolutely sure. Now, how are things going with your dad these days? The two of you getting along any better?"

She shrugged. "We do all right sometimes. I can tell he prays every day that I'll disappear. We have to go have dinner at his girlfriend's house tonight. He's begging me to be nice to her."

Jerry sat forward. "That statement, Courtney— he prays that you'll disappear? What makes you say that?"

"Well, I'm not what he had in mind, you know."

"Explain, please?"

She sighed heavily. "We did okay when my mom was alive. He loved my mom so much, but so did I, and she loved us both and so… Well, we had a good time together. Taking care of me without my mom around—it isn't what he thought he'd have to do."

"I'm sure," Jerry said. "Just as you didn't think you'd be living with him without your mom. But how does he make you feel he'd like you to disappear?"

"I disappoint him a lot."

"How?"

"You know how," she insisted. "It's obvious. I looked like a freak, my grades were bad, my friends were bad… I let him down. I wasn't easy."

"Was, was, was," Jerry said. "What's changed?"

"I changed my hair for one thing. You should've seen his face—he thought he'd won the lottery. I wear riding clothes because that's what I have now. That sort of thing."

Jerry's lips moved as though he tried not to smile at her. "I bet if you dug around in the closet, you could find those old Goth clothes. If you root around in the bathroom, you'll find the black nail polish and lipstick. Which leads me to a question—how long have you been Goth?"

"You act like you know what Goth is!" she said with derision.

"I know you think you're a complete original," he said with a laugh. "How long?"

"A year, I guess."

"A reaction to your mother's death?" he asked.

"I don't understand the question," she said immediately.

"Yes, you do. A reaction to your mother's death? Did your adoption of the Goth style have something to do with your mother's death?"

"Sort of, I guess…"

"You guess how?"

She looked down into her lap. "Everyone was ready for me to get over it, that she died, and I couldn't."

"Everyone?"

"Lief was getting over it—he wasn't up prowling the house all night, wasn't staring so hard he looked like a dead body. He laughed on the phone, went to meetings about his scripts. My friends at school didn't want to hang out anymore—they said I was depressing. Everyone was getting over it. But me."

"So…?"

"So I thought if I just dressed in black, in Goth, I wouldn't have to put on some show about being all happy when I wasn't all happy!"

"Ah!" Jerry said. "Brilliant!"

"Brilliant?"

"Absolutely brilliant! What a perfect solution! You know, Courtney, you are definitely not the weirdest kid who comes to see me, but you might be the smartest. You know exactly what you're doing."

"Yeah, that's what you think…"

"At fourteen, knowing exactly what you feel and why

you feel it is still a process. But you're acting on instinct to defend and protect your feelings, and that's a leap ahead of your peers."

"I'd rather be five-six and stacked," she said with a pout.

He couldn't help but chuckle. "All in good time, Courtney. I'm confident that will come. Let me get back to something important—the disappearing thing. Have you ever *wanted* to disappear?"

She shrugged and thought for a second. "Back when I was living with my real dad, Stu. Yeah, I was kind of hoping I'd just die."

"And now?"

"Oh, I don't want to die," she said. "I'd never do anything like that. I'm only a little crazy, you know."

"Actually, I don't find you crazy at all. I think you're quite stable. Now, about dinner tonight…"

"What?" she said.

"This girlfriend of your dad's…"

"Some woman visiting here from the Bay Area. Visiting for a long time, like she might even stay. She's a cook of some kind. He likes her and he really wants me to like her."

"How do you know that?"

"He said she invited us to dinner and would I please go easy on her."

"And he said that because?"

"Because when I met her at her Halloween party a while ago, I didn't go real easy on her. But she didn't go real easy on me, either. When I asked her what her muffins tasted like, she asked what I like and I told her pork chops, potatoes and gravy and she said then I'd like the muffins. Trying to trick a kid—cheap shot."

He laughed again. "Is it possible you've met your match? She might be almost as smart as you are."

"Well…"

"Can you go easy on her? Give her a chance? Find out if you actually like her before you put a curse on her?"

"What do I care?" she said with an insolent grimace.

"Just put yourself in his position. It should be easy for you—think of yourself and how much it's meant to you to have Amber as a friend, to have better grades, to have a new look that gets the attention of the most handsome guy at the stable. All that feels good, right? So if someone wanted to make enough trouble for you so you couldn't have those things, that would be very disappointing, right?"

"I don't get what you're saying," she said, because it was true.

"I'm saying that your dad—"

"Lief," she corrected.

"I'm saying that Lief has been very lonely since his wife died and it would be a good thing for him to have friends. To have an adult relationship. Just as it's good for you to have teenage relationships—boys *and* girls. It balances things out for the family."

She leaned toward him. "I don't *have* relationships with boys!"

"Maybe not yet," Jerry said. "But you wouldn't find it sporting if Lief did something to humiliate you in front of Gabe, the handsome one."

She thought about that for a moment.

"I'm just saying, don't make it impossible for Lief to have a friend," Jerry said. "He's earned it. It doesn't make you any less important to him."

She thought some more. Then she said, "And if he decides he loves her or something?"

Jerry shrugged. "So?" he asked.

"I don't want a new mother! I'll never have another mother!"

"Good terms," Jerry said, tripping her up yet again by agreeing with her. "Make those your terms. You'll be receptive and accessible and friendly—but you draw the line at having a new mother. If this woman who is having you to dinner wants to take the place of your mother, you are within your rights to tell her no, thank you. You are definitely within your rights to say you're only interested in having friends. How does that sound?"

She grimaced. Actually, it sounded very practical.

"Chances are she doesn't want to be your mother, but rather just be on good terms with you. Kind of like Amber wants to be on good terms with your dad so you two can enjoy your friendship. It's not very complicated."

After a long, thoughtful moment, Courtney said, "I think I'm being brainwashed here. I should call someone, like the police. Get deprogrammed."

He laughed at her. "So tell me about the puppy. Spike. Do you get to bring him home pretty soon?"

Kelly knew how to slip most of the bones out of a raw Cornish game hen. It had to be done the day before roasting or baking, then refrigerated, then stuffed, then baked. She pulled out the spine and ribs, but left the leg and wing bones so there was something to hold the bird together and give it shape.

She had an amazing rosemary dressing for the little birds. Because Picky Courtney was coming to dinner, she was keeping it simple—buttered peas and baby glazed carrots rather than anything as "exotic" as brussels sprouts. She'd serve appetizers, hard rolls, chopped salad and, for dessert, chocolate pie. And if the little twerp was difficult, she'd offer her a hot dog!

"I think your talents are wasted on sweet relish and chutney," Jillian said, observing the boneless hens being stuffed.

"It takes a good chef to do all these things. Sauces aren't easy, canned goods are dicey, if the flavor is going to be right. Besides, as sous chef, I was more of a supervisor than anything else. Creating a special dinner for five—it's a treat." Then she looked at Jill and said, "Help me with Courtney. Please. Especially if she likes you."

"Are you worried about it?"

"I'm worried about Lief being miserable. He gives her so much and I suspect he asks for very little in return."

"Don't worry, Kell. I have a secret weapon."

"Oh?"

"Colin Riordan, king of the wild men!"

Kelly frowned. "Okay, I'm not sure what that means, but don't hurt her."

"Promise," Jill said with a laugh.

Less than an hour later, when the sun was lowering in the sky, the table ready, Jill and Kelly on the porch with their glasses of wine, Lief pulled up. When he and Courtney got out of the truck, the sisters couldn't keep their mouths from dropping open in shock and wonder. That little stinker was *stunning!* Her hair was smooth, dark auburn and swept her porcelain jaw in a sleek wedge. Her lips were pink! Her nails were not black! And though she was tiny, she did sinful justice to a pair of tight dress jeans, shiny boots and a denim jacket.

Courtney kept her eyes averted, but Lief couldn't help smiling as he approached the ladies on the porch.

"Courtney!" Kelly said before she could stop herself. "This is a whole new you!"

Courtney merely shrugged.

"Kid, you look amazing!" Jillian said. She ran a hand over her own dark, layered locks. "Who did that? Tell me it was someone within driving distance. I have to have the name!" She looked at Kelly, smoothing her own hair along her cheek. "I could do that, couldn't I?"

"Annie did it," Courtney said. "My trainer. I mean, riding instructor. She's a beautician and has a shop in Fortuna. So you like it?"

"Like it?" Kelly said. "If I didn't have to spend an hour taming all these wild curls, I'd pay a lot of money to get that cut."

"Well, I don't," Jill said. "Can you believe we weren't adopted? One curly blue-eyed blonde and one dark horse with straight hair! I could do that cut—but I'd have to grow a lot of stuff out first!"

Remarkably, Courtney laughed. "You don't have nearly as much to grow out as I did. I mean, come on—pink, purple, burgundy and ink-black."

Kelly sat forward. "What made you do it?" she asked, sincerely curious.

"I scared the horses," she said, with a smile.

And Kelly noticed—shining, straight teeth. Underneath that scowl was a beauty. "Naw," Kelly said with a laugh. "I heard they were color-blind." She nodded at Courtney's feet. "I like your boots."

"Yeah, great boots," Jill agreed. "If I didn't have to wear rubber in the garden, I'd copy those, too."

There was the tooting of a horn as Colin came speeding up to the back porch in the garden mobile, basically a golf cart with a flatbed back that Jill and her assistant used to get themselves and supplies between gardens. He stopped right in front of Lief and Courtney.

"Hey," everyone said as he got out.

"Courtney, wanna drive?"

She was stunned silent for a minute. "Seriously?" she said.

"I have to go with," Colin said. "I mean, it's Jilly's

buggy. But you can drive as long as you're not too crazy."

"You bet," she said, jumping into the garden mobile.

Colin took a moment to show her reverse, forward, power and brakes. Then they backed away, turned around, and Courtney jerked toward the road that went between the trees to the back meadow. Then she found her comfort zone and, with a squeal, went as fast as the cart would take her.

"Can I help myself to a beer?" Lief asked.

"Of course, but what happened to her?" Kelly asked. "I almost asked where Courtney was!"

"I suspect the good-looking guy at the stable, but it could be the Hawkins family or maybe even the counselor. Who knows? Do I care? It's the first time I haven't lived with an alien in over a year. I'll be right back."

While Lief was getting his beer, Jill and Kelly watched the garden mobile disappear through the trees. Then they only heard it; they couldn't see it. After just a moment, they heard Courtney's high-pitched squeal and Colin's deep laugh. Then they heard that again and again and again as the sounds got farther and farther away. Lief was back on the porch with his beer, listening along with them. "What's his secret?" he asked Jill.

"He doesn't really care for kids that much," she said. "Therefore he doesn't treat them like kids, but rather like short adults. Seems to work like a charm."

Lief took a long pull on his beer. "Wow. I'll try to remember that."

Within a few minutes the garden mobile reappeared, running full speed toward the house on the road between the trees. Colin was leaning back, one big foot propped up on the dash, holding his hat on his head with a hand. Courtney, however, was leaning into the steering column, grabbing it with gusto, sailing past the house down the drive to the front.

Lief, Kelly and Jill burst out laughing when the vehicle had passed.

"Think she'll be willing to give it up so Colin can have dinner?" Lief asked.

"Oh, sure," Jillian said. "It won't be long now."

"How do you know? She looked pretty happy in control of that thing," Lief pointed out.

Jill tilted her head. "It's going to run out of gas. Pretty soon."

Ten

After Courtney's wild ride in a garden mobile, Kelly hosted her at three successful dinners, all within the space of two weeks. If she wasn't mistaken, Courtney was actually pleased to be there. True, she was considerably friendlier and more outgoing to Jillian and Colin, but Kelly understood that. After all, they weren't threatening her position with her father. And she was civilized, if cool, toward Kelly. She even seemed to like the meals Kelly prepared, though she had a tiny appetite.

Courtney loved the garden mobile, and she loved Colin's painting just as much. For a guy who didn't take to kids, he certainly had a way with Courtney.

Tonight would mark their fourth dinner together— the five of them. Then it was suddenly reduced to a threesome as Colin and Jillian announced last-minute plans to meet Colin's brother and sister-in-law, Luke and Shelby, at a restaurant in Arcata for a nice dinner out. Apparently Colin's mother, Maureen, had arrived early for the Thanksgiving holiday and was babysitting Luke's son, little Brett.

"Will you manage?" Jill asked.

"Sooner or later we're going to have to find out if she's going to let her father have a girlfriend." Kelly fanned her face. "My arms are aching from holding him off!"

Jill just giggled. "Good luck with that," she said.

Kelly made a decision. She'd make it one of the best dinners ever. If she was flying solo, she was going to figure out how to win Courtney over. The menu was already geared to a teenage girl's tastes—ravioli. Courtney was not impressed by her culinary achievements; in fact, there didn't seem to be anything about Kelly that impressed her.

Kelly didn't want much, nor did she expect much. They didn't have to be best friends, she and Courtney. But before she could let herself fall in love with Lief, she had to at least be on level ground with the girl.

She lit the fire in the kitchen hearth, cut some colorful mums from the front walk and put them in a vase on the table, set a beautiful table with two plates on one side and one on the other. Her place was closest to the stove and work island for convenience in serving. She warmed freshly baked bread, tossed the salad and uncorked the Shiraz to let it breathe. Finally Lief came to the back door, smiling as he let himself in.

And he closed the door behind him.

"Where's Courtney?" she asked, frowning.

"We're on our own. She's at the Hawkins farm,

helping with the puppies. Apparently mamma dog had a litter a bit too large to keep them all plump and happy and a little hand-feeding help is needed."

"Oh. Then I'll be sure you take some of this ravioli home with you."

"She's spending the night," Lief said. His eyes warmed, but his smile was devilish. "God bless the Hawkinses."

"Whooo boy," she said, a little breathless. "Well, sit down. I'll serve!" She removed the second plate from his side. First, she poured the wine. Then put the salad on the table along with the basket of bread. Then out came the ravioli in an earthen casserole dish. "The left side is three-cheese, the right side is veal."

He sat behind his plate. "And let me guess—you made your own pasta?"

"Of course," she said, sitting across from him. Then she lifted her glass and toasted, "To the puppies."

He raised his glass and met her eyes across the table. Then he put down the glass. He stood and moved his plate to her side of the table and sat down next to her. He turned in his chair so that he was facing her, then lifted his glass again. "To the most beautiful chef in the western hemisphere." And he sipped.

Then he leaned toward her slowly and gently touched his lips to hers.

He lifted her plate and served her a small portion of ravioli. "We've had a little alone time, but do you realize we've never had a meal, just the two of us?"

"I guess that's right," she said.

He took care of his own serving of pasta. "Nothing about this relationship has been exactly routine," he said. "I never gave single parents enough credit."

"Your wife was a single parent when you met her," Kelly reminded him.

"Yes, but a single parent with a babysitter!" He cut a ravioli in half with his fork, speared it and lifted it to his lips, blowing on it. Then he brought it to her lips. "Careful," he said. "I'm sure it's hot."

She blew on the veal and pasta bite, conscious that he served her with his left hand while his right rested lightly on her thigh. When she took the morsel into her mouth, he bent his head to kiss her neck. "Mmm," she hummed, and not strictly in appreciation of the food.

She returned the favor, blowing on a hot ravioli for him, smiling as he accepted it into his mouth from her fork. "Dinner is going to take forever…" she said softly.

"No, it's not," he said, spearing another bite-sized piece for her. "We probably won't even put a dent in it. Just enough time for me to tell you a few things. Like how happy I am that you walked out on that restaurant and came to the mountains." He followed the bite with the lightest of kisses. "If someone had told me I'd find a woman like you in a place like this, I never would have believed it."

"Well," she said, lifting her fork to his mouth, "I could say the same thing."

"I know I come with baggage," he said, feeding her.

"Difficult baggage. Thank you for understanding. And for trying so hard. It's going to work out, Kelly. It has to."

"How do you know?"

One corner of his mouth lifted in a half smile, and he gave a little shrug. "I'm thinking of making her a cash offer. Or maybe I could just buy her a Lamborghini?" She laughed at him, knowing he was not that kind of father at all. "I'll do anything," he said. "One more bite," he said. "Then when you've had enough, we could take this wine to the third floor." He ran his hand along her thigh to her butt. "I've never had a proper tour of the third floor."

"And what would make it proper?" she asked him, arching one brow. She tore off a small piece of bread and fed it to him.

"We could do it in the nude." He grinned at her. And he fed her a piece of bread.

"I suppose I've held you off just about long enough," she said, feeding him one more bite. But what she thought was that *she* couldn't really wait any longer.

"I sleep with you every night," he said. "It's not intentional, but it happens all the time. I can feel you, taste you, smell you. Every night, in the middle of the finest dreams a man could wish on himself, I explore every inch of you. I feel like a sixteen-year-old boy. And I can't wait to fall asleep."

She felt a zing of electricity pass through her, quivering its way down to her panties. "Do you think you can stay awake a little while tonight?" she asked in a flushed whisper.

"For the real thing? Long enough to be sure your dreams will be as sweet as mine have been?" he said.

That was all it took for her to stand up. Ready. But he pulled on her hand, sitting her back down. "I know you worked on this meal all day. We're going to put it away, then take our wine upstairs."

"Right," she said in a daze. "Right."

She slipped the main course and salad into the refrigerated drawers on the bottom of the work island while he folded foil around the warm bread. They each held a wineglass, and he grabbed the bottle, but they hadn't made two steps up the staircase before they stopped to kiss. Two more steps brought them together again. Another three steps and... "Climb!" she ordered. "We're going to be covered in Shiraz!"

He didn't move. "Not a bad idea," he whispered.

When the wine was safely sitting on the bedside table, Kelly fell with Lief onto her bed, and lying there, they worked at the buttons of each other's shirts. She laughed softly between kisses. "We feed each other, undress each other..."

"Do I need a condom?" he asked her.

"Pill," she said. "Not to mention, no man in such a long time..."

"God, what a relief," he whispered. "I have one. And I already know once isn't going to be enough."

"Promises, promises," she murmured, catching his bottom lip gently between her teeth.

He spread her shirt wide as she did the same to him. He caught the front clasp of her bra and freed her breasts, instantly filling his hands with them, then his mouth, drawing on one nipple and then the other. Kelly threw her head back and groaned in sheer delight. But her hands were already on his belt, the snap, the zipper. She was so intent on her chore she barely noticed her own pants were slipping down over her hips, and before they'd passed her knees, he had his fingers on her, slipping into the moist folds, working her until she was nearly in tears. She grabbed his wrist, stilling his hand. "Listen," she said. "I don't want to disappoint you."

"You can't, sweetheart."

"I'm not experienced. Maybe I'm the reason it always seemed like I'd been just wasting my time."

He shook his head and gave her a light kiss. "Not this time," he said. "We're going to take our time."

"Then get rid of these," she begged, pushing at his jeans. "Please!"

Lief pulled away just enough to take off his boots and jeans, then to return the favor, freed her of what remained of her clothing. But then he stopped moving. Kneeling between her legs, he could only look at her, admire her. He ran a big hand from her chest, over her belly to her velvety pubis. "I knew it," he said. "A real blonde. Real everything," he added, going after those wonderful breasts yet again. He felt her hand as she found him, grasped him, stroked him. He rose to her lips, kissed her deeply and whispered against her open mouth. "In my dreams it's always slow and careful and I make you come a hundred times before I can let myself go...."

"Don't make me wait," she begged.

"Making you wait is probably the secret weapon," he said, stroking her into a fever. "And I want points for that because I'm half-insane, needing to be inside you…"

"I don't want the dream," she said breathlessly. "I want the real thing."

He found her and entered her with great care, moving into her deeply. When she had taken all of him, she gasped. He held himself still for a moment, then lifted her legs at her knees, bending them. "You're going to help me, sweetheart," he whispered. "We're going to find that sweet spot." He pulled back just a little bit. "Come to me," he said. She pushed back against him. "Ah," he said. "That's my girl. You know what you want…" She dug her heels into the bed and answered him, thrust for thrust. He plunged himself into her again and again. She pulled him in, rising against him. And he pushed and pumped. Then he slipped his hand between them, stroked her even as he rode her, and her moans turned to urgent cries. He braced one hand on the bed and worked his magic with the other while she raked her nails down his back, grabbing his butt and pulling him into her harder, faster. A low growl escaped him as he worked her body feverishly, their hot and wet union making her gasp for breath and hold on to him as though she'd never let him go.

Then he felt it. She half rose against him, her eyes wide, her lips parted, her breath caught. He could feel the shattering orgasm grip her, and he covered her open mouth with his, pushing his tongue inside as he delved as deeply as he could into her, rocking her, completing her, finishing her. Then he'd reached the limit of his endurance and let himself go, pulsing in a powerful blast that let him empty himself inside her. Their groans mingled in each other's mouths. Their climaxes blended inside their bodies, and it lasted longer than anything he could ever remember. And it left them weak, satisfied and breathless in each other's arms.

A long space of time had passed when Lief said, "Oh. My. God."

Kelly pulled on his rear end harder, keeping him right where he was. "That's good news," she said. "I don't think it was my fault."

He pulled back a bit. "That was incredible. That lasted an hour, right?"

She laughed. "Don't look at the clock," she warned him.

"Are you all right?"

"Oh, better than all right. In fact, better than I've ever been before..."

"I hope we're still alone in the house," he said. "I think you screamed..."

"That was *you!*"

"No wonder it sounded so loud," he said. "If I stay right here, right inside you like this, I'll be ready again in just a few minutes."

"*Twenty* minutes," she said. "I read it somewhere."

"Does complete sexual satisfaction make you laugh?" he asked, smoothing the hair away from her face.

"Apparently."

"Can I stay with you for a while?" he asked.

"Yes. Stay just like this until I say you can leave."

"I want to stay all night."

"Then no more screaming," she told him. Then she laughed.

"Really, I bet that was you."

"It doesn't matter. I just know that if there's screaming in the middle of the night, I don't want anyone from the second floor to break in to save us."

"I love you," he said, kissing her nose. "I didn't think it could happen, but it happened so fast it almost knocked me out."

Her laughter stopped, and she grew serious. "I love you, too," she said. "I hope we don't screw this up. I mean, there's a lot at stake."

"A lot," he agreed. "Because I want to make a life with you, and I don't want to ask you to make big sacrifices in order to do that. I want to make you happy."

And it came to her that fast, all the things that stood between them and happily ever after. Could she be happy canning sauces made from Nana's recipe folder? Would Courtney cut them some slack or prove to be a constant challenge? Could she make it in Virgin River? Because as she lay in his arms, all she wanted in the world was this man, this quiet place in the mountains and a little peace of mind.

She smiled at him. "We're going to worry about this later," she said. "Because right now I'm naked, happy, and in no mood to overthink anything."

"Good plan," he said, nuzzling her neck. "It must

have been twenty minutes…" He moved his hips; he moved inside her.

"Not even close," she told him.

"Close enough," he said, rocking inside her, filling her again.

Kelly wanted the night with her man to never end. She learned that he could be so many things—slow and deliberate, a little wild and crazy, playful, serious. Not only did he touch every part of her body, he touched her heart. Her emotions.

After about three hours in bed, they shared a shower and went back to bed, lying quietly and close, talking. Sometime around eleven they heard distant voices downstairs and finally the closing of Jill and Colin's bedroom door. Just after midnight Kelly and Lief dressed, or mostly dressed. Lief pulled on his jeans and socks, leaving his shirt open, and Kelly wore leggings and an extra-long sweater. They crept downstairs to the kitchen. Lief lit candles on the table, and Kelly pulled out the uneaten dessert—her best tiramisu. They sat at the table, their chairs facing. Lief pulled her legs over his thighs, and in the candlelight, they fed each other bites of tiramisu. There were still embers in the hearth from hours ago, and they could see the starlight in the clear November sky on the horizon over the trees.

"Do you miss the city?" he asked her.

"Not at all," she said, shaking her head. "Especially when I look at that sky. The last couple of days I spent there, I realized I hated my apartment and my job. I love

San Francisco, but I can go back there anytime. For a visit, at least. Do you? Miss the city?"

He shook his head. "I was always a little out of place there. I'm more comfortable in a place like this. I'm happier around fields, streams and trees than freeways and high-rises."

"But your work…"

"There are people in L.A. I have to work with from time to time, the agents, producers, etcetera. But I can write anywhere."

"Are you working at all?" she asked him.

"Barely. I've been sketching, outlining, making notes. It's not much of anything. The hardest work I do looks like fishing. Typing isn't the hard part, it's thinking." He fed her another bite. "I want to spend every minute with you," he said. "And I can't."

"I know."

"I have to move slowly with Courtney… I have to set an example. I don't want her to get the impression it's all right for her to have wild sex whenever she feels like it."

"But it's all right for you?" she teased.

"It's actually healthy for me," he said with a smile. "And when she's forty-two, she can do anything she wants. But right now, one day at a time."

"If you aren't careful, she's going to wear black lipstick and dye her hair seven different colors…"

"I hear that happens. And there's another thing— holidays are coming up. I'd like to spend them with you, but I think for Thanksgiving I'd better take Courtney home to my family in Idaho—a visit before Spike comes to live with us. She hasn't seen them in a long time, and I'll be honest, I'm anxious for them to see her looking normal. I'd like to take you with me, but I'm afraid it's too soon..."

"I understand, Lief. I'm a big girl."

"You might be the best thing that's happened to me in a long, long time. Thank you for understanding."

"Of course I understand. Now, since you're going to be unavailable most of the time, take me back to bed and be the best thing that's happened to me in about an hour."

"My pleasure," he said, standing and reaching for her hand.

Life felt brand-new to Kelly. Like a couple of bad kids, they stole moments alone at Lief's house while Courtney was in school or at her friend's house. They hadn't scored another whole night together, but there was no mistaking a new glow in his eyes and the satisfied flush on her cheeks.

Time in the kitchen was much more pleasurable for Kelly during the November wet and cold. She kept the kitchen hearth blazing and the stove or ovens running. The county health inspector had visited, passed her with flying colors, and now it was just down to paperwork— her official permits would arrive by mail soon. She had stacked crates of her specialty sauces, relishes and chutneys in the unfurnished dining room, and now, while it drizzled outside, she was indulging her favorite pastime of baking breads and rolls, some of which she would give away and some that would be frozen.

Colin had her labels printed for her, and she added business cards to the supplies. Jillian, a former PR executive, put together a four-color brochure, and Kelly set about the task of making a list of people she could send some complimentary jars to. There were about a dozen stores and delis in the general area that she would hand-deliver her goods to. There were also shops and restaurants in the Bay Area where she was a known chef. She thought they would be receptive to the gift and might even wish to order more. While her bread baked, she boxed up packages for delivery or shipping.

During this time of year, Virgin River exploded with duck hunters, and one of them was Lief Holbrook. He wanted to go out a couple of times with Muriel and Walt and had invited Courtney to come along. "Ewww," she said. So Kelly generously offered to be Courtney's go-to girl while Lief squatted behind a bush at river's edge with a duck whistle in his pocket.

"It's not like I need a babysitter," she said indignantly.

"Of course you don't, but you might need a ride somewhere or something to occupy your time after school. You can help me bake bread if you want to—it's fun."

"Whatever," came the inevitable reply.

"Or you can watch TV or watch Colin paint or maybe even drive the garden mobile for Jillian, who works rain or shine."

"That sounds a lot more interesting than bread," she said.

And Kelly thought, *It's going to be a long, long courtship!*

"Are you sure?" Lief whispered to her when Courtney was out of earshot.

"Maybe if I actually spend a little time alone with her, things will improve between us."

"You do understand that it's not about you, right?"

"Are you sure? Maybe she just doesn't like me. I don't claim to have any instincts about kids, especially teenagers."

"Trust me," he said. "It's all about her. As much trouble as she gives me, I think it makes her nervous to think about sharing me. Plus there's likely a little bit of her being afraid her mother will be replaced or forgotten."

"We'll work it out," Kelly said, though she wasn't all that optimistic.

"If I get lucky, do you want a duck?"

That made her smile. "You would not believe what I can do with a duck."

On the day Kelly picked Courtney up from school and brought her out to the Victorian, it was drizzling—great weather for ducks. So Courtney wasn't real interested in driving around in the garden mobile. She went upstairs to the sunroom to see what Colin was painting, and Kelly started on more bread—she was doing a few glazed, twisted French loaves.

She was into the kneading when Courtney came

down to the kitchen. She pulled up a chair at the work island and watched.

"Want some dough?" Kelly asked.

She shrugged. "Sure. I guess."

"I'm making a few loaves that look like a braid." She separated some dough, sprinkled a little flour on the island in front of Courtney and handed her the dough. "When I baked bread at the restaurant, which was pretty rare for me, I could make as many as a hundred loaves. We usually had our bread delivered from our favorite bakery, but now and then we did it ourselves. I love making bread. Lots of things in the kitchen smell good, but almost nothing beats bread baking."

The whole bread-baking thing obviously didn't interest Courtney because she asked, "What do you like about my dad?"

Kelly's eyes snapped up. Courtney was kneading away at her ball of dough, not looking at Kelly. "I... ah... Well, he's a very nice man. What do you like about him?"

"Me?" Courtney asked. "Doesn't really matter, does it? It's just the two of us, anyway."

"You must know what you like," Kelly prompted.

"He's pretty nice, sometimes. But he's strict with me and he can't be strict with you. But if you get married and have kids, you might not like how strict he is with them."

That caused Kelly to stop kneading. "Um, a thought like that has never once crossed my mind."

"About how strict he might be with your kids?" Courtney asked.

"About getting married and *having* them!"

"Oh. You'll probably think of it pretty soon. My real dad did that—got married, had a couple of kids."

"Seriously, Courtney—never crossed my mind. Not once."

"Well, what *did* cross your mind?"

God, Kelly thought. Talk about baptism by fire. "Well, let's see. I thought, what a nice guy that Lief Holbrook is. And handsome, too. And very talented— I watched one of his movies so far but it made me cry so much I haven't watched another one."

"*Deerslayer,*" she supplied. "My mom loved that movie."

"Well, I was impressed, but I cried my eyes out."

"What else?" Courtney asked. "About my dad? Do you like that he's *rich?*"

"He's rich?" Kelly asked.

"Well, duh."

"I guess I never thought of that," she said. "Well, I've been friends with rich guys before. I didn't steal their money and run." She grinned.

"Well, then, what else?"

"I don't know. He can make me laugh—he's funny. That's a big plus. And I'm a chef and I think today he's going to bring me a duck."

"Gross," she said.

"I won't make you eat it," she said, laughing in spite of herself. "I'll fix you a hot dog."

"I don't even want to *see* it!"

"Well, I might have to cook it when you're not staying for dinner then," she said.

"Are you going to *pluck* it?"

"Of course I will. I know how to clean a duck, goose, hen, capon, squab, turkey, pheasant—"

"All right, I get it…"

"Quail," she added. "Anything on webbed or three-toed feet, but I rarely had to. I had a fantastic butcher that specialized in fowl. Besides, hunters are usually responsible for prepping their game. I'm assuming your dad is going to pluck."

And then Kelly concentrated on rolling out three long strips. She was aware that Courtney watched her. She tried to slow her hands down as she braided the strips, on the off chance Courtney wanted to copy her movements. Then she wiped her baking sheet with a thin coat of butter, brushed the top of her loaf with a little beaten egg and put it aside to do the next.

She glanced at Courtney's project. A little uneven, but by all accounts, not bad. "Nice," Kelly said. "Want me to bake it and send it home with you?"

Courtney looked up. "Do you get that I don't want a mother?"

Well. Kelly couldn't help it, she smiled. "Would you like a baseball bat to say that with?"

"Honestly," Courtney said.

"I do get that. You will always and forever have only one mother, Courtney. And I'm very sorry for your loss.

I lost my mother when I was young. I understand it's not easy."

"Did your father marry someone else then? And have kids?"

Oh, Kelly felt very bad about this. But there was no way around the truth. "My father died first. When I was six."

"Oh."

"There was an accident. We were all in it—me, Jillian, our parents. Jillian and I weren't hurt. My father was killed and my mother was paralyzed and was in a wheelchair for the rest of her life. When I was sixteen, she passed away. We were raised by our great-grandmother, who was quite elderly when she took us in. And when I was twenty-five, my great-grandmother passed, but she was very, very old. She lived to her nineties."

Courtney was quiet for a long, clumsy moment. "Yes, I'd like to bake the loaf and take it home."

"Absolutely," Kelly said. "You're going to love it."

Eleven

Two days after the baking and hunting, Courtney spent a little time with Jerry Powell. It was her regular weekly appointment. She found it so strange that when Lief told her she was looking great, she figured he was just screwing with her, that what he really meant was that she was looking *normal*. When Kelly and Jillian said it, they were just sucking up. When Gabe Tahoma said it, she felt like a cute little girl, not on par with someone he would want for a girlfriend. But for some reason when Jerry Powell told her she was looking good, it mattered. And she believed him.

"Well, you look older, that's for sure," he said.

"I'd like to look taller," she said.

He chuckled and said, "I'd like to look just a little shorter. How's life been treating you lately?"

She shrugged. "I'm not suicidal."

"I love the way you throw me these freebies, Courtney. And I'm very happy about that. Does that mean you're marginally happy?"

"Yes. Marginally."

"Which are the happy parts this week?"

"Well, I'm getting the puppy pretty soon. Right after Thanksgiving. When he's about seven weeks. I didn't know when I picked him out that he was going to be the biggest one in the litter."

"Are you ready for the puppy?"

"Ready?"

"I mean, do you have supplies for him?"

"Oh, yeah. Some. Collar, bowls, leash, chew toys, bed." Then she made a face. *"Cage."*

"What's up with the cage?" he asked. "I mean, the way you said it sounded pretty unhappy."

"Lief says the dog has to be in a cage when we're not home or watching him. He said the dog will destroy things and pee and poop on the rug."

"I think that's a true statement, Courtney," Jerry said. "Puppies are chew monsters for a couple of years. Not to mention the other issues."

"But a cage?"

"I think it's referred to as crate training…"

"It's still a cage!"

"Courtney, have you looked this up on the internet? I think the whole crate-training philosophy is as much to keep the puppy safe as the house."

She dropped her chin. "So it says…"

"But—as long as you're attentive, you can have him out. Right?" Jerry asked.

"Right," she said, not happy. "I hate to think of him

trapped while I'm at school. That's not how they do it on the farm."

"I know. But that's a farm. This is going to be a house dog without a pack to raise him. Correct?"

"Coooo-rect," she said, sarcasm dripping from the word.

"So. Anything else on your mind?"

"Lief has a girlfriend now for sure."

"Oh?"

"Well, I knew it was coming. We were having dinner there way too much for it to be just an ordinary friend."

"You like her?"

"Not that much," she said. "I mean, she's all right, but nothing special. But I know it's a girlfriend because *he's* happier. *Lots* happier."

"Isn't that good?"

She shrugged. "I told her what you said to tell her," she said. "That I do not want a mother."

"I see. How'd it go?"

"Fine," she said, glancing away. "She's not looking for a daughter..."

"She said that?"

"Not exactly. Sort of."

"Care to elaborate?"

She gave a deep sigh. "I mentioned something about her marrying my dad and having kids of her own and she said that had never once crossed her mind. I guess she doesn't want to be a mother. To anyone."

"Well, there's that possibility," Jerry said. "Or it could

be it hasn't crossed her mind because she hasn't known your dad that long. Maybe she doesn't want to have children of her own. But how did she respond to the idea that you are open to friendship?"

Courtney was quiet for a while. Jerry was altogether too patient. He did this a lot, made it clear he wasn't going to let it go. He waited. And waited. Finally she said, "Might've forgotten to mention that."

"Well," Jerry said, "I'm sure she got the message you intended."

"It happened before, you know. My real dad got a divorce from my mom, married someone and had a couple of kids, she didn't like me, he liked the new ones better, I was in the way at their house, and so on. He was pretty much done with me."

"Do you think this situation—your dad having a girlfriend—is reminiscent of your previous situation?"

"Why not?"

Jerry's turn to shrug. "I suppose it could be, but we have to remember that we're all individuals. Could be entirely different."

"Well, I don't think I'm ready to take a chance on that," Courtney said.

"Tell me what you're most worried about."

"Seriously?" she asked with a laugh. "I mean, *seriously?*"

He gave a nod. "Seriously."

"Well, worst case, Lief decides he needs a life, so he sends me back to my real dad, who doesn't want me, who has the wife from hell who screeches at him all the time and two little boys who pull my hair, spit on me and steal my stuff."

"That sounds horrible," Jerry said. "Have you told Lief about that?"

She laughed a little wickedly. "Listen, he made me go back a few times after I told him about it...."

"I see," Jerry said. "Did you ask him why?"

"I knew why," she said. "After my mom died, he didn't want to be stuck with me, that's why. Especially once I started my Goth impersonation."

Jerry leaned forward. "Courtney, if you want to stay with Lief and don't want to go back to your dad's house, wouldn't it make sense to be a little nicer to the prospective girlfriend?"

"Are you kidding me? I get any nicer, she's moving right in. And once she moves in, I play second chair, don't you get that? I don't mind that as long as I'm just left alone, but I don't want to go back to my dad's house."

"You seem to think you have this all figured out..."

"I know I do."

"I'm not sure you have it figured out accurately, however. I want to suggest something to you. I think we might try a little family counseling—you and Lief. An open dialogue, to kind of sort through your anxieties. About relationships and your future."

"Ah... I don't think I'm ready for that..."

"Can't really hurt anything," Jerry said. "It might help."

"Right, and I'd be ganged up on by the two of you, who *both* think this girlfriend thing is a good idea. Naw. I can't do that now. Not now. Things are kind of...okay. I don't want to mess with it while it's okay..."

"Courtney, you should talk to Lief about this stuff. He might be able to reassure you, and if he can reassure you, things could be better than just okay for you."

"I don't know about that. It might just work him up. Get him mad or something."

"Well, you're planning a trip together, right?" Jerry asked.

"To Idaho to his family's farm. We're driving. His parents, brothers, sister, nieces and nephews. Lots of them live around there, but we're staying on the farm."

"Is the new girlfriend going?"

"No," Courtney said. "Just me and Lief."

"Ah," Jerry said. "Long car ride. That could be a good time for you and Lief to have an honest discussion about the things that worry you. Will you at least consider it?"

Courtney frowned. "I'll think about it. But to be honest, the thought of bringing it all up just makes my stomach hurt."

"I understand. The theory behind counseling is that once you actually talk about these things, the stomachache goes away."

"Don't you tell him, Jerry! Remember, you promised!"

"I never break a confidence, Courtney. But why would

you harbor all this fear inside when you could throw your cards on the table, deal with it and move on?"

"Because," she said firmly. "I have it under *control!*"

Lief wouldn't ordinarily endorse Courtney taking a day off from school unless she was sick, but she hadn't missed any school this year so he went to the principal and asked permission to take her out on the Wednesday before Thanksgiving to accommodate the drive to Idaho. Then they packed the truck on Tuesday night and left it parked in the garage so they could leave very, very early. He dragged Courtney, her pillow and a throw, whining and whimpering, to the truck before five. It was going to be at least a seven-hour drive.

He had also packed sodas on ice, a thermos of coffee, water, some power bars, cookies and sandwiches. It wasn't a route heavily populated with restaurants.

It was ten before Courtney roused. "Good morning," he said with a smile, and then he quit talking. He knew her pretty well by now—both the old Courtney and this newer, more unpredictable Courtney. He gave her plenty of time to get adjusted. He was never sure which Courtney would wake up on any given day.

"Ah," she said, stretching. "Thanks for letting me sleep. Is my hair all wonky?"

He chuckled. "It looks fine. When you're hungry or thirsty, I have food, cola and bottled water."

"Oh, you didn't suck it all down while I was sleeping?" she asked with humor.

"I managed to save you some."

He concentrated on driving while she woke herself up, had something to eat and drink. Then he said, "We only have a couple of hours left."

"Good," she said.

"I hope you're not too bored while we're there," he said.

She just shrugged. "I'll be fine."

"My brothers' and sister's kids and grandkids won't all be there—but my cousin Jim lives nearby and he has some horses. We could drive over one day and saddle up a couple—I'm sure he wouldn't mind. You and I—we could have a ride. If you want to."

She sighed heavily.

"Bad idea?"

"Listen, there was something I was meaning to tell you, but it's a secret, okay?"

His heart dropped in his chest. He never knew what to expect. "Sure," he said, wondering if that was a promise he could keep.

"I'm afraid of horses. Oh, I'm okay with Blue now. And I kind of got used to a couple of the others. But I'm not a natural, all right? I mean, I don't regret the riding lessons. I'm glad I did it and I think I should keep doing it. But I'm not that good yet. I couldn't control a horse I don't know. And I usually get the runs when I know I'm going to have to get up on the horse."

Lief gave a bark of a laugh. "Really?" he asked.

"You think it's *funny?*" she asked, insulted to her core.

"I think it's funny you didn't tell me and you've been putting up with the runs!"

"I think Lilly Tahoma knows. She said she was glad to get me fresh, with no bad habits to unlearn. But don't expect me to run around the countryside looking for a horse to ride."

"Courtney, when you ride Blue, is it okay?"

"Oh, I love Blue," she admitted. "She'd never throw me or stomp me. Not on purpose, anyway. But it took me a while to feel all right with her."

"I totally understand," he said. But then he laughed again.

"Okay, I don't think you're that understanding if you're still laughing…"

"Court, don't you think I had plenty of fears when I was your age?"

"Like?"

"Geese," he said. "We have a lake on the farm that used to fill up with Canadian geese every spring and fall—on their way south, on their way north. I used to ride my bike to the bus stop and I couldn't get past that lake without those sons a bitches chasing me and pecking me to death! My brothers could turn on 'em and chase them back to the lake, but they knew I was scared to death of them and they would *not* let up!"

"Seriously?" she asked with a laugh. "Geese?"

He frowned at her. "Hey, geese are mean and they're as big as dogs! And they *honk!*"

She giggled. "Does anyone know about this?"

He peered at her, sensing he'd just told her something

that leveled the playing field between them. "*Everyone* knows. And in case you're interested, I'm not afraid of them anymore."

She laughed at him. "Good for you. My horse phobia is still between us. And I'm not so sure I want to go riding."

"Up to you," he said. "Totally up to you. But I'm going to drive over to Jim's to say hello to the family. Come with me. If something happens to change your mind, we'll ride."

"Like what could happen?"

"Well, he could say something like, 'This is old Gert and she can barely walk, but she can still take a light rider. She just goes real, real slow.'"

She liked that; he could tell by her laugh. When she was little, when her mom was alive, she'd thought he was hysterical. He could always make her laugh. He'd fallen as much in love with Courtney as Lana. One night when he'd held Lana, she'd said to him, "If anything should ever happen to me, please watch over Courtney. Stu is a fool who married a mean stupid fool and I want to know my little girl is okay." He had said, "You don't even have to ask!"

"Listen, Court," Lief said. "You could get bored, I realize that. But I have a huge favor to ask."

"Oh, boy," she said, sliding down in her seat.

"It's about my mom," he said. "She's getting really old. She won't slow down, that's for sure, but she's eighty. She's not going to last forever. I call her, you know. A couple of times a week at least. And you know that call she makes Sunday mornings before she heads to church? She's so old-fashioned. She allows herself only that one long-distance call a week even though we've all told her she doesn't have to worry about the charges anymore. But on that Sunday call she wants to know two things. How I am, how you are."

She was quiet for a moment. "Really?" she finally asked.

He nodded. "She's been so worried about you since your mom died. If you could be nice to her, I'd appreciate it. Every time I see her I think it might be the last time. You don't have to pretend, but if you could just treat her extra nice, maybe call her Gram like you used to, I think it could make her feel good. I'd take it as a personal favor."

Again, the quiet. And then she said, "I could do that. But there's a condition…"

"Ferrari? Porsche?"

She giggled. "I want to see the lake where the geese are. But we're staying in the truck."

"Done," he said. "Thanks, Court."

Lief's mother had been expecting them; she was ready for them. "I'm so happy, so happy," she said, embracing first Courtney and then Lief. "I think people will come by later, just to say hello, then come back tomorrow for turkey."

"Fantastic," Lief said. Then his dad came tottering into the kitchen, his newspaper in one hand. If his dad was in the house, the newspaper was attached to his hand. "Dad," Lief said, pulling him in for a hug. "How've you been feeling?"

"Good. Pretty good," he said. Then he peered at Courtney. "Well, young lady," he said.

"Well yourself," she answered. But she granted him a smile.

"He has the arthritis," Lief's mom said. "Both knees, both hips."

"Ain't much," Gramp said. "Picked too dang many potatoes, I guess. That's what I get for my trouble—arthritis."

"Are you hungry? We could make up some sand-wiches."

"I'm fine, Mom. Ate in the car. Snacked all the way, in fact. Court?"

"Nah. Thanks anyway."

"Well, then, pour yourself some coffee. Courtney, there's sodas. I best get back to this baking, get it all done so I can concentrate on the bird tomorrow."

"Aren't the girls bringing things?" Lief asked, refer-ring to his sister and sisters-in-law.

"Sure, sure, they bring. They want to bring it all, but what sense does that make? What am I going to do with myself if they bring it all? I do the bird, the bread, and decided I wanted some cookies on hand for the little ones. Son, go get a cup of coffee."

"I'm going to bring our bags in first," he said. "I'll be right back."

There was a big butcher block work island in the kitchen that was probably as old as she was, and she stood there, her hands in a bowl full of dough. Courtney stood opposite her. "What kind of bread?" she asked.

"Just my basic sweet dough. Nothing so fancy. I'll make some rolls, couple of loaves, maybe put some aside for cinnamon rolls for breakfast…"

"Did you ever make a twisted French loaf?" Courtney asked.

Gram looked up. "Don't know that I have, Courtney."

"Want me to show you how?"

Surprised quiet hung in the air. Finally Gram said, "That would be so nice."

"Well, I can't remember how long to bake it," Courtney said, dipping into the flour canister to sprinkle some flour on her work space. "And I'll need a beaten egg for the glaze."

Gram pushed the dough toward Courtney and went to the refrigerator. "We can figure out the baking time," she said, getting out an egg. She cracked it in a bowl and beat it with a fork.

"And do you have a brush? It's best to brush it on."

"Course," she said. "Let me watch how you do that."

So Courtney kneaded and rolled out her three strips, like three fat snakes, then carefully braided them while Gram watched. She sealed the ends and had a perfect braided loaf.

"I declare, you're gonna make yourself into a baker!" she said. Then she pushed the beaten egg and a brush toward her.

"We have to put on a cookie sheet first, and that's the hard part. Sometimes it wants to fall apart."

"Greased sheet?" Gram asked.

And Courtney remembered how Kelly had done it. "Yes," she said. And a moment later she slipped her small hands under the loaf and transferred it. Then she brushed the top with the egg glaze. "There we go."

"As I live," Gram said. "Aren't you the clever one. That's so pretty. Should we make us one more?"

"Sure," Courtney said.

"Then we best get on the cookies."

"I don't actually know how to make cookies. Just the kind you buy in the tube, already made, and put on the cookie sheet or in the microwave."

"Pah, we want the real thing," Gram said. "Let me get my file out. If you can read, you can cook. I didn't know you had an interest in baking."

Courtney shrugged. "I really don't. I just picked up a few things, that's all. Besides, there's nothing on TV anyway."

"That's a fact," she said. "Nothing on that box worth watching day or night. Not unless you like those asinine real-life things."

"You mean reality shows?" Courtney asked.

"Asinine, if you ask me. People shouldn't be watching other people while they're just living their lives or trying to solve their problems. And the very idea you choose a husband or a wife on the television! The very idea! What happened to acting? If there isn't acting in it, I can't be bothered."

Courtney laughed at her.

"Now, let me see—I think peanut butter and chocolate chip," Gram said. "Does that work for you?"

"Works for me. But there's rolls to do."

"We'll do 'em first. Let's make another one of them French things."

"You got it, Gram," Courtney said. "I shouldn't have gotten myself into this. We're going to be busy all day."

"Well, kiddo, that's the way I like it. Busy all day. Now you tell me when you get hungry and we'll take a break and eat something."

"I'm kind of looking forward to the cookie dough," she said. "Besides, don't you and Gramp eat at about four o'clock?"

"Not quite that early," she said. "That's for the old folks. I'd say more like four-thirty."

Courtney laughed. "You can make it all the way to four-thirty?"

"You wait till you're eighty, young lady. You won't be able to keep awake for those late meals like you used to."

"I guess that is just around the corner," Courtney teased.

And so they baked all afternoon. Then at exactly four-thirty they had a macaroni-and-cheese casserole with ham along with some sliced tomatoes and asparagus. Then after dishes, Aunt Carol, Lief's sister, dropped by without her husband, just to say hello, and right behind her came Uncle Rob and Aunt Joyce. They didn't stay long, just long enough for some pound cake and coffee. And sure enough, by eight o'clock, Gramp was nodding off in his chair with his newspaper in his lap and Gram was still banging around in the kitchen. Courtney and Lief were watching TV. Sort of.

"I think I might be able to stuff down another piece of that pound cake," Lief said, heading for the kitchen.

Courtney thought maybe she'd eaten more today than she'd eaten in a month, but she stood up and followed him anyway. Before she got to the kitchen she heard him say, "Mom, Mom, what's the matter?"

Courtney just waited outside the door. "Old women," Gram said with a self-recriminating sniff. "Sentimental old fools…"

"What happened?" he asked. "Did you get your feelings hurt or something?"

"Hurt? Mercy, no! I got 'em *restored!* I was so afraid I was gonna die before I saw that sweet child come back to her joyous self. Lord be praised!"

"What's this talk about dying? Aren't you feeling well?" he asked gently.

She laughed through her tears. "Lief Holbrook, I'm feeling *eighty!* I could be gone by morning."

Courtney could hear him hugging her. "I think you'll make it till morning."

"You better hope so. I'm in charge of the bird!"

Thanksgiving day in Silver Springs, Idaho, was a full house, though not all the Holbrooks could be there. Some nieces and nephews of Lief's who were grown, married and living in other states didn't come, but there was still a full table. These old-fashioned country folks liked to set two tables, one for the grown-ups and one for the children. A major rite of passage was moving from the little people table to the big people table; this year Courtney sat with the adults.

People seemed happy to see her; that was a relief. She saw the lake and there were even some geese on it, a stopover on their way south. Cousin Jim's farm hadn't changed but he did have some new animals—a couple of geldings he'd taken off a neighbor's hands when the neighbor's farm sold. Not ones she felt ready to ride. Lief went hunting early on Friday morning and again early on Saturday morning, both times with his brothers and brother-in-law. They stayed mostly on the farm—plenty of ponds and lakes nearby. He got himself two ducks, both of which he cleaned and put on ice to take back to Virgin River with him.

She texted Amber all weekend. Sounded like Amber's holiday was just about the same—older brothers, younger nieces and nephews, lots of people at the farm.

On Sunday they headed home. Gram made them coffee, turkey sandwiches, cookies. They didn't leave at the crack of dawn, but rather after a good breakfast. And the first couple of hours of the drive was pretty quiet in the car.

"I was real impressed with your behavior, Courtney. Thanks."

She sighed. "I don't know why we can't just live there. It's not like she's getting any younger, you know?"

"I know," he said. "I'm going to have to make it a point to go more often."

"Why can't we just live there? Near family?"

"Well, I thought about it, but in the end I decided I didn't want to get too far out of California, since I still will probably have to go to L.A. now and then. I still have occasional meetings for scripts. I found a house I thought we'd like and just made a decision."

"There are airports. What if we made a new decision?"

"Moved to Silver Springs?" he asked. "I like where we are. And you've gotten along pretty well."

"Is it about Kelly being there?" she asked.

"I like Kelly, you know that. And to be honest, I didn't think I'd ever meet a woman I'd like. But also, I don't know what her future plans are. When she got here, she planned to stay awhile, then find a position in a restaurant. That she didn't want to live with her sister forever, was practically the first thing she said, so I can't say I'm staying in Virgin River because of Kelly. Look, I don't think we should move to Idaho, but I think we should go back to visit more often. Is that okay?"

"Sure," she said. "Whatever."

Twelve

Lief had never done so much texting in his life. In his parents' house with the paper walls and with Kelly's cell phone reception in Virgin River iffy at best, he didn't want to talk on the phone, say personal things and be overheard by Courtney. His parents were half deaf, but Courtney had inhuman hearing. So he shot Kelly message after message. Sometimes she shot them right back, sometimes they came a bit later. He felt like a kid, secretly texting during class. At least there was communication, but he wasn't sure how this younger generation could stand it—it was so unsatisfying.

On Monday morning he made coffee, put the cooler with the ducks in it in the back of the truck while Court was in the shower, ate a bowl of cereal and looked at his watch fifteen or twenty times.

Which didn't escape Courtney's notice.

When he dropped her off at school she said, "Bet I know what you're going to do today."

He hoped she didn't see the dark stain on his cheeks.

"I'm going to take the ducks to Kelly. Unlike you, she gets very excited about ducks."

"Eww," she said. "Gross."

So, the old Courtney was back. Well, he hadn't expected charming Courtney to last forever. But that wouldn't keep him from being grateful she'd obliged him with his mother and from knowing she was capable of being sweet when she wanted to be.

He drove a little fast to the Victorian, didn't bother with the cooler containing the ducks, but gave two short knocks and opened the back door. Kelly turned from the sink at the sound. The air between them crackled. His heart beat a lot faster, just looking at her, those rose lips, pink cheeks, thick blond hair. "Where is everyone?" he asked.

She smiled. "Denny's not coming to work today. Jill and Colin went to Redding for art supplies." She swallowed.

Then she ran into his arms, shoving his jacket off his shoulders. Her lips met his lips, her arms clasped his neck. Her mouth opened under his, tongues tangled, breathing quickened, and he could feel her heart thud in her breast. "God, I missed you," he said.

"It was the longest holiday weekend I've ever spent," she said.

He lifted her, and her legs went around his waist, his hands holding her up under her butt. He laughed against her opened lips.

"Funny?" she asked.

"I guess we can't do it on the table," he said. "Or against the nearest wall."

"Pretty risky, near those windows, the way folks in this town drop by."

"Ten years ago I could've carried you up three flights, just under the sheer power of wanting you. Now? I'm afraid I'll fall..."

"And hurt us both?" she asked, kissing his neck, his ear, his cheek.

"And not get laid," he said with a chuckle.

"How fast can you get upstairs if you put me down?" she asked.

"I have an advantage. My legs are longer." He put her on her feet. "You better run or I'll have your clothes in shreds."

"God," she said, her feet touching the floor. She put a hand against his cheek. "I think this whole event is going to take under three minutes."

He looked into her liquid blue eyes, smiled and said, "Go!"

With a shriek she turned and ran for the stairs, Lief right behind her. She was completely out of breath when she got to her bedroom on the third floor and flounced on the bed. Lief slammed the door—better to be safe than stupid when living in a commune—and was right on top of her, his mouth on hers. He rotated his hips slightly, pressing into her.

"Hm, ready already?" she asked.

"I've been ready all morning." He lifted her shirt over her head, so happy to find her braless. He pressed her breasts together and plunged his face into their full softness. Then his hands were on her pants, opening the snap, slipping down the zipper and pulling them down her legs. He knelt on the floor beside the bed to get them all the way off and, being in that position, had a thought. He spread her legs, kissed her inner thighs, separated her farther and put his mouth on her.

"Oh, don't," she said.

He lifted his head. "Why? You love this."

"I can't last and I want to wait for you!"

He grinned at her, putting a large hand over her breast. "Don't worry about me, honey." And back he went, exploring her with his tongue, following his movements with his thumb's firm pressure. She went off like a rocket, clenching and vibrating as she pushed against him.

He gave her a moment, then slowly rose to look into her eyes. "I love it when you do that for me," he said. "You are one hot, sexy woman, and I love you."

"Then take off your clothes!"

Grinning, he unbuttoned the shirt, then the jeans, then kicked off the boots. Then he hovered over her, still smiling. "Tell me what you want, honey."

"I want you inside."

He ran a knuckle along her soft ivory cheek. "You realize that once I'm in there, I have maybe ten strokes in me. I'm pretty hot."

"I think that should be enough," she said, reaching to put her arms around his neck to hold him close. "For now."

He plunged his hands into her soft hair, found her mouth with his, entered her in one long, smooth perfect stroke and growled low in his throat. Then he started to move, and she started to move in concert against him, taking him in. She released a little whimper, sucked hard on his lower lip, and it happened again. She froze, clenched, looped a leg over his waist to hold him inside her, and she came in cascading waves. "Mmm," he said against her mouth. "Mmm, honey. That feels so good." And he found he couldn't wait her out. He pumped his hips a couple of times and released, his throbbing climax bringing a delicious moan from her.

And then they were still, holding on to each other, recovering.

A minute later he lifted his head, looked into her eyes, and they both started to laugh.

"That was a good two and a half minutes," she told him.

"I'll be better next time," he said. "How far away is Redding?"

"Plenty far," she said. She ran her fingers through his hair. "I hated being away from you. I understood how important it was, but I missed you so much." She slapped his muscled backside. "I missed this."

"It's always good, but when you can't wait, it's better. Fun. How'd I get so lucky to find you?" he asked.

"Makes no sense. I was running away from my life. This shouldn't have happened. But I'm so glad it did. And thank you for staying in touch through the weekend—I wondered about you every minute."

"All that damn texting stuff—I can't live like that. I mean, a message now and then like 'pick me up' or 'new president elected,' that I can understand. I needed to hold you, to hear your voice." He kissed her. "To taste you, to feel you under me."

"This is the best part," she said, snuggling closer. "When we're joined like this and talk…"

"Let's talk about how much I worship this body," he said, kissing her neck, breast, lips. "What a perfect fit. Can we stay like this until we starve?"

She laughed at him. "Anything that makes you happy."

His rich brown eyes grew warm, and he brushed her hair back. "It makes me happy when I can make you happy. When I can make you cry out, when you're so satisfied you can't sit up." Then he smiled and moved inside her. He was ready for more. "This time, sweetheart, we'll go slower. I can't get enough of you."

"I don't expect special treatment," she whispered.

"Yes, you do."

"Fine. But only because it's you and everything you do to me is special."

It took some willpower to give up the bed after making love for a couple of hours. They showered, dressed and went to the kitchen for lunch. The ducks Lief brought went in the refrigerator while Kelly made them a couple of sandwiches. They filled each other in on the details about their long weekend apart. Kelly had been invited to join Colin and Jill, Colin's family and the gathering that took place at General Walt Booth's house. "Very nice extended family," she said. "Walt is Shelby's uncle. Walt's daughter Vanessa is Shelby's cousin. Muriel was there, of course."

He told her how delightful Courtney was. "Almost like the old Courtney—sweet-natured and funny. I'm embarrassed that you rarely see that side of her."

"I'm hoping that changes soon," she said.

"And I'm hoping you remember how to get to my house."

"Why is that?"

"Because Spike is coming to live with us this week. I can only leave him for a few hours or less at a time— he's going to be in training. Or I'm going to be in training—we'll see which it is."

It was unusually sunny and warm, so they put on jackets and took their coffee outside to sit on the porch. They were talking about whether she should freeze one or both ducks when the sound of footfalls coming up the drive could be heard.

When the man came around the corner of the house, Kelly gasped. It was Luciano Brazzi. He stopped when he saw Kelly. She shot to her feet when she saw him.

"Luca!"

"Bella," he said in his deep, heavily accented voice. He nodded his head in a brief bow.

"What are you doing here?"

He reached into a worn leather satchel he carried over one shoulder and pulled out a cell phone. "Ah, Bella.

There is so much to explain. You and I—we were tricked and lied to."

"What?"

Luca looked between Kelly and Lief. "I'm afraid I'm interrupting, I apologize. I couldn't call ahead—I had the address, but no phone number. I parked in the front of the house and rang the bell, but no one came to the door. And I heard laughter, so I followed the sound. If there's a time we could have a private conversation—"

"What?" she asked, still a little stunned. "Oh, Luca, this is Lief Holbrook. Lief, Luciano Brazzi, an old... friend of mine. Luca, come and sit down. I'll get you a glass of wine."

"I can come back," he offered.

Kelly leaned to look around the house. "Where's your posse? All your assistants?"

"I'm alone, Kelly. If you'll tell me when I can come back to talk to you alone, I'll busy myself until that time..."

"Now," she said. "We can talk right now." She turned to Lief. "Will you excuse me? I think it's important I have this conversation."

Lief took her hand. "If you'd like, you can go inside to talk and I'll wait here on the porch. In case you need me."

She smiled at him and gently placed her palm on his cheek. "I'm perfectly safe, but thank you. I'm sorry to cut our day short, but you can go and I'll call you the minute I'm finished talking with Luca."

He gave a nod. Then he leaned forward and gave her

a brief, deep kiss, just in case this interloper had any doubt about who had claimed her. She loved him for it and gave him a little hug.

"I'll call," she repeated. Then she ushered Luca into the house.

"Ah! Bella," he exclaimed, taking in the kitchen. He gestured with an arm wide. "I see at least one reason why you're here!"

"This is my sister's house, Luca, and I'm visiting. Is your driver waiting?"

"No driver, no assistant, no valet. I'm alone."

She pulled a chair out to seat him at the table. "When was the last time you actually drove yourself?"

He sat down. "I've been spoiled, but I'm not incompetent. I drove myself. The minute I found out where you were, I came."

"Wine?"

"Please," he said. He put the phone on the table, and she recognized it as the one she lost. "Perhaps you should have a glass as well, sweetheart."

She had to concentrate to close her mouth. "Perhaps," she finally said in a stunned whisper.

A moment later she was sitting at the table with him.

He raised his glass to her. "To better times…"

She answered the toast with her glass but immediately said, "Explain, Luca."

He pushed the phone toward her. "My cell phone was stolen," he said. "I suspected it was lost. I get preoccupied and careless. My assistant immediately replaced it and I called you at once with the new number." He pulled his phone out of his pocket and clicked on to the text screen. "This is the response I got, on my new phone, from you."

I'm very unhappy with the limbo of our relation-ship and it's causing me great stress. I'm taking a few days away from work to think this over—please give me space to do that. Just a few days and then I'll call you. I ask you to please respect this request. Love, Kelly.

"I didn't send this."

"I realize that now," he said.

"Olivia came to see me, at work. She thought we were sleeping together and asked me to stop. She told me *you* sent her, that she was often sent to clean up your messes, that you wouldn't be taking my calls any longer, that you were finished with me."

"So I'm told," he said. "I learned this very recently."

"Luca, I tried calling you, sending you texts, emails. I even got in touch with Shannon to get a message to you! You should have come to the restaurant."

"Oh, I did that, of course. The very next day. I was told you took some time off for personal reasons, for a family emergency. Something about going out of town to help a family member. I was promised a phone call when either Durant or Phillipe heard from you. I knew your only family was your sister, but I also knew she had moved to some small town and was no longer in the area. I continued to try to reach you, and finally, after a very frustrating two weeks, I went to your flat to confront you. But you were gone."

"What about my emails to you?"

"Shannon, obviously taking her instruction from Olivia, screened my mail on the office computer and deleted anything from you. When I looked for email on my phone, there was no new message from you. It never once occurred to me to check deleted emails. We were tricked."

"How did you find out?" she asked him.

"I found your phone in Phillipe's desk. I was using his office recently, was looking for a ruler to line my paper, and found this." He put a hand on the phone.

"Why, Luca? Why did Olivia do this? *How* did she do this?"

"She had far more control of the business than I ever realized. I didn't know she controlled so many of my people. She was obviously threatened by the prospect of anyone ever replacing her, both in her business and social stature. Bella, everything I told you was true— we've been living separately under the same roof for twenty years. We were always on the best of terms. I thought she was devoted to our business even if she wasn't in love with me. And yes, we were trying to negotiate a divorce. I thought we were doing so ami- cably. Certainly she was asking me for the earth, but I had no problem with that—I'm a fair man and she's the mother of my children. Even if her motivation was strictly selfish, there was little doubt she worked like a crazy woman, both as my partner in business and as head of our family." He shrugged. "I'm old-fashioned. It was always my intention to see she was taken care of."

"But she said there were other women! That there were children outside your marriage!"

"Women, yes—my marriage was over and sometimes I was lonely. From time to time, with the greatest of discretion, my eye wandered. But not for a long time, Bella, I promise you. And there were never children." He shook his head. "So many lies."

"Unbelievable. What if I hadn't left the restaurant? We'd have found her out!"

He laughed remorsefully. "We'd only have learned that she tried to drive you away by lying to you and asking you to end our friendship. She would have played the desperate, injured wife. She's been making excuses about not feeling the divorce was right, that we should continue as we were for the sake of the family, but I wouldn't go along with that idea. I never found my phone—I'm sure it's at the bottom of a river. It was finding *your* phone that pried open all the lies. One confession led to the next."

"Who confessed first?"

He lifted a brow. "Who do you suspect? Phillipe, of course. Under the threat of losing his position and never finding another one in the Bay Area. Next it was young Shannon, in a flood of tears. Then some of the accounting staff admitted they answered to Olivia. Durant was also her man. That doesn't even account for household staff."

"What did you do to Phillip?" she asked.

"Oh, I fired him on the spot. He accused me of not keeping my word and I confessed that he was right." He grinned a bit evilly. "But not until he told me where he mailed your last check. How could I keep a man like that around? He'd sell me to the devil!"

"Olivia said she lifted your phone from the nightside table…"

"No, Bella. I don't have proof of this, but I believe I left it in the car. We were riding into the city together and I remember using it en route. Shortly afterward I couldn't find it and had the driver tear the car apart in search of it."

Kelly rested her forehead in her hand. "She must have worked very quickly after that," Kelly said.

"Very quickly, with Phillipe agreeing to steal your phone from your purse while she talked to you in his office."

Kelly laughed lightly. "And shortly after that, I was taken out of the kitchen on a stretcher!"

"What?!" Luca said, sitting forward with a shocked look on his face.

"It didn't have all that much to do with you, or with Olivia for that matter. Her visit was a blow, but at that point I didn't even know my phone was gone. I thought it fell out of my purse in the kitchen."

"Bella, what happened to you?" he asked, grasping her hands.

"Oh, Luca, I wasn't going to survive in that kitchen. The stress was too much. I'm not as stubborn or hard-headed as you are—Durant was eating me alive and Phillip was constantly conspiring against me. And that was before either of them knew our friendship was special." She gave a shrug. "I crashed in the kitchen. Grabbed my chest, could hardly breathe, passed out cold."

"And now?"

She waved her hand at Jillian's kitchen. "Now? Clean bill of health, feeling well, rested and I have very little stress in my life."

"And the man?"

She smiled fondly. "A wonderful man. I'm sorry, Luca," she said, shaking her head. "I'm no longer available, even if you are."

"Ah," he said, dropping his chin. "This is the worst of what Olivia has done to me. She took you away from me."

"Not really. I wasn't really yours and you were never mine. Your life is too complicated for me and it's far too late for you to have a simpler life. And for that matter, I may not be able to work things out with my very special man for similar reasons. But I'm going to try, Luca."

"It makes me very sad," he said. "I don't know where I've met a more perfect woman."

"What's happening with Olivia now?" she asked. "Did you leave her in the Bay Area to wreak havoc on your home, family and business?"

"No, darling, no. She's in lockdown," he said with a

smile. "That's what we used to call it when the children were in trouble and we removed all their entertainment as punishment—no cars, no phones, no TV, no friends. Bank accounts are frozen, credit accounts on hold, lawyers and auditors on the premises taking an accounting, many people terminated. I called all the children, explained that the thing we'd been talking about for years was taking place—there *would* be a separation and divorce. I promised them it would be fair, amicable and wouldn't affect their plans. I hope I can count on that, but there are no guarantees."

Whew, she thought. Certainly not with Olivia backstage, orchestrating all kinds of melodrama and deceit, it could be a horrible ordeal. But that wasn't her problem. It was even more evidence that she wasn't cut out to take on a man like Luca.

"I should leave you," he said. "You have a good life here, that's obvious. And there's a special shine in your eyes. I only wish I'd put it there."

"You know I care about you. That I wish you well."

He lifted her hand to his lips and kissed the backs of her fingers. "Thank you, sweetheart. I think I've put you through enough. Me and my complications."

"What will you do? Drive back to San Francisco today?"

He shrugged. "Slowly, perhaps. I might stumble on a hidden gem in restaurants or something along that order. I'm in no hurry. I have too much to think about and I found I liked the driving. It felt good to be in control once again."

"Don't go," she said, squeezing his hand. "Stay over. There's a guest room. Jillian and Colin, my sister and her partner, will welcome you. We'll cook together tonight, though you'll have to make do on what I have in the kitchen. We'll eat, drink wine, sleep well, and tomorrow you can drive back."

"What about your very special man?" he asked.

"I'll call him, invite him to join us."

"He can do that without being jealous?"

She laughed softly. "He's neither Italian nor a temperamental chef. If he's available, he'll do it with class."

When Luca opened the refrigerator, he exclaimed, "Duck!"

"From the wilds of Idaho," she explained. "But there's one small complication—Lief will be bringing his fourteen-year-old daughter and she thinks duck is gross. Probably because he shoots them and plucks them himself."

"Hah! A minor inconvenience. Does she like pasta?"

"I assume so," Kelly said with a laugh.

"Good, we'll fix her up. And we'll enjoy duck! How would you like it? Honey-orange glaze? Cassoulet? Confit?"

She laughed at him, watching his excitement grow as he considered the possibilities. "I don't have juniper or allspice berries on hand for confit, Luca. I do have bacon and sausage if you feel like cassoulet. Or we can rub it down with garlic, stuff it with wild rice, serve it with vegetables…"

"Do you have sherry?" he asked.

"Yes."

"And merlot?"

She frowned. She recognized the sherry marinade—so Italian—sherry, oregano, garlic, rosemary, basil… "What do you need the merlot for?"

"To drink!" he said, lifting his hand in the air.

And she burst out laughing. Ah, she remembered now—there was so much about him to love. He was so full of fun, of life! And she also realized, not for the first time, that didn't put her *in* love with him. They were birds of a feather in the kitchen and it was wonderful, but not necessarily right anywhere else.

The cooking commenced. She was more than happy to take orders. He entertained himself so thoroughly, walking her through each step even though she already knew it all by heart. Once she said, "Luca, I know the recipe." And he said, "Pay attention, my darling Bella! I could throw you a curve! And it could change your life."

She just laughed—as if a new twist on perky sherry duck could change her life!

Colin and Jillian came home after a long day away shopping. After introductions, Colin stowed his new art supplies in the sunroom and was back in the kitchen. He sat at the table for a while, laughing at the choreography in the kitchen. Jillian went out to her greenhouse and returned with a basketful of lettuce, leeks, a few small tomatoes and some skinny green beans. Luca snatched it out of her hands and tossed it all in the sink to wash, cook and serve—Kelly couldn't wait to see how.

Lief and Courtney arrived next, and the moment they were all seated comfortably, Luca had an antipasto tray sitting before them, made out of the contents of the refrigerator and cupboards. He had warmed one of Kelly's frozen French loaves, exclaiming proudly on the texture and aroma, and added that to the table. He poured olive oil and a few spices onto bread plates for dipping. He put Courtney at the head of the table, completely blew off her pique, and never set a place for himself.

Next he served them duck liver appetizers, deviled eggs spattered with inexpensive caviar and cheese and tomato slices. He had always said the true measure of a chef is what he can bring out of the cupboard at last notice. He continued to serve and pour, talking nonstop as was his way, until he had everyone laughing and swooning over his food. Courtney was brought a small casserole of her very own macaroni and cheese, Italian style, which she couldn't keep away from everyone else. As their forks constantly threatened her casserole, they had her giggling!

By the time Luca delivered the duck to the table for a viewing before carving, even Courtney was impressed. He applied a sharp knife to a few key places and the meat, usually tough and gamey, fell away from the bone.

"Aren't you going to sit down, Luca?" Jillian finally asked.

"Why? I eat constantly. My passion is to bring it to your mouths. *Mangia!*"

He never stopped talking, joking, prodding, stopping just short of spooning the food into their mouths. Even Lief was enjoying the performance, and for Luca, every meal he prepared *was* a performance. Of course it was no small matter of reassurance that Kelly sat beside Lief and often had a hand on his thigh.

But she was reminded by Luca's good mood, his joy, his humor and his energy that it was *cooking* that set him right. It was not his fame or wealth, not his many restaurants nor his picture on the labels of specialty foods, but creation in the kitchen. He might indeed be fond of her, proud of her, but he was *not* in love with her any more than she was with him. He was in love with his craft. And it would sustain him.

Finally, even though everyone at the table was stuffed to the button-popping stage, he brought out the tiramisu.

"I had nothing to do with this," he announced. "Except that I'm sure I showed her the recipe and method to such perfection!"

"Always taking credit," Kelly said with a laugh.

It was nine o'clock before the gathering broke up. Courtney had school the next day, Jill had the garden, Colin had things he wanted to do, and, as Kelly pointed out, Luca had to get back on the road.

But that didn't prevent Kelly and Luca from sitting up with a new bottle of merlot. He picked the bones of the duck carcass, congratulating himself with every bite. And he also had opened the precious jars of her sauces, relishes and chutneys, raving about each one as he tasted.

"There is a fortune here," he said.

"Hopefully there's enough to pay the rent, though I won't turn away a fortune."

"If you had the right factory and backing, a fortune," he insisted.

"Right now, I'm just testing the market. I already know it's good—it comes from my great-grandmother. It's always been good."

"Let me take some back to San Francisco and show them around, see if you find a market there."

"That would be lovely, Luca."

He grasped her hand and said, "All the things I promised—your own kitchen, your own trademark, your own restaurant—anytime you want to take me up on that, you have only to call me. I will have you in place in a day."

"I won't work in another restaurant like *La Touche,*" she said. "It's suicide."

"You will choose the sous chef, the manager, the staff, the line chefs. And you will make the rules," he said.

"Thank you, Luca. Your faith in me means a great deal."

"And production of these recipes? I'll pay and pay well. I'll supply the production—we'll work out a contract so you never have to worry about the rent again!"

"The recipes are precious to me," she said.

"I understand," he answered with a nod. "I want you to know, I wasn't just talking—I meant it when I said you had my support. You could be a success without it, but if I can be a part of it…"

"I'm happy here," she told him.

"If you're ready for a change in a month or a year, in two years, it doesn't matter. Call me. In the meantime, I'll have one of the new interns put together a distribution list for you for northern California. I'll write a letter of endorsement you can use."

"That would be so generous. Thank you."

They sat up drinking and talking until well after midnight, and still, Kelly was up in the kitchen at six the next morning. Luca followed soon after, ready for coffee and something to eat. By seven they were standing on the front porch, and his car engine was running.

"I mean it, Bella. No matter when you call me, I will not let you down again."

"Thank you, Luca. That means a lot to me."

He leaned toward her for a kiss and she obliged. He sucked in a deep breath, pulled her close, covered her mouth with his and worked his magic.

But for Kelly, it was like kissing an uncle. After two years of fantasizing unspeakable passion, it was nothing like their last kiss. What happened to the thunderheads?

It was over for her. Luca was a friend and mentor. She adored him, admired him. And didn't want him as her partner, lover or even fantasy anymore.

Finally he let her go. He smiled into her eyes and said, "Nevertheless, I will support you in your success."

And she smiled back. "Thank you, Luca."

"Call if you need me. If you need anything, at any time. If you ever decide to leave the mountains, just let me know. I will put you to work."

She nodded. "And good luck with the family. And all that."

"I believe we could have made a good couple, Bella."

"Maybe," she said. "It must not be meant to be."

He gave her a melancholy smile, a brief salute, and was off down the drive.

The first thing Kelly did after breakfast, after she assumed Courtney was off to school, was drive to Lief's house. She was a little surprised he hadn't come knocking at her door, but then he knew Luca was staying over.

When he opened the door and saw her, he was smiling broadly. "You read my mind," he said.

"I have so much to explain to you," she said. And over coffee at his kitchen table, she told him the whole story as Luca had told her—stolen phones, fake messages, lies.

At the end of the long and complex story, Lief enfolded her in his arms and said, "Ah, God bless Olivia Brazzi!"

Thirteen

Frequently heard around the Holbrook household these days was, *"Courtney!* If you take Spike out of the kennel, you have to *watch* him!" Spike was absolutely the cutest chubby little blond puppy that ever lived. He had a round soft belly, floppy little ears, black eyes and a precious little yip for a bark. And he was a pooping, peeing, chewing machine.

As long as she was constantly reminded, Courtney was coming along as a trainer. The second eight-week-old Spike came out of the kennel, he had to be taken outside. Immediately after eating and drinking—outside. During a pause in romping and playing—outside!

The one really dedicated to the training part was Lief, which surprised him not at all. Courtney was more dedicated to the snuggling part. Since it had been a very long time since there had been any snuggling between Lief and Courtney, he was glad he'd gone along with this idea.

One thing Courtney was beginning to understand—

when she went to Amber's house and took Spike with her, he was locked in a pen with the other few remaining puppies in the barn. Their dogs were not house dogs, and they weren't really sentimental about them. Spike's mother had special privileges for birthing and nursing, then was put out again. That being the case, Courtney didn't take Spike with her. She didn't like him trapped outside in the barn in the cold night.

For Lief and Kelly, this all meant making love on the sly, during school hours, at Lief's house, often to the background music of a wailing puppy who didn't feel like being in his kennel.

"I much prefer your screaming and wailing to his," Lief told Kelly.

One thing he had to admit—just having the puppy, though sometimes a giant pain, had a positive impact on Courtney's attitude. She was definitely nicer to him. And her appearance and grades continued to improve. She was building some body mass from the riding, and her appetite had improved as well, probably because of the exercise. Amber came to their house for homework more often than Courtney went to Amber's, largely because of the puppy.

That creepy Goth girl was becoming a mere memory.

Courtney was lobbying to go to Idaho for the Christmas holidays. Lief wasn't sure the whole puppy thing was a good idea. "You have to remember, I come from a farm very much like Amber's farm. Gram and

Gramp might want to lock him outside or put him in the barn."

"But you can just tell them that he's a house dog, not a farm dog, and they'll be okay."

And the other thing was he'd been hoping to spend some time with Kelly over Christmas. Not the whole time, but at least some.

Without a hint or provocation, Courtney said, "Do you just want to stay here so you can be with Kelly? Because I'd rather be with *family!*"

Sometimes she was so hard to anticipate. Before her mother's death, she'd liked going to the farm. Afterward, she'd not only hated it, she wouldn't talk to anyone when they were there and she seemed to take great pleasure in acting and looking as weird as possible. Now they were back to family taking priority.

"Just let me think about it, maybe talk to Gram about it. Or maybe we can get a dog sitter or something..."

Lief, being a smart man with pretty decent instincts, seldom did things for which he had regrets. That's why he couldn't believe his own stupidity when he sent Courtney's dad, Stu Lord, Courtney's freshman school picture. It was completely unnecessary; they hadn't heard a word from Stu in forever. Not since Stu gave up even his weekend visitation last spring, if he remembered correctly. He had let Stu know they were moving and Stu had not responded to that either.

Truthfully, he'd sent the picture because he was proud. A proud dad. She'd been lovely in the picture and looked happy. And Lief remembered that the last time Stu had seen her she was pretty scary looking. He wanted Stu to see that his biological daughter was as pretty as her mother had been, was smart, was healthy. He wrote a brief note:

> *Straight As, horseback riding twice a week, feeling much better about life these days and has made a very nice adjustment to living in the mountains. Hope all is well at your end. Lief.*

Then on the morning of December 10, the phone rang. It was Stu.

"Hey, Lief, how you doing, man?"

"Getting by. How about you, Stu?"

"Great, thanks, just great. Thanks for sending the picture, Lief. Damn, the little munchkin looks terrific, doesn't she? And you say she's got her schoolwork back up to where it should be?"

"That's right, Stu. She's been working hard."

"Fantastic, and now that she's straightened out, we'd like her to spend Christmas with us. We're going to Orlando. Family vacation. I'd love it if my daughter came along. Sherry would love it, too."

He didn't even have to think about it. "We already made our plans, Stu. In fact, Courtney was the one who asked if we could go back to the farm, my family's farm, for Christmas. She's gotten real close to my mom."

"Well," he laughed. And he *did* laugh it. *Well-hell-*

hell. "You guys might have to plan to do that next year instead. Because Sherry and I and the boys want her with us. We haven't seen her in a long time."

"You haven't called her either, Stu. We haven't heard shit from you in months. In fact, last time I talked to you—I think it was last April maybe—you said you were all done putting up with Courtney and she was all mine. And Stu—I took you up on that."

"*Well-hell-hell,* that isn't going to cut it, pal, because I have custody. I'm the custodial parent. Remember that little detail? So break it to her, sonny. I want her here by the eighteenth. We head for Orlando on the twentieth. She'll have a great time."

"I don't think so, Stu. Courtney isn't going to want to do that. And you and Sherry pretty much chewed her up and spit her out already. She's had enough."

"Here's the deal, Lief. You can do this my way or you can flat out refuse, in which case we're talking custodial interference and I let the law take over. After that, I guess she lives with us permanently."

Lief felt like the wind was knocked out of him. "Please don't do this, Stu. Please. It's taken so much work to get Courtney back on track. I don't think she can take any more uncertainty or confusion. Please, Stu."

"Then I guess it makes sense to have her here by the eighteenth. It's just Christmas. Make her return reservations for January second. Then she can go back to the mountains. Or…? You don't want to fight this out, do you, Lief, old pal?"

His voice came in a mere scratchy breath. "Please, Stu… Come on…"

"Nah, this is what it is. The eighteenth. Let me know when to pick her up."

Stu hung up. And for the first time since his wife died, Lief wanted to break down in a bone-deep cry.

Lief called his lawyer before doing anything else. When Lana died, though it only compounded his grief, he knew he'd have to let Courtney go to Stu if that's what Stu wanted. Fortunately, Stu had a second marriage and family and it wasn't that important to him, so Courtney went back and forth for a while. Stu was agreeable to a joint custody arrangement with Lief, but Stu remained the primary guardian.

Then came that awful day Stu had said he'd had enough of Courtney. It should have been the best day, but the agony it caused his little girl had pushed Lief over the edge. Lief's fatal mistake had been in not taking legal action to ensure his custody of Courtney right then. What he'd done instead was pull Courtney in, told her she didn't have to go back to Stu's house, not even for a weekend visit, and begun at once looking for a place out of the city. A place away from the noise, confusion and Stu.

Today when he called the lawyer, he was informed that Lief would not only be breaking the law by refusing to let Stu see his daughter for the holiday, but it might make Lief's petition for custody more difficult. "As I see it," the lawyer said, "Courtney is close enough to an age of responsibility that a judge would hear her preference on where she'd like to live and with whom. If you cooperate now, that will go down easier. Hard as it might be to go along with this, it's probably in your best interests, both yours and Courtney's."

"She's not going to see it that way," Lief said.

On instinct, he drove out to see Kelly. One look at his angry face and she said, "Uh-oh. What's wrong?"

"Do you have a little time to talk? I have to talk to someone. I'm going to drive to Grace Valley and talk to the counselor, but I have to sort it out first."

"It's Courtney, isn't it?"

He shook his head. "No. But it's going to be, I know that. It's her father."

Kelly frowned. "You've so rarely mentioned him, I didn't think he was a factor." She pointed to a stool at the work island and poured him a cup of coffee. "What's happening?"

"I should never have turned my back," Lief said. "I know this will be hard for you to envision, but before Lana died, Courtney was the sweetest, kindest, most loveable child. There was almost never a problem. Discipline was easy with her. But then her mother died and her life became hell. Not only was the poor kid a puddle of grief, but she started living with Stu, her surviving parent, and visiting me every other weekend. And at her father's house, she was treated worse than a dog."

"How, Lief?" she asked. "Was she abused?"

"Stu has a bitch for a wife and two little brats for kids. I think his boys are maybe seven and ten right now. Two years ago, at five and eight, they were horrible, undisciplined monsters. The entire household was one screaming, fighting mess. Courtney would come home for her weekend with me in tears, begging not to be forced to go back there, but my hands were tied. Once she even had a child's bite mark on her leg! A bite bad enough that I had to take her to the doctor. The clothes in her suitcase would come back ravaged and stained—not with food but with things like marker, paint, bleach. One of the little bastards cut her hair while she was asleep. It was a nightmare."

"Why would her father let that happen to her?"

"He was absent. He's a producer, mediocre at best, and his hours were long or he was on the phone or computer. Sherry, the stepmother, didn't watch the kids— just told them to go play, told Courtney she was a big girl and to stop whining. I've never been able to figure out why Stu wanted her around at all—he didn't spend any time with her, didn't protect her. I paid child support for the privilege of having her a couple of weekends a month, but surely that wasn't enough of an incentive for big-shot Stu. And you can probably guess what happened—Courtney changed. She started to look different. She started to act out, to fight back. By the time her hair was seven different colors and she looked like a little horror flick, Stu was ready to negotiate—she could live with me most of the time, visit him once in a while. For the next year she lived with me, visited Stu, kicking and screaming the whole way.

"There were things I noticed much later, after I had her back, things I should have noticed right away, but I'm not an experienced father," he went on. "She stopped crying about six months after her mom died, about six months after being tortured at Stu's house. She stopped smiling, too. I regularly checked her internet hits and found she researched suicide. She didn't eat enough to keep a bird alive and had no guilty pleasures, like ice cream or chocolate. She was failing in school. Things like that. And then one day about a year and a half after Lana died, it all came to a head. Courtney called me from her dad's house and said to come and get her—her stepmother had told her to get the hell out and stay out or she'd put her in foster care. She said she was going to run away if I didn't come. She was sleeping on the floor because Sherry's mother was visiting and her head was bleeding from getting hit with a toy truck."

Kelly gasped and covered her mouth.

"And I lost it. Lost it. I was there in thirty minutes. Courtney answered the door and I told her to show me where she was sleeping—sure enough, a sleeping bag on the toy room floor. I asked her to show me her regular room—it was a guest room made up for the grandmother, the closet and drawers and bathroom full of the grandmother's clothes—Stu hadn't even provided a room for his daughter. Bleeding head from a toy truck? One about big enough to ride! I heard the TV and found Sherry and her mother doing yoga to the TV in their screening room while drinking wine and giggling because they were tipsy. I told Courtney to wait by the door and I went to Stu's home office, yanked him out of his chair by his shirt, dragged him to the toy room, to the guest room, to the screening room, to the front door to take a look at the back of Courtney's head, which later took three stitches. And then he told me to get the little freak out of his life, he'd had it with her constant complaining. And I slammed him up against the wall, called him a lot of horrible names and threatened his life."

Kelly was quiet for a moment. When she finally did make a sound, it was "Whew."

"Yeah," he said, looking down. "Big-time Hollywood producer shouldn't mess with a farm boy. We're raised a little scrappy out in the country."

"My God, Lief. I had no idea how traumatized she's been."

"Completely. I brought her home, got her right into counseling, though I couldn't see that it helped much. I started looking for a house out of town and found the one I'm in now. It took me five months to get in it. And believe it or not, Courtney's come a long way since last spring."

"Looks like she's come a long way since I met her.

At least she doesn't ever have to go back to her father's house."

"Well, there's the problem. Stu called me this morning. He wants her for Christmas..."

"Don't!" Kelly said.

"I called my lawyer—I'm in a box. Since Stu pretty much threw her out, I knew I had her. All I wanted at the time was to get her some help, get control of the situation, and I never legally changed our custody arrangement. I should've done it while he was seeing her as a weird little freak who was more trouble than she was worth—he probably wouldn't have given me any trouble. I'll do that now, of course, but it's not going to get us out of Christmas. Stu says they're taking a family vacation to Disney World. Hopefully she can get through it. I'll talk to him again before that—I'll make sure I know where they are, make sure he knows I'm going to be nearby in case there's a problem, make sure he's not putting her on the floor in the kids' toy room."

"You think she'll go?" Kelly asked.

"I'll take her. I'm not sending her into the lion's den. I'll take her and stay in the same hotel..."

"Good," she said. "I mean, bad for Christmas, but there are other Christmases ahead..."

"It's my fault," he said. "I've contacted Stu twice in the past year—mostly out of guilt from promising to kill him. I called him and told him we were moving so he wouldn't accuse me of kidnapping, and I sent him Courtney's recent school picture. She's all cleaned up—no more Goth. Her smile looks real. I scribbled a note—that she was doing well and her grades were back up to As. If I'd just left it alone, left him thinking she was a wild, troublesome Goth character, I probably wouldn't have heard from him." He took a breath. "But like him or not, he's her father. I thought I had a responsibility. Damn it. Damn my parents for all that responsibility talk when I was growing up!"

She smiled at him, though her blue eyes were a little liquid. "Well, good for you. And you'll be just down the hall in the same hotel so you can rescue her if things get crazy." She shook her head. "I had no idea."

"There's been these times recently that amaze me," he said. "Like when she was showing my mother how to make a twisted French loaf, I saw the old Courtney. I love that kid, Kelly. She's my daughter."

Kelly straightened. "She was showing your mom a twisted French loaf?"

He nodded. "I know she learned from you…"

"Wow. I thought she pretty much hated me."

"I think that's just her fear and lack of confidence…"

"You realize I can't help you with any of this, don't you? I can sympathize and be an ear, but that's about it. First of all, I have no experience, no insights. Second, Courtney really doesn't want my help. She puts up with me—that's all. But if she liked me even a little, I'd go with you. If you had any trouble from the bad people, I'd be happy to kick ass and take names."

"I think she'd appreciate that..."

"She trusts you, Lief. If you tell her you're going to be nearby, I'm sure she'll be okay."

"I'm sorry about all the melodrama. None of it is her fault, not really."

She reached for his hand. "I know. Maybe we'll get through it yet."

"And I'm sorry about Christmas,"

"Not to worry. I'll stay busy. Maybe I can help out— would you like me to take care of Spike?"

"He's a load," Lief said.

She smiled and squeezed his hand. "It'll give me something to do. Maybe it'll get me some points with Courtney."

Once Lief left Kelly, she immediately started dragging vegetables out of the cooling drawers and refrigerator. After she had a big pile on the work island, she realized that she instinctively did this when she was at loose ends.

So much of what Lief had told her was shocking to her.

Courtney's problems were so much bigger than hers, that was for certain. That poor kid, just not old enough to understand the dysfunction of the adults who were supposed to take care of her. And who could blame her or fault her? Kelly didn't have to like her to realize she barely had a fighting chance.

Second, Lief's commitment and the weight of his

obligation kept growing. And yet, for the sake of a troubled young girl, she wouldn't have it any other way. But this would definitely change things, going forward. It would be very hard for Kelly to be a part of that family. It just might not be possible.

Kelly and Lief had begun to talk a little bit about how they might see each other over Christmas. Jillian and Colin were going back east. One of the Riordan brothers was assigned to the Pentagon; it seemed Luke and Shelby would go also, leaving Shelby's uncle Walt to check on the cabins in their absence. They had asked Kelly if she had any interest in going along, but she'd declined immediately. She had been looking forward to a rather quiet holiday, some of it with Lief. Perhaps with Lief and Courtney.

But not if they would be in Orlando.

Being a little lonely wasn't the worst thing. She'd be busy. Perhaps she could help out with chores around the gardens in case Denny, the assistant, wanted to take some time for the holidays. She'd cook, can and bake. That's what she did if she was lonely. If she was troubled or uncertain.

Why couldn't she fall for a man who was free to fall for her?

"No!" Courtney said. "No, you can't make me!"

Lief had talked to Jerry Powell, who'd encouraged him to break the news as soon as possible, not only to give Courtney time to get used to the idea but also time to talk to Jerry about her concerns at her next appointment. The minute he got her home from school that day, he broke it to her.

"I'm not going to make you, Court. I'm asking you to put up with this one last time and I'll get my lawyer working on a change in that custody agreement so that you won't have to do it again."

"Please," she said. "Please don't send me!"

"I won't send you," he said. "I'll take you myself. And I'll find out where you're staying in Orlando and I'll go. I might even go on the same plane, stay at the same hotel. I won't let him get away with anything."

She put her hands on her hips. "I bet you're just saying that. I bet it made your day—freed you right up to spend Christmas with your girlfriend!"

"Why would you say that? No," he said, shaking his head.

"Why? Because I remember it made you pretty damn mad when Stu decided to stop having custody or visitation—you were pissed. You threatened to kill him for doing that to you!"

"No!" Lief said. "No, Court! I wanted to kill him for treating *you* that way!"

"That isn't what it sounded like," she said, turning abruptly to walk away from him.

He grabbed her arm and spun her back. "Is that what you think? That I was mad about getting you back full-time?"

"That's how it looked. First thing you did after my

mom died was send me to Stu. Then Stu sent me back
and said, no—she'll live with you, visit me. Then he
said, 'Just take the little freak' and you had him up
against the wall, telling him you were going to kill him.
And then—all the way back to your house, you were
like *purple,* you were so pissed! You think I'm too fucking stupid to figure out no one wanted me? That I had
nowhere to go?"

Lief sank weakly to the couch in his great room.
She'd been a witness to the whole thing. How could she
not understand any of it? In his head he heard himself
telling her she shouldn't be saying *fucking*....

But she was gone. The door to her room slammed.

He felt like the bones in his body had melted. She
couldn't really have misunderstood to that degree, could
she? He tried to run the film of the whole year following
Lana's death in his mind, and it was clear as yesterday,
but he couldn't see it from Courtney's perspective. His
wife had died of an aneurism while at work; he'd been
called to come to the hospital, though she was already
gone. He'd had to pick up Court from school and try to
explain through his own choking tears. It was such a
dark blur—holding his little girl, crying with her, bury-
ing her mother.

And after that—packing her off to Stu. Hating that
son of a bitch as Lief only got her for a quick weekend a couple of times a month. After all, Stu hadn't
raised her; he'd never had her longer than the occasional
weekend.

Finally he stood up, forced himself to lift his chin, and went to Courtney's room. He didn't knock. He opened the door to find her on her cell phone. "Call whoever that is back," he said. "I need ten minutes."

She clicked off and looked up at him expectantly.

"It wasn't like that," he said. "The worst day of my life was when your mom died. The second worst day was when your father said, 'Well, I guess Courtney comes to live with us now.' I had to fight him, Courtney, to get weekend visitation. I had to pay him child support to get you two weekends a month. That day you called me to come for you, the day I got violent with him, I wanted to kill him for letting you be treated that way, for talking about you the way he did, for shoving you away when he should have put his *life* on the line to keep you safe! To make sure you knew you were loved and wanted. I swear to God."

She lifted her chin. "Looked like you were pissed off because he told you I was your problem from now on," she said.

"I should have killed him for saying that. He should never have let you feel that way. He was wrong."

"And I have to go there? To spend *Christmas* with him?"

"I will take you myself. I'll stay close, my cell phone on at all times, and if things aren't perfect, I'll get you out of there. Please trust me."

She looked down. "Funny you don't just take advantage of the vacation," she said. "You and the girl-friend."

"And it's funny you don't give her a chance. She's a good person. She wants to come along—camp out in Orlando where you are. She said one false move and she'd be happy to kick some ass."

She widened her eyes. "She said that?"

Lief nodded. "Not that many people are like Stu and Sherry. I hope to God they've changed."

"I don't know if I can do it," she said. Then she shuddered. "They're awful."

"Last time," he promised. "The lawyer is working up some paperwork asking for custody. Permanent custody. And I'll be close by, I promise."

"What about Spike?"

"I'll make sure he's taken care of. I'll find someone to take care of him before we go."

"Okay," she finally said. "But I think it's a bad, bad idea."

Fourteen

On the sixteenth, Kelly arrived at Lief's house at four in the afternoon, her arms laden with groceries. A second trip to her car brought her back with gifts for Lief and Courtney. While Lief and Courtney were pulling the last of their things together to pack, Kelly was cooking a special farewell dinner for them.

Too bad it couldn't be a joyous occasion.

Kelly didn't add her gifts to those still under the tree; she put hers on the table. Then she got busy—Courtney loved pasta, and Kelly had some to-die-for meatballs that she'd made ahead and added to her great-grandmother's sauce. By the time she was fluffing up a salad, Lief had joined her in the kitchen.

"How can I help?" he asked.

"You can pour us each a glass of wine and keep me company. I brought some gifts—nothing so much. Just a holiday thought."

"Kelly, you're an amazing woman, all you're doing

for Courtney and I when you're being abandoned for Christmas. I'd give anything to take you with me."

"And you should, too. I was trained in one of the meanest kitchens in San Francisco—I could take the bastard!"

He chuckled as he poured wine. He put a glass in Kelly's hand and clinked his against hers. "If I play this right, there won't be any more holidays like this."

"The most important thing is that Courtney understands she has some security in you." Spike came prancing into the kitchen, loose again, a pair of folded socks hanging out of his mouth—socks that had been left in Lief's suitcase. Lief picked him up. "Two important things," Kelly amended. "That she feels secure and that I keep the dog alive!"

"The big challenge for you will be not killing him. When he's not whimpering in the kennel, he's in trouble."

She leaned toward Lief and, over the puppy's head, gave him a kiss. "I have ear plugs."

"Are you sure you don't mind staying here for him?"

She shook her head. "It only makes sense. That big old house will swallow me up. Besides, I'm going to sleep in your bed. With any luck I'll smell your after-shave on the pillow."

"Will you spend some time in Jillian's kitchen?" he asked her.

"I'll go over there once in a while. I might do some cooking. And I'll be sure to keep an eye on things, just to make sure all is secure. Believe me, I won't have time to be lonely with two big houses and a naughty puppy to manage."

"I might call you fifteen times a day," he said.

"There are two landlines and a cell," she said. "Just be careful you don't get yourself arrested for stalking."

Courtney was understandably subdued during dinner. "Will you play with him sometimes?" she asked Kelly.

"Every day," she said. "By the time you get home, he'll sit up to shake hands."

"Well, let's clear the table and open a few presents. Courtney, Kelly brought you something."

Courtney shook her head. "I don't want to open anything until I get back. I just want this to be over."

Kelly almost said, *As we all do!*

"Courtney, Kelly has gone to a lot of trouble for us—"

"No, it's okay. Let's all wait. That's a better idea. Let's get through this and celebrate a homecoming when it's behind us. How about that? I like that idea."

Before the table was even cleared, Courtney stood up. "I think I'll just take Spike to bed now."

Kelly stopped her before she could leave the kitchen. "Courtney, listen. I'm sorry you have to do this—your dad told me how hard it is. You'll have your cell phone, right? Make sure my numbers are programmed in. If you ever wonder how the puppy's getting along, call me."

"Have you ever actually *had* a dog before?"

Her tone was so abrasive, Kelly had to fight the urge

to stiffen indignantly. Instead she smiled and said, "No, I haven't. And I thank you for letting me do this. I look forward to it. I'll be very careful with him."

Courtney just shrugged and left them alone.

"Maybe when she sees that we're both on her team, things will improve," Lief said.

"Maybe so," Kelly said. But she was thinking, *If it doesn't improve a lot, I'm not signing on for this.*

She didn't stay late, though leaving Lief's arms wasn't easy. She told him to spend that last night at home with Courtney, in case she felt like talking. When she got to her own bed on the third floor of the Victorian, all she could do was toss and turn. She had a feeling this thing she had with him wasn't going to make it. He had another woman in his life, a more important one. She didn't mind falling second, but she couldn't survive as persona non grata.

Lief and Courtney set out for the six-hour drive to San Francisco on the seventeenth, and it was a morbidly quiet drive. He tried to reassure her from time to time with statements like, "I know you won't enjoy this visit as much as I'd like you to, Court, but it's not dangerous. Worst case, highly annoying."

"Right," she said.

"Listen," Lief said, "if there's anything about this that's dangerous, you need to speak up! Have your dad or stepmom ever done anything to physically harm you? Ever hit, ever put you in dangerous situations, ever—"

"The only dangerous thing is that I have to stay under

the same roof with those carnivorous boys. And no—
nobody touches me funny, either! But I have to tell you
the truth, it goes way beyond highly annoying. I've had
medical treatment after a couple of visits with them!"

There was no arguing that. "Do you carry hairspray?"
he asked.

"Yes."

"Hairspray," he said. "Right in the eyes! And fight
back! Call the police! Do not let anyone hurt you."

She sighed heavily. "Are you sure you'll be close?"

"I will follow you all the way. I got all the information from your dad, booked a ticket on the same flights
and a room at the Disney Hotel. We're solid. He wasn't
at all happy about it, either. He says if I interfere, there
will be trouble. The good news is—it's Disney World.
There will be a million people around. If you need help
and you don't see me standing six feet behind you, all
you have to do is shout."

"Thanks," she said meekly. "You sure Spike's going
to be all right?"

"Sure, honey. Kelly's not only a good, responsible
person, she likes him. And he's cute. Besides, she's
going to be all alone."

"What about her sister and all those people?" she
asked.

"Gone for the holidays. It's just Kelly. They invited
her along, but she didn't want to impose. She volunteered
to take care of the dog so he wouldn't have to go to the
vet's kennel."

"Oh," she said. "I didn't know she volunteered. I thought you asked her."

"I told you—"

"Yeah, yeah, she's nice," Courtney interrupted.

"Listen, we'll have a good dinner in San Francisco, then a little shopping. You might as well have some vacation clothes. We don't fly to L.A. until midday tomorrow, so we have lots of time to relax. We can enjoy ourselves."

"Sure," she said, biting her nail down to the quick.

As much as Lief wished Lana were still alive, he was glad she didn't have to see this. Watching Courtney suffer ripped his heart out. Lana had somehow managed to get around Stu most of the time, keeping Courtney's visits to his house down to a bare minimum, but for his life, Lief couldn't remember how she'd done it!

After checking in to their hotel, Lief took Courtney shopping. It was like dragging a ball and chain, but he managed to get her interested in a couple of shirts, capris and hoodies. Not much, but something. They chose an Italian restaurant, somewhere Courtney could get a cheese pizza and nothing exotic. They shopped a little bit afterward, but she just couldn't relax and enjoy herself.

For all the times Lief had nearly fallen to his knees to pray she'd just stop sniping at him, he couldn't bear her silence.

When they got to L.A., he rented a car. He stopped off at her favorite burger restaurant to be sure she had something solid to eat before dropping her at Stu's, but she only picked. "Look, all we can do is get this over with," he said. "I have an appointment with the lawyer tomorrow—he's going to get together the paperwork. I'm filing for permanent custody. We'll file the second we step off the plane after this ordeal. Let's try to get through it, Court. I'm sorry, but that's all we've got."

"I know."

He carried her bag to the front door. She rang the bell.

"Court?" he said, causing her to turn. He put down the bag and opened his arms to her. She rarely hugged him anymore, rarely showed physical affection. But with watery eyes, she filled his arms and hugged him hard. "It's going to be all right. We'll get past this."

"Promise you'll be there," she whispered.

"Promise."

The door opened and Stu stood there, a beam. "Welcome, Courtney! Long time! You look great! Ready for a little vacation with the family?"

Courtney just looked down and entered the house, pulling her suitcase behind her.

"Thanks, Lief," Stu said. "Guess I'll see you late on the second."

"You'll see me sooner than that. I was able to get tickets on your flight, reservations at your hotel. I'm going to be nearby in case Courtney needs me. No more bite marks, no more stitches, no more abuse."

"Whatever," he said dismissively. "Kids have their issues. Siblings fight sometimes. I can't be on top of 'em every second."

"Well, you'd better be, Stu."

"Lighten up, man! I'm taking her on a goddamn vacation! And I can't keep you from following us, but you'd better keep your distance or I'll be calling my lawyer!"

Great, Lief thought. *He can talk to my lawyer.* "I won't get in the way unless she needs me."

"She isn't going to need you. Stay out of my face while I vacation with my family!"

Courtney waited inside the door until Stu turned to her and told her where she was to sleep. Turned out she got the guest room—bed and everything.

"Want anything to eat?" he asked her.

"No, thank you," she said. She pulled her suitcase to the bedroom and closed the door behind her. The house was fairly quiet; no greetings from the stepwitch or the boys, which suited her just fine. She checked her iPhone for messages and shot a text to Amber. *Haven't been beaten or fed to the dogs yet. Off to a good start!*

Amber wrote her right back. *Don't be so dramatic! Try to have some fun!*

"Shows what you know," she said aloud.

She didn't even open her suitcase; she was a little afraid to get comfortable, to let her guard down. She put in her earbuds and listened to some music from the phone. Every now and then she'd hear one of the boys shout or run down the hall, but she was left strictly alone. Maybe they'd just let her tag along, enjoy a little of Disney on her own. Lief had given her money and the emergency credit card—one that he had in her name in case she ever ran into a worst-case scenario and needed cab fare or even a plane ticket. If Stu and Sherry just left her alone, maybe she would enjoy a little trip to Orlando.

Late that night she texted Lief. "I'm sleeping in a bed and no one has bothered me."

He texted back immediately; he hadn't been asleep either. "Just do your best and let me know if you need me."

She decided she *was* going to give it her best. Maybe when this was over Lief would be really proud of her and that would be the end of this back and forth crap. She didn't want to ever go through this again! With her earbuds in her ears, she fell asleep listening to the music stored on her iPhone; she slept in her clothes. She didn't leave her room once, not even for the bathroom. Sunlight was brightening the room when she woke up; the battery in her iPhone was dead from having it on all night. She sat up and rubbed her eyes. She'd slept on top of the covers, not even burrowing into the bed. She rooted around in her bag for her recharger and plugged in the phone before even walking out of her room to the hallway bath.

There was an awful lot of activity in the house, but she thought that was probably normal. When she finally made her way to the kitchen, she saw there was luggage by the front door.

"Well, sleepyhead," Sherry said cheerfully. "I was

just about to wake you. You must have been awful tired to sleep so late."

"What time is it?" she asked. She didn't wear a watch; her iPhone was almost permanently attached to the palm of her hand. That was her time source.

"My gosh, it's after seven, and we have an early start today! I hope you didn't completely unpack! We need you and your suitcase ready in fifteen minutes!"

Courtney frowned. "For what?"

"For our trip, silly!" And then Sherry grinned.

"We're not leaving till tomorrow," Courtney said.

"Last-minute change of plans, pumpkin," Stu said as he came into the room, holding his coffee cup. "It's all good—we'll get there a day early."

They were awful dressed up for a travel day. Sherry was wearing a designer sweat suit—it might've been silk—gold sandals and lots of jewelry. Her red hair was teased and spiky, her fingernails long and coral, her toenails matched. Stu looked pretty slick himself, for a short bald guy. "You told my dad the twentieth."

Stu immediately frowned. "Okay, now, that really hurts. I'm your dad, pumpkin. I know the guy's important to you, but could you cut me some slack here? I'm taking you on a first-class vacation. I want you to enjoy yourself and your family. Can you let me be the dad?"

"You told Lief the twentieth," she persisted, thinking *what is this pumpkin shit?*

"Last-minute great deal on tickets, that's all," he said, standing up to his full five-foot-six. "I'm sure he'll figure it out."

She decided she'd just call Lief from the airport if her phone had charged enough. So far things weren't disastrous.

"I don't have time to shower," she said.

"Just wash up a little and change," Stu said. "We have a car on the way. We're going to get the fun started!"

Courtney had a very bad feeling about this, but she was also backed up to the wall. Their bags were sitting at the door, they were all being nice to her, and all Stu seemed to want was to be referred to as her dad. She could do that. But the bad feeling just wouldn't go away.

A fancy car with a uniformed driver showed up; Stu was doing this up big. When they arrived at the airport, he had the driver transfer the bags to a skycap. Stu took charge of the boarding passes and IDs and ushered them all to the first-class lounge. He told the boys to sit at a table, and there was a slight shoving match as they did so. Stu barked, "Boys! Remember our deal?"

They stopped at once, hung their heads and sat down quietly. Boy, she had never seen anything like that before. Maybe things were changing—Sherry was cheerful, Stu was disciplining, the boys were almost human.

A few minutes later, another couple came into the lounge, all smiles upon seeing the Stu and Sherry Lord family. They had two small children with them, probably about three and four years old. There were lots of hugs and handshakes, and then the woman, a very pretty woman, came right up to where Courtney was sitting, bent at the waist to be on eye level with her, and said, "You must be Courtney! I'm Ann Paget! I can't tell you how much I appreciate this, Courtney! The au pair quit without notice and here we are, stuck! Believe me, Dick and I will make it well worth your while—I promise!"

"Huh?" she said, completely confused.

"And this," Ann said, bringing forward the children, "is Alison and Michael. This is Courtney, kids. Say hi!"

"Hi," Michael, the older one, said. The little girl just stuffed her hand in her mouth and buried her head in her mother's thigh.

"Aw, it's early," Ann said. "They're usually much more friendly and outgoing." Then she laughed. "That's something you'll have to watch! These two will walk off with any stranger!"

"What?" Courtney said. She actually found herself thinking she wanted to *stay* confused, but the sick reality of it was coming through. "I don't understand," she said hopefully.

"Courtney," Stu said. "Come with me a second, honey." He took her arm rather gently, pulled her out of her chair in the first-class lounge. She looked over her shoulder to see Sherry herding Ann and Dick Paget to the bar for Bloody Marys as Stu led her farther into the lounge. He sat her down on a sofa far enough away from the group so that they wouldn't be overheard. "Here's the deal, Courtney. These people are very important to my business. He's a well-known director. If I get him for this film, it could set me up for life. I'm ready to make a deal with you—help me out with this and you never have to have anything to do with me again. Screw this up for me and I'll make sure you never see Lief Holbrook again. I have custody. I'm your biological father. He won't even get weekends."

"Help you out how?" she asked with a scowl.

"You call me dad, you help watch the kids. That's it. We all have a good time and when it's over, Dick and Ann will give you a big wad of cash for some babysitting. That's all."

"I want my dad!" she said.

"I'm serious, Courtney. If you screw this up now, I'll fight Lief for permanent custody. I'm your biological father. I'll win."

"After doing this to me?" she asked.

"Doing what? Taking you on a sinfully perfect Hawaiian vacation? I'm sure the courts will lock me up for it!"

"Hawaiian vac— We're supposed to go to Disney World! My dad has tickets on the same plane and a room at the same—"

Stu was smiling. "Here's how it is, sweetheart. Help me out here. Help watch the kids so Dick and Ann can have some fun. It won't be that bad. And after it's over, you go back to the mountains with your knight in shining armor and I'll leave you alone. I need this, Courtney. Like I've never needed anything."

"I don't even babysit! I hardly ever have!"

"Come on, you're a smart girl. Ann and Dick will

never be far away. Just play with them, keep them out of trouble. It's not like you have to change diapers or feed them!"

She looked at the boys. "Them, too?"

"They don't need that much watching. Besides, I told them both if you complain about the way they act even once, they're finished. If they're good, I'll take them on the Disney Cruise. Now, you'll have to give me your cell phone."

Her eyes welled. "No," she said, pulling away from him.

"Will you stop acting like I'm a kidnapper? I'll call your dad later, tell him where we are. Courtney, I swear to you, if you do this for me, I'll never bother you again. It won't be bad, I promise. Ann and Dick are good parents. They'll be watching their kids most of the time anyway—they just need a hand keeping the kids busy and out of trouble. So we can talk, so we can go out to dinner and stuff."

"Why?" she asked, shaking her head. "Why did you do this? You tricked me and you tricked Lief!"

"You heard her—the au pair quit. They were going to cancel and I already had two first-class condos on the beach. I need this director, Courtney. Work with me here."

"I need to talk to Lief first…"

"No. That's a deal breaker. You have to promise not to bring him into this—he'll never go along with it and I need this time with the Pagets. You work with me, help me out, or we fight it out in court and you have to put up with us for the rest of your life."

She felt a tear run down her cheek. To her absolute amazement, Stu wiped it gently away with his thumb. He'd never paid much attention to her, much less shown gentle affection.

"Listen," he said softly. "I'm desperate, all right? I have some serious money problems and one small shot at working it out. I don't want it to be this way with us, but I need a couple of breaks here. Call me Dad. Keep the little kids out of trouble so Ann and Dick can focus on business. That's all I need, honey. Please."

Part of her wanted to do it now—start screaming. Ask for help. Tell anyone who would listen that he had tricked her and was taking her away against her will. *To a sinfully perfect Hawaiian vacation…?* She might succeed in causing them to miss their flight, but after that? Could he be telling the truth? Just go to the beach with these kids in tow, do a little babysitting while the parents go out to dinner, and this nightmare part of her life was over?

"How bad can it be, huh? Ten days at the beach in exchange for me giving up custody? Come on."

"But I have to talk to Lief."

"I told you, pumpkin. You know he's not going to go along with this. He'll screw up my deal and I'll be fighting him in court for years. But you'll spend those years living in my house, I guarantee that." He held out his hand. "I'll call him later and let him know where we are. Phone please."

She was torn. She didn't really believe him, and she didn't trust him. She wasn't sure that if she did this for ten days, he'd set her free. But she was absolutely certain that if she *didn't* play his game, he'd make her suffer somehow.

She put the phone in his hand. When Lief didn't hear from her, he might alert the National Guard.

"Thanks, pumpkin. I owe you for this and I promise I'll come through. Now go splash a little water on your face and get in the game. This is all going to come out the way you want it to."

She sniffed and watched Stu walk to join Sherry and the Pagets at the bar where they had a Bloody Mary just waiting for him. And she went to the bathroom to get a grip, to talk herself into her ten-day sentence.

At the bar, Ann faced Stu with concern. "Is there a problem?" she asked. "Is Courtney having second thoughts?"

"Well," Stu laughed. "She's only fourteen, remember. She wanted to be sure she'd get her fair share of beach time, too. I'm sure it'll work out that she'll have plenty of fun."

"Of course!" Ann said emphatically. "We always made sure our au pairs had their own time!"

"There you go," Stu said, lifting his glass. "To a perfect vacation. And a perfect friendship!"

The ten-day sentence began with Courtney sitting in coach with four kids while the two fun couples enjoyed first-class. The little ones were well-behaved, thanks

to being used to babysitters and the abundant supply
of books and portable DVD players with their favorite
movies and snacks. Aaron and Conner lasted about an
hour before they started kicking the seats in front of
them, scraping and making too much noise. Courtney
knew she was taking a chance, but she couldn't help
herself—she exacted a little revenge on Stu and Sherry.
When the flight attendant asked her if she was responsible for the boys she said, "Actually, I'm the au pair for
these two little angels. The parents of those two are in
first-class. Maybe you should get them?"

Stu came back, warned them sternly, frowned at
Courtney and went back to his party. He had to come
back three more times. He leaned his face close to
Courtney's and said, "You're pushing me."

"Quote—'they don't need that much watching,'"
she said. "End quote. Indentured servants only have
two hands." Then she smiled into his annoyed eyes and
mouthed, *I hate you so much.*

She did what was expected of her for six hours; Ann
and Dick came to check on their kids but never had to be
called out of first-class. By the time the plane landed in
Maui, Courtney was exhausted, hungry and near tears,
but Ann was impressed.

Stu had a stretch limo waiting, and Courtney helped
herd all the luggage and children to the car. When they
reached the condos, they parted company, and Courtney went with Stu, Sherry and the boys to their condo
to settle in. Before they even had their luggage dropped

off, Sherry walked next door and said to Dick and Ann, "Drinks on the beach in a half hour!"

"Oh, I don't know," Ann said. "The kids might need a nap after that long plane ride."

"Courtney will watch them. Won't you, sweetheart?" Sherry said.

She straightened her spine. "I didn't get food on the plane," she said. "They don't serve food in coach. Just in first-class."

"Oh, darling," Ann said. "You must be starving! I'll have something sent up to you and the kids from the beach bar immediately. Can you get the kids settled or do you need my help with that?"

She thought for a second. Ann was as selfish as Sherry, but wearing a 'nice suit.' "Just go," she said wearily. "*Mom?*" she said, the word souring in her mouth. "Please take the boys with you so they don't wake the little ones."

"Courtney," Sherry answered with a laugh. "They can't go to a *bar!*"

"I can't handle all of them at nap time."

"They'll be fine on the beach," Stu said.

Ann wrote down her cell phone number and put it by the hotel phone. "Just call me if there's any problem, Courtney. I'll come right up."

Courtney eyeballed the phone, then shot a glance at Stu.

"Go ahead, everyone," Stu said.

When the room was clear but for Courtney, Stu and the two little kids, Stu said, "I'm going to call Lief, tell him where we are. If *you* call him, the deal's off. You'll be moving back in with me."

"I should tell him I said I'd do it."

"I'll tell him. Just don't let me down and I won't let you down."

Two hours later, a pizza was delivered to the condo where Courtney was babysitting two children who, after sleeping on the plane, were not at all tired.

This time, she thought to herself, Lief *is* going to kill him. She was looking forward to it. If she survived this.

Lief's appointment with his lawyer was very encouraging. With Courtney's strong desire to live with Lief in Virgin River along with the accompanying issues of bites, stitches and sleeping on the floor while everyone else in the family not only had a bed but their own bedrooms, this should be a slam dunk. Not to mention the fact that Stu had kicked her out, given her up to Lief. After all, she was fourteen-and-a-half years old, not four-and-a-half. And she wasn't choosing to live with Lief because she could get away with murder—since living with him her appearance had changed dramatically as had her grades. She had new friends and new and healthy hobbies such as riding.

"Unless Stu fights you on this, I don't see a problem," the lawyer said. "Could take us a while—courts move slowly. But she shouldn't have to go back to him."

So Lief texted her. *Good news. Lawyer says we're*

going to be fine. Finish this visit on good terms and we'll have our custody.

About four hours later she texted back. *thanx. U R the bomb. Having fun. TTYS*

It didn't feel right. First of all, her responses were usually immediate. Even a half hour or hour seemed too long, but four hours? And Courtney didn't text things like, "You are the bomb," which had gone out a long time ago. And TTYS, for "talk to you soon," was a more adult acronym.

As soon as he'd gotten her response, he'd texted right back, *You all right?*

Great. Later, came right back at him.

So he went to the airport the next day, fully expecting to see the entire Lord family in the boarding area, ready to go. When he didn't see them, he assumed they were running late. But as boarding time neared, he became more worried. Then as most of the passengers got on the plane and departure time approached, he went to the gate agent and asked if they had already boarded.

"I'm sorry, sir, but I'm not allowed to give out that information," she said.

"Can you check and see if my daughter, Courtney Lord, is on the plane."

"Listen, I'm not supposed to—"

He took out his wallet and flipped it open. There was the most recent picture of Courtney. "I'm her stepfather, but she lives with me full-time. Her mother is deceased and she's supposed to take this trip to Orlando with her biological father and his new family—she didn't want to. Help me out here. I promised her I'd be nearby if she needed me. I'm not getting on the plane until I know she's there."

"Sir, this could be just one giant—"

"What?" he asked. "Scam? To get on a plane full of people with a terrified fourteen-year-old girl? "

The gate agent thought for a moment, clearly weighing breaking the rules against helping a person who came off as believable.

"Take the picture out of the sleeve, please," she said quietly.

He did so. She clicked around on her computer a bit, then carried the picture away from her podium. She showed it to the agent who was checking in the boarding passengers. Then she went down the Jetway. Five really awful minutes passed before she came back and said, "I didn't see her. No one remembers seeing her. I don't show the name Lord on the manifest."

He closed his eyes, his mouth opening with an unspoken *Oh, dear God,* his head tilting back. He took the picture from the gate agent and said, "Thank you. I have to get my bags off the plane."

"Aren't you going to board now, Mr. Holbrook?" she asked.

"No. I have to get my luggage off the plane and find my daughter," he said.

Once he had his luggage, he phoned his lawyer. He tried Courtney's phone and Stu's, but was sent to voice mail both times. He called the hotel in Orlando; they wouldn't tell him if there was a reservation in Stu's name, but they would say no one by that name had checked in.

Then he called Kelly. "He tripped me up again," he said. "I can't find Courtney and she's not taking my calls. Neither is Stu."

"Oh, my God," Kelly said. "What are you going to do?"

"I don't know. Call the police, I guess. I'll call you in a while."

Fifteen

Kelly was feeling a little lonely. Spike wasn't quite enough company to sustain her. She tucked him into his kennel on his soft bed with a chew toy. Then she exchanged her sweat suit for a nice pair of jeans, boots, crisp white blouse and heavy wool blazer. She went into town to the bar, but she didn't go empty-handed. She took a big batch of Christmas cookies, some for Jack's family, some for Preacher's. She found the place empty.

"Wow, did I rent the place out for a private party?" she asked jokingly.

"Well, missy, nice to see you," Jack said. "We had some of the regulars for dinner earlier, but hunters are rare about now. Everyone's home wrapping the presents and decking the halls. Just a few days till Christmas."

"I brought cookies for you and Preacher," she said, putting a couple of large covered plates on the bar.

"Thank God for you," Jack said. "We had some

cookie donations, but none of them made it home with me. Mel can't bake. And I don't have time."

"She can't bake at all?" she asked.

"At all," he confirmed. Then he turned and banged on the wall to bring Preacher out. "Have you eaten?" he asked Kelly.

"Yes, thanks. I just thought I'd drop in for a little bit of brandy on a cold December night. Brandy and company. Courtney's puppy and I have totally bonded, but he hasn't learned to talk yet."

"That's right, you're on your own," Jack said. Preacher came from the back, wiping his hands on his apron. He wore his usual frown until he saw her, then grinned happily. Jack went on, "The Riordans are in D.C. with Sean and Franci, and Lief is out of town. You know you have a standing invitation at the Sheridan household. Don't worry—I can cook even if Mel can't."

"And you're always welcome at our house," Preacher said.

She chuckled. "Thanks, boys. Just a little brandy will do it for now. I also have an invitation from General Booth."

"Then let's just have a drink," Jack said. "No one around to make us work." He brought down a snifter for her brandy, which he poured first, and a couple of shot glasses for himself and Preacher. Before anyone drank, he asked, "You doing okay, Kelly?"

"I'm getting by fine. It's quiet, but I haven't lived with anyone in my entire adult life and Jill and I could barely scratch together a holiday meal before she came

to Virgin River. This is nothing new. It's just that I..."
She cleared her throat. "I miss Lief."

"Have you heard from him?"

"I have," she said, taking a sip. She needed to see
a friendly face after Lief's alarming call. "Remy," she
said appreciatively. "Thanks, Jack. Very nice. Yes, I've
heard from him several times. He ran into some trouble.
He got all the travel information from Courtney's dad
but when he got to the airport, none of them were on
the flight they were supposed to be on. He'd booked
himself on it, as well. Of course the hotel in Orlando
wouldn't tell him if Stu's family had reservations there,
but they hadn't registered yet as of this morning. Lief
doesn't know where they went. He doesn't know if it's
just a different flight and different hotel or a whole different place. Courtney's not answering her phone. He
can't find them."

"Jesus," Preacher said. "That's horrible. What kind
of bastard does something like that?"

"Well, in this case, the kind of bastard who's the
custodial parent and doesn't want anyone in his business. Lief texted Courtney's phone immediately asking
where she was and got no reply. He's called Stu's phone
repeatedly, even trying the 'unknown caller' option—
he's not taking calls. She's either having a wonderful
time or he's not letting her use her own phone."

"Lief must be half-crazy," Jack said. "Is he still in
L.A. or did he go to Orlando?"

"He's not budging till he figures out where to go."

"He's not coming back?"

"Are you kidding?" she said with an unamused laugh. "Not without Courtney. I think he's living between a rental car and the airport. He's been to talk to their neighbors, called the police, asked for help from a detective, tried to bribe airline personnel... That almost got him arrested. And it's Christmas week—no one wants to get involved now. It's not exactly kidnapping. It would be hard to even argue custodial interference since he gave Stu permission to take her on vacation. Everyone he talks to tells him to relax, it's her father, she'll be back soon. Etcetera." Kelly put down her snifter and rubbed her temples. "I feel for him. Feel for them both. But this is seriously bigger than I am."

"Been there," Preacher said, lifting his glass.

"You have?" she asked him.

"When I met Paige, she was married and already had Chris. She came in here one night on the run from a bad husband. Took a lot of doing before all that could be left in the past and we could start a life."

"A *lot* of doing," Jack confirmed.

"I thought the kids were both yours," she said.

Preacher shook his head. "Really, I didn't think I'd ever marry and have kids. It's a pure miracle."

"So let me ask you something," Kelly said. "How old was Chris? Did you have trouble getting on his good side?"

"He was only four. We got along fine from the start, but not because I had any idea what I was doing. It was Paige I had to win over. She'd been in a real bad abusive relationship and was pretty worried about making another mistake like that. Takes a lot of patience, Kelly. Patience and maybe blind faith."

"While you were having this patience, did you ever get very, very lonely?" she asked.

Jack and Preacher were both quiet for a moment.

"Come to our house for Christmas dinner, Kelly," Preacher said. "I'll even let you help in the kitchen if it makes you feel better."

She laughed at him. "Nah, it's not that. I'm used to being alone. It's just that however this all works out, I have no idea how to convince Courtney I won't take her dad away from her. That poor kid has been through so much. Who knows where she is now? And I don't want to stand in line to be the next wicked stepmother."

"She's a little prickly," Jack said. "Teenagers are like that anyway. Even the ones who haven't been through a lot."

"Right now I'd be so happy to deal with all her little prickly thorns if I just knew she was safely in Lief's care." She took a sip. "They need each other so much."

And I need him a little too much, she thought.

Lief had exhausted almost all his ideas; it had been a very stressful couple of days. It seemed there was no help for a stepfather who'd been duped. He couldn't imagine what Court might be going through, kept from him like this. Was she thinking that he'd broken his promise to be nearby in case she needed him? And he was panicked to think *where* she might be, though he was relatively certain Stu couldn't have taken her out of the country. Lief had her passport in the strongbox at home along with her birth certificate.

He tried one last idea. Walt Booth's number was listed, and he called it. Walt picked up on the second ring. "Walt, it's Lief. I'm calling from Los Angeles and I need to reach Muriel. It's urgent."

"She's right here. Hang on."

When she came on the line, Lief explained what he was up against.

"Why, that bastard," she said. "How does a person do something like that when a child is involved? How can he sleep at night? Don't you worry. I'll find him!"

"He's not answering his cell phone, but here's the number in case you can find a way to get through."

"Oh, I'll get through. I'll get a patch through a studio or agency line. When Muriel St. Claire wants to make a movie, people tend to take the call. And even though it's just a few days before Christmas, I want a meeting. I'll offer to fly in, wherever he is. Just sit tight and try not to panic."

"God, why didn't I think to call you two days ago? Thank you."

"Keep the phone on, Lief," she said.

Less than an hour later his phone rang and it was Muriel. "He's in Maui. Kapalua Beach in some condo. Got a pen?"

"Ready," he said.

She gave him the address. "Can you get there, Lief?"

"I'll get there if I have to swim," he said. "Listen, I owe you."

"Just go get your girl. I never did like Stu Lord. He's an ass."

Lief turned in his rental car and headed straight to LAX, determined to eat and sleep in the airport until he could find a flight. He had to wait several hours and couldn't get a nonstop into Maui, but he was headed in the right direction and was grateful he could find anything at all this close to Christmas—the airport was mobbed.

Courtney had done three days of babysitting, counting their travel day, and was exhausted, even though Alison and Michael were good children and their parents were usually close by. Stu said he'd talked to Lief, and Lief had said to tell her to try to have a good time, that he wished he was at the beach. "Didn't he ask to talk to me?" she had asked.

"Courtney, I asked him not to interfere and I promised him you were fine," Stu said. "He warned me that I'd better be telling the truth and agreed to leave it alone. After all, I am your father."

"I don't believe you!"

"We have a deal," he reminded her.

"I'm sick of babysitting!"

"Well, you decide what you want, Courtney. Life in L.A. or the mountains. It's up to you."

So she held out, and after just a couple of days she was feeling tired and bored. She wasn't going to last through another week of this—chasing little ones, eating with them, reading to them, playing with them, falling asleep on the couch in Ann and Dick's condo, right next door to Stu and Sherry's condo, until Ann and Dick came back late at night after dinner, a little drunk. And Ann would cheerfully say, "Courtney, our last au pair would at least pick up the house before we got home."

"But I'm not an au pair and I never wanted to be one!" she said.

"But you're doing so well. The children love you!"

This was almost a practical joke.

At least she didn't have to watch the older boys very much; Stu and Sherry let them run wild and kept tabs on them during the day. They hired a hotel service at night since Courtney babysat in Ann and Dick's condo next door. Thankfully they didn't want to hang out with a three- and four-year-old.

She kept trying to figure out how she was going to get out of this situation without the penalty being a life sentence with Stu and Sherry. Every last idea went through her head, even just running away and living on the streets. She thought about ditching right now—she had that credit card. She wouldn't mind sitting at the airport until she could get a flight, even if it took days. But she'd have to at least tell Ann and Dick; she couldn't leave Alison and Michael unattended—they were completely innocent. If something happened to them, she'd probably get life in prison. And if she alerted the Pagets, that would alert Stu. And while Ann and Dick seemed polite enough, always remembering to say please and thank you and smiling while they gave orders, they were not at all interested in watching their own kids. They were obviously quite accustomed to having full-time help.

She just wanted off this island so bad.

She was at the hotel restaurant for breakfast with Alison and Michael, as usual. They sat at a table on the other side of the room from Stu and Sherry and Dick and Ann; the adults didn't want to be bothered or summoned unless it was absolutely necessary. The older boys were done eating and had taken off for the beach. While she and the Paget children were finishing up, an older couple she'd seen for the last few days sat down at the table next to them.

"You sure have your hands full, young lady," the gentleman said.

"What a nice big sister," the silver-haired woman said.

"I'm not related to them," she said.

"Oh? Pretty nice babysitting job, I guess," the man said.

And that fast, she knew she was done. Lief would have to find a way to get them out of this custody mess. She was not living with Stu.

"Excuse me, do you by chance have a cell phone?"

"Sure thing," the gentleman said. He plucked it out of his shirt and handed it to her. "It's not an international call, is it?" he teased.

"'Course not," she said. She punched in the numbers and waited. "Oh! Dang! Your voice mail! Dad, Dad, it's me! I'm in Maui at Kapalua Beach. I know we're not supposed to even be here! Stu told me if I called you, he'd find a way to never let me see you again. He said he'd make sure I'd regret it! I want to go home." Then her voice grew a little panicked because she'd done it—called him! Nixed *the deal*. "Please, come and get me! He took my phone away and told me I'd better not call you or else! Don't call me back on this phone—I just borrowed it. Just come! Come and get me! Please, Dad. Please!" She swallowed back tears. "Please," she said one last time.

She clicked off and handed the phone back to the man. Both of them, the man and his wife, were looking at her in open-mouthed horror. Shocked.

"Thanks," she said meekly.

"Sweetheart, do you need help?" the woman asked.

"I need my dad," she said. "When he gets the message, he'll come."

"Are you in trouble? In danger?" she asked.

She shook her head. "I'll be fine until my dad comes." Then she wiped the kids' faces and said, "Come on, you two. Let's go to the swings."

Courtney glanced over her shoulder to see them looking at each other in disbelief. They conferred briefly. She just went to the playground. Maybe Lief was okay with her being on this trip, like Stu said, but if she called him she knew he would come.

Stu would just have to live with it; they'd all have to watch their own kids. She was so outta here!

Courtney had been chasing the kids around the play area and pushing them on the swings for about an hour when she noticed a blue-uniformed police officer walking toward her. His partner seemed to be standing on the walking path behind him, talking into his radio. The gray-haired couple from breakfast were standing with the officer on the path. And she thought, Crap! They'd called the police! Now that was going to really piss Stu off!

She hadn't been kidnapped, she thought. Just tricked. But by her own father. She should have started screaming at the L.A. airport.

"Hi, miss," the police officer said. "How are you?"

"I'm fine," she said, pushing one child, then the other in the swings.

"I'm wondering if you need assistance," he said. "I'd be happy to help if you have a problem."

"Why?" she asked.

"We received a call saying you were being held against your will by someone," he explained. "That couple over there heard you call your father and beg him to come for you because someone wouldn't let you call him? Is there a problem of some kind you want to tell me about?"

"I just needed to call my dad, to tell him to come and get me. I could get back to California on my own, but no way Stu would let me go. But my dad will come for me. My stepdad, actually, but I've lived with him for years. I've even lived with him since my mom died, but my real dad brought me here to babysit for his friends so they can party and my dad...my *step*dad, who I live with, probably doesn't even know where I am. Stu said he called him, but I just don't believe it. Stu...my real dad...said he was taking me with the family to Disney World and brought me here to babysit instead. That's all I need. Is for my dad to come and get me. Stepdad. But my stepdad is my *real* dad!"

The police officer frowned. He must have been completely confused.

And Stu Lord, who was totally blind and deaf while his sons were tearing up the beach or acting like professional wrestlers in the coach section of the airplane, was running toward them because there were cops around Courtney. He was out of breath when he reached them.

"Officer," he wheezed. "Did my daughter do something wrong?"

"Just offering our assistance, sir," he said, giving his hat a slight tip, He turned to look at Courtney. "Which one is this, miss? The father or the stepfather?"

"The father. He said he was taking me to Disney World for Christmas, or so he told my dad—my stepdad, technically—but instead we came here so I could babysit for his friends."

"Is that right?" he asked. "And what is it you need?"

"Well, I need to let my dad know I'm here and that I want to go home. I only got his voice mail. I bet Stu didn't call him and he's half crazy trying to find me. Stu lied to him once, I bet he lied twice. And then I need to not babysit—I didn't agree to do this and I've been the full-time help for these kids for days and I am totally *shot!*"

"Well-hell-hell," Stu laughed. "I guess the little munchkin needs a break. I'll take it from here, Officer. Sorry you were bothered…"

"Was there some talk about punishment if you tried to call your father?" he asked Courtney. "Er, that would be stepfather?" he corrected, peering at Courtney.

"He took my phone," Courtney said. "I was supposed to call my dad every day so he knew I was okay, but Stu took my phone away. And he said if I called my dad, I'd never get to live with him again, not even on weekends."

"We're on vacation, Officer. I thought we should have some vacation rules, like no texting, that sort of thing…" Stu attempted.

And then here were Sherry, Ann and Dick, wondering what was going on. "Is there a problem, Officer?"

"I don't think so, sir. These your children?"

"The little ones, yes," Ann said. "And Courtney is our au pair!"

"I am *not!* I don't know anything about being an au pair and I didn't ask to be!" Then the older boys were there, panting, smelling gamey from running on the beach, crowding in, curious. "Those are Stu's boys," Courtney said. "My half brothers."

"And you're watching the four of them?"

She nodded. "Mostly the little ones. From wake-up to at least midnight."

Sherry laughed cheerfully. "Officer, she's being paid!"

The police officer frowned. "How old are you, miss?"

"Fourteen," she said. "Look, all I wanted to do was *call* my dad! That's all."

"Call your dad? Stu's your dad!" Dick said.

"Yes, but I haven't lived with him in a long time, like forever. He hasn't called me or sent me a postcard since he threw me out last year. He said he wanted to take me on a fancy Disney vacation but what he wanted was someone to babysit so he could do a deal with you. Now can I please just have my phone back?"

"Officer," Stu laughed. *Off-His-Ster-er-er.* "Obviously we have a disgruntled teen here and I assure you I can make it right in no time. She needs a break, some fun in the sun, a little—"

"Sounds like she needs to call her dad. The one she lives with."

"We'll definitely take care of that, but right now we're getting ready for a big meeting with a very important actress." He cleared his throat importantly. "Ever hear of Muriel St. Claire? She's meeting us here today as soon as the studio jet can get her here. Now I'll take care of Courtney, I promise you, and—"

"Courtney!"

She pushed aside the police officer and saw Lief jogging down the walking path, lugging his baggage. He dropped his bags and ran toward her.

"Dad!" she yelled, and she bolted for him.

He grabbed her up in his arms, and for the first time in so long she couldn't remember, she cried. She *sobbed*. She buried her face in his neck and let go. She hung on to him so fiercely, she was amazed he could breathe.

"Oh, honey," he said, holding her tightly. "It's okay. I'm here. It's okay."

Lief lifted his head. One police officer was talking to an older couple and simultaneously writing on his pad. The other was watching Lief and Courtney, hands on his hips. The couple with Stu and Sherry were staring with open mouths. Sherry was frowning and Stu was tapping his foot.

He put Courtney on her feet. "Court, what happened? Why are there police?"

"That couple with the gray hair? I borrowed their phone to leave you a voice mail. I guess they called the police."

"Are you okay?"

She nodded and wiped her tears. "He brought me here to babysit this director's kids so they could make a deal. He said if I didn't, I'd have to live with him forever. That I'd never even get weekends with you."

"Is that so?" Lief said. "Not if I have anything to say about it!"

Holding Courtney's hand, they walked toward the gathering.

"Well, your timing couldn't be worse," Stu said. "There's a lot going on today and none of it concerns you, Holbrook. So if you would kindly—"

"Officer, I have a joint custody agreement with this

man. I have a copy in my suitcase. He brought my daughter to Maui without my permission. Without my knowledge."

"You can go to the station and file a complaint and we can certainly direct you to family court," the police officer said. "I don't think you're going to get that settled right before Christmas. Lots of domestic issues right around the holidays. I'm not going to write a citation for this unless we have some abuse situation. Why don't we try to settle this amicably so we can all just have a nice holiday?"

"I'd love to, Officer," Stu said. "But I have a meeting with—"

"Dick, that's Lief Holbrook. He won the Oscar for *Deerslayer,*" Ann said in a stage whisper.

"Oscar?" Sherry said. "He did? For what? He's just a writer!"

Courtney rolled her eyes. Sherry—not the sharpest knife in the drawer.

Dick's hand shot out. "Lief, Dick Paget. We met Oscar night, I believe. Great to see you again."

Lief was scowling. He didn't take the hand. Courtney tugged on his shirtsleeve, and he bent down slightly. "They think I'm their au pair," she said.

"Is that a fact?"

"Well, not exactly," Dick said, taking back his rejected hand. "We thought she wanted to babysit, that's what Stu said. We were paying her for her help, of course."

"Look," Stu said, "do whatever you want. You want

to take her home? Take her home. I'm not going to argue about this. All I wanted to do was bring my own daughter on the family vacation to Maui—a treat! If that's not okay, sue me! Do what you want, but right now I have to set up for a meeting with Muriel St. Claire. I don't have the time or patience to discuss whether Courtney's in the mood to help out with the kids!"

Lief just shook his head. "You moron," he said to Stu. "How do you think I finally found you, since you wouldn't take my calls? I called Muriel, asked her to track you down, tell you she wanted a meeting for a film." He laughed. He looked down at Courtney. "Where's your luggage?"

"In the condo. Stu's."

"Do you have a key so we can get it?"

"Yes."

"Let's get out of here…"

Stu reached out and snatched at Lief's shirtsleeve. "Wait. What about Muriel?"

Lief couldn't believe this guy. "She's a good friend of mine. I asked for her help in finding you. She was all too happy to help. She asked what kind of a bastard would do something like take a child like that. And then she said she thinks you're an ass. I guess that means the meeting's off." Lief looked at the police officer. "Are we free to go?"

"Is everyone in agreement? There's no further issue with who is the parent in charge?"

All heads shook, even those bystanders who had nothing to do with Courtney's custody.

"Thank you," Lief said. Then he turned with Courtney, and they walked away from all the commotion.

It was very late in Honolulu when Lief called his
house in Virgin River. A very sleepy Kelly picked up,
and he said, "Hey, babe. Mission accomplished. I have
Courtney back. We got to Honolulu and she's asleep.
I'm out on the patio. Can you hear the surf?"

"I think I can. What time is it there?" she asked with
a yawn.

"Midnight. It's been a very long couple of days. Stu
nabbed her, manipulated her and tried to strike a deal
with her to act as babysitter to another couples' pre-
schoolers so he could work a movie deal. This is why
so many of his deals don't work out very well—he's an
idiot." He explained how Muriel had helped him flush
Stu out. "His biggest concern was that we get our issues
handled so he could have his meeting with Muriel. You
should have seen the look on his face when I broke it to
him that she'd set him up."

She laughed into the phone. "Oh, sorry. It was probably inappropriate to laugh."

"I'll tell you what, if Stu gives me any trouble about
keeping Courtney with me after what he tried to pull,
I'm going to fight dirty. I don't know exactly how, so I
hope it doesn't come to that."

"Are you all right?" she asked.

"I'm tired, relieved, and I miss you like crazy. I've
got the hotel's travel agent working on flights back to
anywhere in California, but it's a bad time of year for

this last-minute travel. I fed Courtney, tucked her in and came outside with a drink." He sighed deeply. "What a circus."

"Thank God you're back in the driver's seat!"

"Kelly, we might not get back by Christmas... The chances of getting a seat on Christmas Eve or Christmas Day..."

"I understand... I wasn't expecting you until January second," she said. "That doesn't mean I don't miss you..."

"You want to know how much I miss you, honey?" he asked. "The only thing missing from my life right now is holding you. Once we get home, maybe life can get a little normal."

She laughed a little. "You think so, huh?"

"Okay, I admit, we have some adjustments ahead. Courtney has been through a lot of emotional turmoil, thanks to Stu. I'm going to get her in to the counselor before school starts up again. But surely there's sanity in the future. The *near* future."

"Boy, aren't you an optimist," she said sarcastically, but he could hear the smile in her voice.

They talked until Lief finished his drink and could barely hold his eyes open. He recharged his phone. It was ringing first thing in the morning. The travel agent got them on a flight into San Francisco on Christmas Eve. Perfect—that's where he'd left his truck in the first place.

Tired as they were, emotionally worn out as this whole adventure had left them, a little laugh at the airport was the last thing either of them expected. While they were waiting to board, who should arrive in the boarding area but Ann and Dick Paget and the little kids. They wouldn't even have noticed Lief and Courtney if Alison and Michael hadn't run up to Courtney, so happy to see her.

"Well, hello," Courtney said. "Going for a plane ride?"

"Going home," Michael said.

"Children!" Ann called. "Over here! Now!"

Ann was looking a little frazzled. Haggard. She kept pushing a lock of limp hair back out of her eyes, and she didn't seem to be wearing her "nice suit" today. She seemed very irritable. Maybe chasing a couple of kids around the beach wasn't really working for her. And Dick was harassing the gate agent about upgrading, though she repeatedly told him there was nothing available in first-class.

Lief had taken the only seats available—they were first-class. He exchanged glances with Courtney and they both tried very hard not to laugh.

Moments later, they started boarding—first were special-needs passengers, then first-class. Ann glowered at them as she and her family passed through the first-class cabin to find their coach seats.

When the gear was up on that flight, Courtney leaned over to Lief and said, for the hundredth time, "I'm never going back to Stu's house. Never."

"Okay," Lief said.

"Seriously. I don't care if the Supreme Court says I have to."

"You won't have to."

"What if they do? What if some judge says—"

"No," Lief said. "First of all, I don't think there's going to be a problem. Second, if by some weird twist of fate there is, I'll find a way to deal with Stu. Maybe I'll get him a meeting with Muriel St. Claire or something." Then he grinned at her. "Anything else worrying you?"

"No," she said, settling back in her seat. "But I wish, you know…"

"Wish what, Court?"

"You know. That it could be just us."

"Huh? What are you saying?" When she just shrugged and looked down into her lap, he nudged her. "What? Be specific."

"I wish you wouldn't get married again…"

He lifted her chin and looked into her eyes. "I haven't made plans to get married. I haven't even mentioned marriage to anyone. But I'm very fond of Kelly and she's been real good to us—I wish you'd give her a chance. She doesn't have to be your friend unless you want her to be. She's *my* friend. But I don't have plans to get married. Not at this point."

"I'll help around the house more," she said. "I'll keep straight As and I'll be so polite all the time you'll wonder if I'm possessed or something."

He chuckled. "That would be nice. What a novel idea."

"And it can be just us?"

"Courtney, I'm not getting married…"

"But you love her. I heard you on the phone. You love her."

There was that superhuman hearing thing again, he thought.

"Yes," he admitted simply. "What did I tell you, Court? If I'm lucky enough to have a girlfriend, it won't make me less of a father. I need friends, too. I need to feel love as much as anyone. But I'm not going to marry anyone until you like the idea as much as I do."

"Promise?"

He sighed. "Promise. But I want you to keep an open mind. Kelly is good for me, she makes me happy. I think under the right circumstances, she could be good for you and make you happy, too."

"But you promise?" she said.

He was quiet for a long moment. "Promise."

Sixteen

Lief didn't tell Kelly about the promise Courtney had extracted from him. He did tell Courtney that he was planning to continue his friendship with Kelly. He had to repeat that he wasn't planning to let it interfere with his relationship with Courtney and he wouldn't be marrying anyone without her approval. At least while she was a young teen, living under his roof.

Guilt about that promise flared in him when he and Courtney got home late Christmas Eve. He found Kelly asleep on the couch, Spike cradled in her arms, snacks in the kitchen waiting for them, a fire still smoldering in the hearth and lights twinkling on the tree.

Lief left the suitcases sitting in the hall and asked Courtney to take Spike outside for a bathroom break. He knelt beside Kelly, smoothing her blond hair away from her brow. "Why aren't you in bed?" he asked her.

"Hm," she said, sleepy. "Oh, I'm fine here. Since I knew you were coming, I put fresh linens on the bed and left out some snacks. I bet you guys are tired."

"You want to guess how much I wish I could just take you to bed with me?"

She smiled dreamily. "As much as I'd like to go?" She sat up. "I'll go and let you guys get to bed."

"You don't have to go. It's late, it's cold. Stay here."

"Are you sure?" she asked, lying back down.

He laughed at her.

"If you feel like company tomorrow, I thought I'd make glazed ham, cheesy potatoes, some green vegetables, pie...."

"It's so much trouble," he said.

"I'd be glad to, but I don't have to. If you'd rather be alone..." she said.

"I would love to spend Christmas Day with you."

"I'm so happy you're home. And that everything worked out in spite of Stu."

Christmas Day was the three of them, Kelly mostly in the kitchen. The dinner was tailor-made for someone like Courtney, though perfectly enjoyable for Lief. He knew that Kelly would have prepared something far more gourmet if not for Courtney—a goose with all the trimmings, maybe. A pudding? Mincemeat pie?

All day long Lief was chasing the puppy to get his sharp little teeth off the Christmas tree lights, the TV remote, his shoes, the edge of the area rug. And he'd yell, "Courtney! If you can't watch him, he has to be in the kennel!"

They had a gift exchange. It wasn't too fancy—a sweater for Lief, a couple of tops and a new pair of boots for Courtney, a suede jacket for Kelly. There was a small box from Kelly for Courtney. The excitement on Kelly's face, like she was lit from inside, when Courtney finally opened it sent such a river of hope through Lief. It was a necklace, a silver necklace with a silver charm in the shape of a dog, perhaps a golden retriever. Courtney gasped when she saw it. She lifted it out of the box and held it up. And then, as if she remembered she wasn't going to encourage this relationship, she put it back in the box and put the lid on. She said, "Nice. Thanks."

And Lief's heart fell.

No one could have possibly been more relieved that Christmas was past than Kelly. First of all, Jillian and Colin came home, and her loneliness was eased. Second, Courtney was busy again; even before school was back in session, she went to see her counselor, went for riding lessons, spent an afternoon and evening at the Hawkins farm. She could have time with Lief, and when there were finally a few hours to string together, she fell into bed with him like a desperate, wanton woman.

When school was back in full swing, she had her lover during the day, like a married woman cheating on her spouse. They spent a few evenings together as well, but there was no privacy at Jillian's house nor at Lief's in the evenings. Still, they could have dinner together, even if it was just the gang. If Kelly cooked at Jillian's, the meal included anyone who happened to be around, often Luke and Shelby as well, and of course, Courtney was always invited. If Kelly cooked at Lief's, it was the three of them.

Courtney was never talkative. She was distant and cold; she couldn't be more obvious—she was not going to warm up to Kelly. She had a smile for just about anyone else, but for Kelly her behavior edged near contempt. Short, one-word responses, frowns or flat expressions, eye rolling and tongue clucking. Kelly was to the point that if Courtney just went to her room and ignored them, she felt it was a good night!

Courtney didn't wear the silver necklace with the doggie charm.

Through the freezing snow and sleet of January, Kelly shipped some of her jars of sauces, relishes and chutneys to people Luca had contacted for her, interested retailers in the Bay Area. She spent most of her time during the icy-cold month experimenting with soups and stews. She invited her friend Laura Osika to the Victorian to have some fun with vegetarian soups—Laura was, remarkably, a vegetarian married to a butcher. They worked together on a few of their meatless recipes.

"How did you end up married to a butcher?" Kelly asked.

"Very simple," she answered with a warm smile. "I loved him."

Kelly only wished love could solve her problems, for she loved Lief so much.

Winter was a great time of year to hang out in the bar kitchen with Preacher because there weren't hunters or fishermen around. They cooked together, exchanged favorite recipes, techniques and menus. Preacher showed her what to do with game, and she showed him what to do with pastry. They had a wonderful time with stews and breads. They decided to have a chili cook-off at the bar, and it seemed to Kelly that half the town showed up. The results? A tie!

On Valentine's Day Lief brought her flowers and a beautiful platinum choker from Tiffany's that he admitted he had ordered from the jewelry store online. He left Courtney at home with the puppy and spent time on the third floor with Kelly, sharing a bottle of wine. But he had to get home.

And then came the rains of March, and Kelly knew it was time to make a change. She held Lief's hands in hers and said, "I don't know when I've loved a man like I love you. You make me feel like the perfect woman. Every minute I spend with you is the best minute of my day, whether we're making love or having a meal or just talking. But those minutes?" she asked, shaking her head. "Not so many in the grand scheme of things. Of every day, every week, I have much too much time to myself, wondering when I'll be able to see you, wondering if we'll ever be able to make this work. Lief, I can't do this anymore.

"I'm going to call Luca, Lief. I'm going to tell him I need a job. Either processed food production for my recipes or a chef's position. Anything he has. I have to have purpose, something to work for. I have to feel valued. Like I'm building something."

"But your sauces and relishes… You are building something… Right here!"

"With a lover on the side who I can meet for a quickie

during school hours?" She shook her head. "It's not working for me, Lief. It's half a life."

"You'd leave here? But you love it here!" he said.

"I do. And I love you. But I can't stay here. I'm afraid of what's going to become of us. I'm afraid I'll actually marry you, completely against Courtney's wishes, by the way. And in a couple of years when the blush of brand-new love and passion settles and all that's left is the chill in the air from your daughter, it's going to be so painful. It's going to hurt me, you, her."

"Please," he said. "Don't give up on us. Not yet. I think she just needs time—when she's more mature…"

"I'm not giving up. I'm going to ask for a job. But when I get a job, I'm only going to visit now and then—maybe we can keep things in perspective that way. Maybe if I live in San Francisco, Courtney will be less threatened by me." She shrugged. "It could take Luca weeks or months to come up with something for me."

"I saw the hungry look in his eyes," Lief said. "He'll have the perfect job within minutes."

"Oh, I'm not leaving you for Luca. You know that! That part of my life, that silly fantasy? Over forever. But I'm lonely here. Jill has her work, her lover, Colin's family… I just stay busy and wait for you to call." She shook her head. "I understand how it is—you're a father first and your daughter needs you. She needs to be sure of your commitment to her. She *will* recover from everything she's been through, I know she will, but it might be a long time. And she might be thirty-five when she's finally ready to let me in.

"We'll stay in touch," she went on. "Maybe you can even escape now and then and spend a couple of nights with me in the city."

"What are you saying?" he asked. "That you'll *wait* for me?"

She shook her head. "Not saying that either, Lief. I'm saying that I'm in love with you, that moving on is so hard for me it breaks my heart, but maybe the time for us isn't right now. Maybe it's later, when your life is more settled and stable. And if later comes and my life hasn't changed too much…" She shrugged. "Maybe it will still all work out. But it's not working out now. And I can't stay here this way. It hurts too much. I feel empty inside…"

"Is this how you break up? End it? Because I'm not ready for that to happen! I'll just tell Courtney that she has to—"

"Sh," she said, putting her finger to his lips. "I'm going back to the city to work as soon as I get a good offer. And I'm not telling you this so you'll have a standoff with your daughter. You have to take care of her. I'm telling you because I don't want you to be surprised. You can't make Courtney accept me. In fact, if you're able to *force* her to accept me, that would be even worse." She shook her head. "What's supposed to happen will happen. In the meantime, I'm going back to work."

"Don't," he said. "Not yet. We'll figure it out…"

She shook her head. "We're the grown-ups who know how to handle tough stuff. Let's act like the grown-ups."

* * *

"I think we're just about done with this whole counseling thing," Courtney told Jerry. "We've been at it for months and there's nothing left to talk about."

"Well," he began with his usual patience. "We might talk about why you're not very happy these days."

"What? I'm happy! Perfectly happy!"

He leaned back in his chair. "Convincing," he said drily.

"Thing is, Jerry, I'm too busy for this. I have a lot of responsibility. I promised Dad I'd keep my grades up, I have to keep an eye on Spike *all* the time, I help around the house and even cook—he loves it when I cook—and now that the snow's melting, I'm riding more."

Jerry glanced outside. It was overcast and drizzling. "Not missing any riding today, are you?"

"Duh," she said.

"This one hour a week might seem like a waste of time to you now, but you might look back on it and find it was productive."

"Seriously, I'm pretty busy…"

"I realize that, Courtney. I have noticed some changes since we started our discussions."

"Yeah, my hair is all one color. I bet you're taking credit."

He disregarded that. "When we started meeting, you called Stu your dad and your stepdad was Lief. Always Lief. Now he's Dad and Stu is Stu."

"Well, after what Stu did to me over Christmas, he's lucky I even call him Stu!"

"Point very well taken. What do you hear from him?"

"You're kidding me, right? We don't hear from him. That doesn't mean we don't know what's going on down there. Dad found out that Stu and Sherry are getting divorced. He found out from the lawyer who's handling our custody thing."

"How's that going, the custody thing?" Jerry asked.

"Stu's signing off on me. And I guess in his divorce, the loser gets custody of those boys." She smiled wickedly.

"Does that give you some peace of mind, Courtney? That you can now safely assume you're permanently settled with Lief? I mean, your dad?"

"Sure," she said. "I guess."

"That's what you want, right?" he asked.

"Uh-huh. Yeah."

Jerry leaned toward her. "What's wrong, Courtney?"

She shrugged. She looked down. "It might not be making him that happy..."

"Why do you say that?"

"He's sad," she said. "He's been sad since we got home at Christmas. Sad almost like he was after my mom died. Not that bad, but still..."

"Have you talked to him about that?"

"Like, what am I supposed to say?"

"How about something like, 'You seem sad. Why are you sad?'"

She shook her head. She really didn't want to do that. She was afraid of the answer.

"Want to have a family session? I could ask him with you present and that would give you an opportunity to listen in a safe place. You wouldn't have to do the asking."

She shook her head again. Safe place or not, she didn't *want* the answer.

"Oh, boy," Jerry said. "You have a very big cork holding back something important. If you'll get it out where we can look at it, maybe we can work through it."

"You say that a lot," she said, an angry edge to her voice. "Get it out where we can look at it! I don't have to look at it! He's sad, that's all."

"Are you afraid he's sad because he now has permanent custody?"

"No!" she shot back angrily. "I know why he's sad! Because I told him he can't marry Kelly!"

Silence hung in the air for a moment. Finally Jerry said, "Was he planning to marry Kelly?"

She shook her head and swallowed thickly. "He said he wasn't planning to."

"Okay," Jerry said. "So, you're both in the same canoe on that subject. Then why is he sad and you're sad that he's sad?"

She took a breath. "He wants me to give her a chance because he said she's a good person. And I said I want it to be just us. Me and him."

"I see. You must have had a very good reason..."

"You know," she said. "The way things go."

"Maybe you could explain that to me in your own words and we could go from there."

She smirked at him. "You know, you're such a sneak sometimes. This is more of that *Get it out there where we can look at it!*"

"Guilty as charged. Got an A-plus in Sneaky 101. So?"

"Things just don't work out the best sometimes, you know? Me and my mom were real happy, then Dad came along. We were all real happy. Then my mom died and Dad sent me to Stu. He said he had to and didn't want to, but that didn't make it easy. Then Stu sent me back. Then Stu tricked me at Christmas and almost gave me a fucking nervous breakdown... Sorry. About the swearing."

"Courtney, you can swear your head off in here. As much as you want. I'm not here to judge. Go on."

"So then I'm back with Dad and what's the first thing we have to think about? How about Kelly? Let's let Kelly come into the family!"

"Don't you like Kelly?"

"She's all right. She's even nice, sort of. She can be funny. I like her sister better but her sister is hooked up to Colin, who I also like. It's not that I don't *like* her."

"Then what is it?"

"What if they get married and something happens? What if Dad dies, then Kelly has me, then Kelly gives me back to Stu, then Stu gives me back to Kelly, then Kelly finds some guy to marry and *she* dies and so on? Huh? You think I feel like doing all that again?"

"Apparently it's the uncertainty of the future that bothers you most. Frightens you."

"Duh," she said.

"Maybe you should talk to your dad about this."

"What's he going to say? That he's not going to die? He can! I think it's better if it's just us. Me and him. We don't need anyone else."

Jerry waited it out, like he was expecting her to say something more. Finally he said, "But you do. Courtney, you do need other people. And right now, one of the things you need to know is what plans your dad has for you if anything should happen to him. Not only is there a possible new woman in your future, but your dad also has family in Idaho. Family you like. As for Kelly, she has family you like. Why don't you try to get some of these questions answered before you put this kind of pressure on yourself?"

"What pressure? It's no pressure on me! If he wasn't sad, I wouldn't be sad!"

"But that's where you're wrong—this situation that you've outlined, just you and him and the rest of the world stay away—this puts an *enormous* burden on you. You're fourteen and a half, almost fifteen. Very soon there's going to be a boyfriend if there isn't already, and he's only going to be the first boyfriend. You're going to get older, spread your wings, go to college, travel the world, find new boyfriends and more best female friends. In a few years, about three and a half, you're not going to be living with your dad every day, every night. You're probably going to be living in a dorm or apartment with girlfriends. You're going to fall in love. You might fall in love more than once. You might go back to your dad's now and then, maybe even for long stretches like a couple of months at a time. But it's your job to build a life outside of your dad's house. And then you're going to want to bring some of that life back to him to share—like your boyfriend, your fiancé, your husband and children…"

"That is not happening anytime soon!"

"Sooner than you think. What about your dad? Don't you worry that he'll be lonely when you start to spread your wings?"

"We can worry about that later…"

"I see. Well, just so you know, they don't allow fathers to live in sorority houses with their daughters."

"Funny. You're so funny…"

"Courtney, you're not only asking him to remain lonely and sad so that you can feel safe, but you're asking yourself to keep all the important people of your future away so you can dedicate yourself to him so you can feel safe. And you'll be lonely." Jerry shook his head. "That's the hard way."

"Then what's the easy way?"

"Tell your dad you've been stressed out about your future, about where you would go and what you would do if anything should happen to him. Talk it out."

"He'll just say—"

"Lief Holbrook lost a young wife in a completely tragic and unpredictable brain hemorrhage. He is *not* going to say it can't happen." Jerry paused. "And if there's the slightest worry that you might be a little afraid of getting attached to someone like Kelly and losing her somehow, you could talk about that, as well."

She just shrugged. And gave a little sniff, though she *wasn't* going to cry.

"You're not unique, you know," Jerry said. "It's not even a teenage thing, Courtney. It's a very normal, human frailty we all have, to be afraid someone we love could be taken from us. And the reality is, eventually we all suffer loss. It's a sad fact of life. There is no way to stop it, really. But there is a way to prepare for it…"

"Let me guess," she said sarcastically, feeling a very large rock welled in her throat. "Get it out there where you can look at it."

"Yes, Courtney, tiresome as you find it. This is what people do to the best of their ability. Not just by talking about their fears and worries, but by being proactive. They have medical checkups, take their vitamins, wear their seat belts, write wills. It really does all begin with talking about it, however. I'd like you to seriously consider that."

"But see, not everyone goes through it," she said. "Even if they talk about it, sometimes it never comes," she said, unable to swallow.

"Yes, Courtney. Everyone goes through it. You can't name a person who hasn't or won't experience loss and grief."

"How about Amber, huh? The only girl in a family that thinks she's the princess? I mean, they're dorky, but really… And she's too dorky to ever worry about anything. Amber's life is so calm and easy, even if she does have a lot of chores."

Jerry lifted a brow. "And doesn't she also have a little brother or nephew in a wheelchair? With a disease for which there is no known cure?"

"Rory," she said in a breath. How had Rory not even come to mind? Because even though he was in a wheelchair, he was so cute and funny and crazy, it was easy to forget he might not live past his teenage years. He could, she knew that. Not likely, though. "Well, thanks a lot. Now I feel even worse."

"When you and your dad understand each other's feelings, you're going to feel a lot better. I'm going to see you in a week. If you want to bring your dad along for a little help in talking about this, you're welcome to do so."

"Not fucking likely," she said. Then she tilted her head and smirked at him. "You said I could swear."

"Absolutely, Courtney. In fact, it's helpful. When you cut loose like that, I know what things you're most angry or passionate about."

She narrowed her eyes. "Sometimes I really hate you."

He smiled a bit. "I get that a lot."

Nothing could solidify that rock in Courtney's throat like shifting her thoughts from her own losses to the potential of losing Rory. She loved that goofy kid! And Amber might seem dorky, but Courtney knew in her heart that far more than dorky, she was sincere and loving and devoted to her family.

And to Courtney.

The very next day at lunch Courtney asked Amber, "Do you ever worry about maybe losing Rory?"

Amber chewed and swallowed and said, "All the time. It's not even a maybe—if some wonderful, scientific thing doesn't happen, we will lose him. And it kills me."

"Does he know that?" she asked.

"Of course he does. He's been in the chair two years—you think he hasn't asked what it all means? Little booger is smart, you know that. He knows more about his disease than the doctors, I think."

"Isn't he scared?"

"Sometimes, but he knows it won't hurt. He knows it will only hurt the ones like us who will have to miss him."

Courtney shook her head. "How do you do that? Talk about it without crying?"

She shrugged. "We already did the crying."

The next day was a rare sunny March day and Courtney's riding lesson was on. She was getting very good on Blue; she could not only move her around expertly and perform a thorough grooming right down to the hooves, but she'd actually washed her down a couple of times.

After her lesson, Lilly Tahoma invited her to ride along the trail with her for a half hour or so before Lief picked her up. Blue was Lilly's horse, but she let Courtney keep her and took one of the other stable horses.

Lilly yammered about how the green growth of spring was beginning to peek through, especially in the foothills, and they were enjoying one or two warm days every week. "And the snow pack in the mountains is beginning to melt, so watch yourself around the river—it will swell. Courtney?"

"Hm?" Courtney said, turning her attention back to Lilly.

"Did you hear what I said about the river?"

"No, what?"

"The snow pack in the mountains is beginning to melt. You should mind the river—it could swell and even flood."

"Okay," she said.

"You've been so quiet. Is there something on your mind?"

"Hm? No, nothing…"

"You don't have to talk about it if you don't want to, but you should never be dishonest. Just say 'it's personal' and that will do it."

"No, there's nothing," she insisted.

"Old Hopi saying—*When you lose your temper, you lose a friend. When you lie, you lose yourself.*"

And Courtney shot back, "When you're nosy, you irritate people."

Lilly chortled. "What is most fun about you, you have the face of a young girl and the sharp mind of a wizard. I apologize. I didn't mean to pry or offend. You're right to correct me."

Courtney sighed. "Sometimes I just flip out. Sorry.

I've been worrying about things. One of them is my best friend's little eight-year-old nephew who has muscular dystrophy. He's in a wheelchair and seems to be doing fine right now, but it's not good, you know?"

"Oh, I'm so sorry. Sometimes life can seem so cruel."

"No kidding."

"How is your friend handling it?"

"She's handling it fine! I'm not doing so great with it."

"Oh, Courtney, there's an adjustment to news like that. Don't be hard on yourself."

"Well, it's not that I'm hard on myself," she said. "You know my mother died, right? I mean, even though I never tell anyone, everyone seems to know."

"I knew, yes. I believe your father mentioned it."

"Well, that wasn't too easy. And I guess I worry about going through stuff like that. It's made me sad." Then she shrugged. "I guess."

"Oh, now, that I understand," she said with a laugh. "I'm an expert at that. I was hurt once and decided never to be hurt again."

Courtney was astonished and looked at Lilly. "Really? I mean, really?"

"Oh, yes. It gave me a chronic sore throat, holding back the tears. *Afraid* of the tears. But the Hopi have another old saying. *Crying will release the sorrowful thoughts on the mind.*"

"Where do you get all these old Hopi sayings?"

She laughed. "From an old Hopi grandfather. I

treasure them now, but believe me, as I was growing up he got on my last nerve!"

"Did you ever hurt so bad inside that you were afraid you'd never stop crying? That maybe you'd die of crying? That the ground might swallow you up?"

"Oh, sweeting, yes! That's why I cut it off! But people don't die of crying—they only get very messy and very tired and in the end, there is sometimes relief. Sometimes it takes a lot of that messy crying to get relief. But it is cleansing."

"What did you cry over? Did your mother die?"

"I never knew my mother," Lilly said. "Other heartbreaks, certainly not the same as yours. Life's path sometimes has many rocky curves."

"Another Hopi saying?"

"No," Lilly said with a laugh. "The unfortunate truth! I've had as many hard times as wonderful times. As I'm older, I flow with it better than I did when I was your age. At least you have that to look forward to!"

"That's good news…" Courtney replied drily.

"I've been meaning to commend you on your progress, Courtney—some of the wonderful news of the day. And I'm wondering—would you consider helping me with some of the much younger girls? Some of them are nervous around the horses and some have a bigger problem—they're *not* nervous and perhaps too brave to pay attention to safety. They could use a role model like you to show them the way."

"Seriously?"

"I couldn't be more serious. I'm very proud of you. I think you could teach us all. Could you help?"

"Sure," she said, her entire mood suddenly brighter.

"It's just about finished, Courtney," Lief said on the drive home from the stables. "The custody filing. I have to appear in court, but it's a mere formality and you don't have to go. This will be the end of it. I will only be gone one night and the Hawkinses said you and Spike can stay with them."

"I don't need to stay with them," she said.

"I took care of it, honey. Pack an overnight, take the bus home from school so you can pick up Spike and your bag. Amber's dad will come for you. Then, if you're okay being alone until I get home late Thursday night, they can drop you and Spike off after dinner. You okay with that? Because if you're not, you can stay with them two nights. I should be back by eleven at the latest. Want to stay a second night?"

"No," she said quickly. "I'll come home."

He chuckled. "Okay. Mr. Hawkins said he'd bring you. You have your key. And…do I even have to say this? No friends over. No sneaking out, no beer, no et-cetera?"

"Gimme a break," she said. "Haven't I been like a perfect child?"

"Truthfully? Yes. Great record. Don't mess it up."

Seventeen

Courtney made a decision to show Lief how totally functional they were, just the two of them. When she got to school she told Amber that her dad's trip was postponed, and it would maybe happen next week, but she wouldn't be spending the night.

"Aw, that's too bad," Amber said. "I was kind of hoping you'd come."

"Well, I could come anyway, but I should stay home and, you know, catch up on stuff. You're doing okay on algebra, right?"

"Thanks to you!" she said, smiling.

"Will you tell your mom and dad? Tell your dad not to come and pick me up?"

"Sure. Wanna do something on the weekend?"

"We could do that," Courtney said. "I'll ask my dad."

And when she got home from school, Lief was gone and Spike was in the kennel waiting for her. Lief had left her a note: *Call my cell for any reason. And here are some numbers in case you have a problem of any kind. Love, Dad.*

Dad. That felt so good, so right. So there was a lot in her life that was kind of upside down, but Lief was her dad and he was getting the papers signed.

They had talked about her last name—Lord. She'd been using Holbrook at school because it was less confusing, but it wasn't her legal name. Lief had told her that after she was eighteen she could have her name legally changed if she wanted to and wouldn't need anyone's permission, not even Stu's. She was planning on doing just that.

The names and numbers under his note included Kelly's cell phone and landline, the number for the town doctor, Dr. Michaels, the number for Jack Sheridan, who could find anyone she might need, Mike Valenzuela, the town cop and the number of the veterinarian in Fortuna they'd taken Spike to for his shots.

She'd only been home a couple of hours when her cell phone rang, and she saw that it was Lief.

"Hi, honey," he said. "Doing okay?"

"Just doing homework," she said. It wasn't a complete lie. She was doing homework, but she wasn't doing it with Amber. She was doing it at home alone. She was thinking about making some mac and cheese, and while she told the literal truth, she knew she was misleading him. She just wanted him to know that they could make it, just the two of them. She wanted him to know she'd stick by him, and he didn't need to be sad anymore.

Regardless of all the things Jerry and Lilly had said

about this, about worrying about the grief and pain the future might bring, it still seemed like the best idea was proving herself competent. And proving to Lief he didn't need anyone else.

"When is court?" she asked him.

"I appear in judge's chambers tomorrow, not open court. Stu signed his documents and doesn't even have to be there. I'll see the judge at nine, be done by ten, have a meeting with the lawyer, then lunch with my agent since I'm here and can't get a flight back till later. Then I'll drive home from the Bay Area. You'll probably be asleep when I get home."

"But will you text me if you have any problem with the judge?" she asked.

"Of course, but don't worry. I've been told that, with Stu's consent, this is as good as over."

"Okay. And will you please wear your seat belt?" she asked.

There was momentary silence. "Courtney, I always wear a seat belt, you know that."

"Right. Yeah. Just making sure."

"You all right, honey?"

"Sure. I think it's time to eat, I'd better go."

"Well, say thank you to Hawk and Sinette for me, will you please?"

"Yeah, I will. Talk to you tomorrow?"

"I'll give you a call when you should be home from school, before I catch my flight."

"Good. Right," she said. "See you later."

Once she had signed off, she felt all proud again.

She felt like this was the right thing to do, to show him they'd be fine without anyone else joining their family. She finished her homework, started water boiling for her mac and cheese, and then she heard the telltale sound of gnawing.

Crap! she thought. She'd forgotten about Spike. He was loose. And it took him about ten seconds to get in trouble.

And then there was a pop, a yelp, the lights in the other room flickered, and all went quiet. "Spike!" she yelled. "Oh, God, Spike!" There was no response.

Courtney ran frantically through the house, looking for him. The yelp had been close, he must have been near the kitchen. She looked behind the couch, in the pantry and laundry room, but she couldn't find him. She called and called, but he didn't come. Then she saw a bit of blond fluff sticking out from behind the entertainment center, and with a gasp, she ran.

She lifted the limp dog; at five months he was large and heavy. But totally limp! And the end of his tail was *black!* The fur was burned! And his lips were black! "Oh God, oh God, oh God," she cried, holding him in her arms.

She carried him with her to the kitchen. He was lifeless, his head lolling. She laid him gently on the kitchen floor while she grabbed the cordless and her list of phone numbers. She dialed the vet.

"This is the Sequoia Veterinary Hospital. Our hours of operation are…."

She hung up on the recording. Whom to call? She

put her hand on Spike's chest and jostled him; she was hyperventilating. She was afraid he was dead!

Well, the vet's office was closed. Not the human doctor! Not the bar! She called Kelly's number.

When Kelly answered, Courtney shrieked! "Kelly! Spike! I think he's dead! My dad's gone! I don't know what to do!"

"Did you call the vet?"

"They're closed! I'm not sure what happened to him! I heard him chewing, heard a noise like a pop, found him with his head behind the bookcase and I think he's dead! He's all limp. His mouth and tail are black!"

"Oh, God, is he breathing at all? Was he chewing a wire?"

"I don't know," Courtney said, beginning to cry.

"Stop crying and listen to me. Do you know CPR? I don't know if it'll help, but you can try breathing into his nose. Not big breaths, but small ones for his small body. Hold his mouth closed and blow into his nose. And I'm on my way! Can you do that?"

"Uh-huh," she whimpered through her tears. "Uh-huh."

"I'm hanging up so I can come over, all right?"

"'Kay," she said, crying. "'Kay. Hurry."

It took Kelly fifteen minutes to get to Lief's house, and all the way there she was wondering, What is Courtney *doing* there? As she understood it, Lief was making a quick trip to Los Angeles County Court to get the final filing on his custody of Courtney. But Courtney and the puppy were supposed to be with Amber. It was just after six, and Courtney had her hands full of dead dog.

Oh, this is great, she thought dismally. *What in God's name am I going to do with this situation?*

When she got to Lief's house, she was doubly alarmed to find the front door standing open. "Courtney?" she yelled.

"In here!"

Kelly followed her voice and found Courtney kneeling beside the dog in the kitchen, Spike on the floor and looking calm and sleepy, but not dead.

"Is he all right?" Kelly asked.

Courtney turned to her, her face pathetic with the tracks of tears, red nose, puffy lips. "He's breathing, but not a lot. And he can't stand up!"

"Holy crap, look at that tail," Kelly said, grabbing the phone. "Where's the vet's number?"

"They're closed!" Courtney said desperately. "I don't know what to do."

"Sh. Just pet him a little and let me listen a second." The recording came on explaining the hours of operation, but after that there was a number for an emergency animal hospital, available twenty-four hours. Kelly scribbled down the number, placed the call and spoke to an operator or receptionist. "Hi. I have a five-month-old pup—Labrador or golden mix—and I'm not real sure what happened to him, but—"

"He chewed wires!" Courtney cried out with a sob in her voice.

Kelly looked at the dog. "Well, that explains it. He

chewed on wires. I think he got a bad shock. He's breathing but his mouth and tail are burned and he can't stand up."

"Is he gonna die?" Courtney cried.

"Sh," Kelly said. Then into the phone she said, "Sure, where are you?" She scribbled on the back of Lief's note. "Okay, we'll be there. Thanks."

She disconnected and looked at Courtney. "Get your jacket, kiddo. He needs to go to the hospital."

"Is he gonna die?" she asked again, desperate.

"I have no idea, but he's not dead yet. Let's take him to the vet. Get your jacket. And maybe a special toy or blanket for Spike."

"'Kay," she said, running to do so.

And Kelly thought again, what the hell? Lief is out of town! They're not supposed to be here.

She looked at the note and list of numbers—hers was there along with others. Not the Hawkinses' number, however.

Courtney insisted on carrying Spike to the car, wrapped in his favorite filthy, demolished, threadbare and frayed blanket. Once they were under way, Kelly said, "Your dad told me he was flying to L.A. but that you would be at Amber's house for the night…"

"I know," she said with a sniff. "He's going to be so pissed…"

"Well, what's going on?"

"I wanted to prove to him that I could handle things. That I don't need a babysitter! But I can't! I might've killed Spike! Because I wasn't watching!"

"Aw, Courtney," Kelly said. "When you're fourteen and as responsible as you are, it's not a babysitter, it's more like company. And an adult in case you need something, like a ride to the doggie doctor. And he's not dead yet, so let's not bury him. Okay?"

"What if I killed him?" she sobbed, laying her head on his fur.

"Well, first of all, you didn't. Puppies, like small children, get into trouble sometimes. You have to be alert. But you didn't feed him the live wires."

"It's my fault. I don't like him to have to stay in the kennel. He's getting big and it's getting too small and I know he's going to learn to stop doing bad things. He goes to the back door now! When he has to go outside! Every time!"

Kelly reached over and gave the dog a caress. "Don't borrow trouble. He'll probably be just fine."

Dr. Santorelli was a silver-haired man in his sixties with a great sense of humor. He gave Courtney a little peace of mind. "Oh, he's had a bad shock, that's for sure. I think he'll be all right. Don't know about that tail, though. He might lose the end of it. That jolt went straight through him and blew out the end of his tail."

"Oh, no," Courtney sobbed.

"Easily fixed, really. He'll have to stay the night, get some IV fluids and some antibiotic and a little oxygen. He's stunned and hurt, but not terminal. I think your biggest worry is whether he's brain damaged from the jolt."

Courtney sniffed. "How will I know?"

Dr. Santorelli peered at her over the top of his glasses. "If he chews wires again, brain damaged."

Kelly put her hand over her mouth to keep from laughing.

"I have Labs," Santorelli said. "I had to take rocks out of one's stomach. Then I had one who ate one of those disposable plastic razors. My fault—I didn't get the shower door closed and she got in there and ate an entire shaver. Had to watch for razor blades to pass.…"

"Really?" Courtney asked.

"Oh, yes. I'll never hear the end of that one. My fault and all. But it was my wife's shaver. One of those scented ones. I think she should share responsibility, personally."

"It didn't kill her?" Courtney asked. "The dog, I mean?"

"Hey, I'm a veterinarian!" he teased. "Everything passed, clean as a whistle." He leaned close to Courtney. "I get the shower door closed now."

"When do they stop chewing everything in sight?" Kelly asked.

"Some never do. Most outgrow it in a couple of years. But some eat the wildest things, you'd almost wonder if they need to eat them. Like rocks, garbage, plastic, wood. The rule of thumb is, watch your dog and figure out what he does. If he's a chewer, replace the bad thing with the good thing. Tell him 'No!' and give him the rawhide. That's a good start."

"He goes outside and not on the rug now," Courtney said, proudly but tearfully.

Kelly instinctively put an arm around her shoulders and pulled her close, holding her, giving support and comfort.

"Listen, you have to watch them, but understand something—they get the best of all of us sometimes. They take off running, chase cars, eat valuable or dangerous stuff, get in fights with other animals, all kinds of things. They're animals, young lady. We love 'em. We don't necessarily trust 'em."

"Will you let Spike out tomorrow?" Kelly asked.

"I imagine so. But I want a closer look at the tail— might need a surgical procedure. And I need to get a little life back in him. He's had a bad shock." He raised a brow at them. "Literally," he added.

On the way home Courtney said, "I guess you could probably take me to Amber's. That would probably be all right."

"It's late," Kelly said. "We don't have to bother them. I'll just sleep on your couch and you get some rest."

"You don't have to…"

"I know, honey. But I think you've had a hard enough night. I don't mind."

"But you don't have pajamas," she said.

"I'll live. Won't be the first time I've slept in my clothes."

"My dad's going to kill me."

"Nah, he'll get over it…"

Courtney glanced at her. "You could've said, 'Oh, we don't have to tell him.'"

Kelly smiled. "No. I couldn't. You have to own it, Courtney. When you screw up you own it, you make amends, you learn your lesson."

"Yeah, I guess. Sooner or later he'd find out anyway. Like when he sees Spike with a shorter than usual tail."

"Yeah. Dead giveaway."

It was quiet in Kelly's car for a long time. Then Courtney said, "It was nice of you to help me out, take me to the vet…"

"You'd do it for me," she replied.

"Well, thanks a lot. I don't know what I would've done."

"Listen, Courtney, if I hadn't answered, someone else would've. Jack or Preacher or Amber's dad… I like Spike. I was happy to help out."

Another long silence passed. Then Courtney said, "You can sleep in my dad's room if you want to."

Kelly reached over and patted Courtney's knee. "I'll be fine."

It was about eleven at night when Kelly heard her cell phone chime, alerting her to a text message. *Where are you?* it said.

She glanced down the hall to see that Courtney's bedroom door was closed and her light off. Then she went to the great room, picked up the cordless phone and called Lief's cell. When he answered, she said, "I'm sitting on your sofa, watching TV. But I had to check the wiring behind the entertainment console before turning it on."

"What?" he asked.

"We've had a little excitement, and I'm spending the night on your couch."

She explained the events of the evening, her story punctuated by Lief continually saying *Oh, God* and *Oh, Jesus*.

"So, the dog will live?" he finally asked.

"It appears so. And so will Courtney."

"Tell her she's in big trouble," he said.

"Sorry, boss. That's above my pay grade. You tell her when you get home. And she's having a sore throat tomorrow…"

"How do you know that?"

"Because I'm calling her in sick to school. We'll go visit the dog or hopefully pick him up and bring him home. I know she was a bad girl, but that bad girl has been through the grinder with this. She's limp as a noodle with remorse."

"Whatever you want," he said tiredly.

"I'll stay till you get home tomorrow night. Then you can do whatever you have to do."

"Well, go find a T-shirt of mine or something. Sleep in my bed."

But it was hard enough to *think* about his bed, to think about his wonderful scent on the pillow. "I'm fine," she said. "Just travel safe."

"There's some brandy in the cupboard above the Sub-Zero, kind of hidden behind the Crock-Pot."

She laughed at him. "Now, I might take you up on that."

After they hung up, Kelly used the kitchen's step stool to root out that brandy, poured herself a small bit in a juice glass and settled back on the sofa, wrapped in the throw. And she was really quite happy watching very old, very late night television reruns. She was almost done with her brandy and starting to nod off when she heard an odd sound.

She turned the volume way down. Yes, an odd sound. The wind whistling through the pines maybe. If Spike were here it could be the sound of him whining in the kennel, but he wasn't here. She threw off the blanket and got up, creeping down the hall toward Courtney's room, listening. Sure enough—little miss was crying. Scared for her dog probably.

On instinct, Kelly just opened the door. "Hey, hey, hey," she said, entering and sitting on the bed. "He's going to be fine. Try not to worry!"

Courtney turned over a bit. "I could've killed him!" she said.

"Oh, honey, he got into mischief. That's why we watch. He's going to be all right."

But she turned back and just sobbed into her pillow.

Kelly lay down on the bed behind her, spooning her. "Wow, you have a major pity party going on here," she said, running fingers along Courtney's temple, stroking back her hair. "We'll pick him up tomorrow and I bet he's not even brain damaged. Probably not any smarter, though, so be warned. You might have to do the majority of thinking in this family for a while."

More sobbing.

"You'll probably be grounded forever," Kelly said, just to get Courtney's mind off the dog.

"Did you tell him?" she asked through her tears.

"Yes. You were right. I think he's pissed. But he'll probably get over it. All we really care about right now is that the dog's okay. Right?"

"Right," Courtney said miserably.

"You'll feel so much better when you know that for sure."

"I have school," she said.

"Nah," Kelly said. "There's a major illness in the family. Hospitalization, even. I'll call you in sick. We'll go together. Pick him up. Bring him home. I'll stay with you till your dad gets back. You'll get through this…"

"It's all my fault," she whimpered.

"We've been through that," Kelly said. "Even the vet had accidents with his crazy dogs—puppies are intrepid! They can find trouble anywhere."

"But my fault for not going to the Hawkinses'. I wanted to prove we didn't need anyone. I wanted my dad to see that he didn't need anyone besides me. What a dummy!"

"Well, you can put that proving thing off a little while, I think. Just a little assistance here and there until you can drive your own dog to the vet, huh?"

"But it was wrong. Jerry was right—it was wrong."

"Who's Jerry?" Kelly asked.

"Oh, the stupid counselor who said we need lots of people in our lives."

Kelly pulled Courtney a little closer. "Listen, you're doing fine, kiddo. Don't take on too much without help, but don't beat yourself up. I think you're doing very well. You're smart, responsible and you love your dad a lot. You get an A-plus."

"But I really screwed up tonight…"

"Nah," Kelly said. "You called me. When you needed help, you called. You get big points for that. And we got the job done."

"But I was trying to keep you and my dad from getting married, and what a dumb thing!"

Kelly was still for a moment. Very still, very quiet. "Honey, didn't your dad tell you?"

"Tell me what?"

"I'm going back to San Francisco. Next week. Oh, I'll visit sometimes, like once a month or whatever. But I'm going back to the city to work."

"You are?" she asked softly.

"Yeah. It's time."

Quiet filled the space in the room. "Well, if Spike and I need you, I guess you won't be around…" Courtney said.

"There are plenty of people around. There's your dad, he doesn't leave often. Jill and Colin. The Hawkinses."

"I guess," she said very softly.

"I do have one suggestion, though," Kelly said. "Might want to change his name from Spike to Sparky."

Courtney's laughter blubbered through her tears.

Spike was discharged, though his tail was indeed a bit shorter. Kelly stopped by the Victorian to get something comfortable for the evening so she wouldn't have to sleep in her clothes again. She showered at Lief's and made some kick-ass mac and cheese for dinner. Courtney went to bed with her puppy while Kelly dug around in the cupboard for the hidden brandy. She was just getting real comfortable on the couch in the great room when Courtney appeared. She was holding her pillow and her puppy, now alert, was standing at her side.

"Aren't you coming?" she asked Kelly.

"Coming?"

"I guess you don't want to sleep in Dad's room, but you could sleep in mine."

Kelly thought about it a minute. Then she said, "I'll be right there."

Lief's flight was a little late. He didn't get back to Virgin River until one in the morning. There was a light left on for him. A note on the counter said *Mac and cheese in the fridge*.

When he didn't see Kelly on the couch, he got a little excited, hoping he might find her in his bed. He carried his bags back to his room. Nope, not in his bed.

He doubted she'd leave Courtney alone, not after

all that had gone on. With the hall light to illuminate Courtney's room, he pushed open her door. There, in her bed, Kelly was curled around his daughter, his daughter curled around her dog. All asleep.

Spike lifted his head. He wiggled free of Courtney's embrace and trotted out toward Lief. When Lief pulled the bedroom door closed, Spike, with a slightly shorter tail, trotted alongside.

"You're not exactly my first choice," Lief said to the dog. "But you'll do."

A week later, it was time for Kelly to go. Kelly and Jill sat at the kitchen table with their morning coffee. The fire was lit, making it cozy. Though the sun came up bright and the sky clear, it was still cold outside. Jill said, "Well, it was a great fantasy, that you'd cook what I grow, sell it under a family label and stay."

"Maybe that will still happen someday," Kelly said. "Just not right now."

"I'm encouraged by the fact that you're leaving your furniture on the third floor. At least I'll see more of you than I used to."

"Luca has lots of properties around the Bay Area. He insists I use one of his small furnished apartments while I think about where I want to live. And why not? He's richer than God, and he's getting a bargain in me. Besides, I want a place like this as my getaway. I'm never going back to the kind of grind I suffered before I walked out on that insane restaurant. People need balance. We can't work all the time."

"And there's Lief," Jill said.

"And there's Lief," Kelly agreed with a smile. "I can't give him up cold turkey. Because I love him. But hey—he won't be neglecting his daughter if she spends the night with a girlfriend once or twice a month! He can drive down to the city once in a while. I'll come up here sometimes."

Jill held Kelly's hand across the table. "I know we never lived together after you turned eighteen and went off to study food, but it's very hard to give you up after having you here for five months."

Kelly squeezed the hand. "You're not giving me up. But Jill, you have your business and your relationship. What I have is too much time on my hands, too much room left over in my heart. I need more than work. I learned that when I fell in love with Lief. I need to feel needed, not superfluous. I need to be a part of something that's vital and growing, not waiting around to see if anything will take root. I've given this enough time. It's no one's fault. It is what it is. This is the right decision for me. I'll come back up for a weekend in two or three weeks."

"What did Lief say when you were with him last night?" Jill asked.

"That he loved me and wishes I could stay, but of course he understands. He was never in a situation like I am. When he met his wife, she had a little girl who instantly adored him. It wasn't a challenge. He still hopes this can work out between us."

The back door opened, and Colin was pulling off

his gloves as he stepped inside. He wore an army-green canvas jacket over a black turtleneck, his hair pulled back into a ponytail. He was smiling. "I completely repacked the back of your car. Now you'll be able to actually use the rearview mirror. You're good to go."

"Thanks," Kelly said. "I'm going to miss you, too. But I think I have to hit the road before you get pudgy."

"You spoiled me, that's for sure. You call us the minute you get there."

"Sure."

"And take your time," he ordered, opening his arms to her.

"Yes, sir," she said, walking into his embrace. "Take care of my sister, Colin. I'm counting on you."

"Jilly's in good hands, Kell. Take good care of yourself. You're always feeding everyone else—remember to feed yourself, too. And I'm not just talking about food."

"Thanks, I'll remember that." Kelly hugged her sister. "Thank you for everything, honey. I was so happy here in your wonderful house. You made it so easy for me."

"You remember, it's always here for you. Always. If you get tired of working for that crazy Italian, you come up here and make sauces and relishes."

"I will."

Colin held the door open for her, letting Kelly precede them onto the back porch. And there Kelly stopped, coming face-to-face with a little sprite a few inches shorter than she was. Courtney looked a little surprised. Maybe nervous. "Well, hello," Kelly said. "I didn't expect you to be up so early. We said our goodbyes. Maybe I'll see you in a few weeks."

Behind Courtney, leaning against Kelly's packed car, his hands in his pockets, was Lief. Beside him, sitting politely, was the dog.

"You can't go yet," Courtney said.

"Courtney, I have to get moving or I'll end up in city traffic—"

"No, I mean, don't go at all. Not yet. There's still things we can try. Like Jerry said we might try some group counseling to see if we're all in the same canoe— he likes to say that. He also likes to say 'Get it out there where we can look at it.' Here—so you can look at it— most of the time when I wasn't so nice, I knew it. I'm not even sure why, but I knew it. I can be a lot nicer. Seriously."

"Why are you doing this now?" Kelly asked.

"I didn't think you'd really go," she said. "Seriously, I thought there'd be at least one more warning."

Kelly hugged her quick and hard. Then she pulled away, looked into Courtney's pretty eyes and said, "Listen, I won't be far. And I'll be back at least every month, maybe a couple of times a month."

"But no," she said. "Don't go."

"Courtney, I'm sorry, but Luca's counting on me. He offered me a good job and I made a commitment to him. He needs me. But I'll visit, I promise."

"But my dad needs you," she said, her eyes welling with tears.

Kelly felt a hand on her shoulder, too big and heavy to be Jill's. Colin's hand. Shoring her up.

Kelly looked at Lief. His posture was unchanged, but he made a slight shrug, barely discernable.

"Courtney, your dad can call me every day. We'll talk. We'll see each other now and then. This isn't a surprise. We talked about it."

"You can't just walk out on him," she said. "You have to give it a little more time."

"I'm not, honey. I'm not walking out on your dad and he understands that. Lief," she said. "Lief, tell her that I'm not abandoning you."

"She's not, Court. She needs to be someplace where she feels she really belongs, where she's counted on and feels useful and appreciated. I understand that."

"This isn't goodbye," Kelly said. "I'll see you soon." She gave her another hug and stepped down the porch steps.

"Okay!" Courtney yelled. "I need you! Sparky needs you! Don't go! Just please, don't go!"

Kelly stopped in her tracks, met Lief's warm and dark brown eyes and his slight smile. She slowly turned back to Courtney, who had her fist covering her mouth and tears slipping out of her eyes.

"Okay, so I really want you to stay," she said softly, then hiccupped. She lifted her chin. "He won't mind, believe me. But it's me, okay?"

Kelly frowned. "Why?" she asked.

"I don't know." She shrugged with a half sob. "Because you just take me as I am, pretty much. Because you're not mean. Because you help." She sniffed and wiped her hand across her nose. "Because you said my dad was going to ground me forever and wouldn't cover for me to get on my good side, but still slept in my bed with me because I was crying. Come on." She pulled the necklace Kelly had given her for Christmas out from the inside of her shirt to show it to her. "Give us a break. Huh?"

Kelly shot a glance at Lief. He just cocked his head to one side as if to say it had nothing to do with him.

She looked back at Courtney.

"You just have to give us one more chance. Me," Courtney said. "You just have to give me another chance, because really I never wanted you to leave, I just... I just worried about not being important around here, like I wasn't important at Stu's house."

"Maybe we should take a breather," Kelly said. "See where we are in a few months..."

"Don't go," she said. "My dad loves you. He told me at Christmas—he loves you. And I didn't really want to, but after Sparky blew his tail off, I knew you were the real deal and I started to love you, too."

"Wow," Kelly said. "You sure made me work for it!"

Courtney laughed through her tears. "Seriously," she said.

"You need to know something, little chick. If I pack my car again, ever, I'm moving."

"I get that," Courtney said.

"Hey," Colin protested from behind her. After all, he

was the one who'd packed the car. She shot him a glare to shut him up.

"So you're staying?"

"I'll give this a try," Kelly said. "If you really think we're in the same canoe."

"I do," Courtney said. "I do. You do love my dad, right?"

"I love him a lot," she said. "And you're really growing on me."

Courtney laughed at her. "You should probably kiss him, then. He's been awful to live with lately."

Kelly approached Lief warily. When she was about a foot away, she asked, "Was this your idea?"

"I had absolutely nothing to do with it. Nothing. Now come here. She's right. You should kiss me."

She allowed herself to be pulled into his arms, met his lips and behind her she heard, "Ewww. Gross." Kelly jumped back and looked over her shoulder.

"Kidding," Courtney said with a laugh.

Looking back into Lief's laughing eyes, Kelly said, "I bet there's going to be a lot of that sort of thing, huh?"

"It's a tough assignment, babe," he said. "Definitely not for sissies. Now come on, lay one on me. I've been hell to live with lately."

Epilogue

Six months later

Kelly and Jill stood on the widow's walk and looked at all the activity below them. Late September was a perfect time of year—most of the garden was harvested and the leaves on the trees were changing, but the branches were not yet bare. The day was sunny, the air cool. Between the garden and the house, large round tables had been erected and covered with starched white tablecloths. The folding chairs were dressed in linen with fancy ties in the back, and each table had lush flower arrangements in orange, yellow, red and some dark plum. There were tall candles that could be lit when the sun went down. There was seating for over a hundred, and guests were milling around, visiting as they held on to long-stemmed champagne glasses. At the far western end of the yard, up against the lilac and rhododendron, there was a trellis draped in white. Next to the trellis, a string quartet.

The front of the Victorian showed cars, trucks and SUVs parked all down the drive. Out of sight from the widow's walk, parked near the back porch, were two large white-paneled vans lettered with a red *BRAZZI* on their sides.

Jill glanced down at her fingernails. "I wore gloves all last week and I think I still have dirt under my nails…"

Kelly inspected them. "I think you're okay," she said. "I have some paprika under mine…"

"Kelly! Jilly! Come down here!" Courtney called. "Luca is here."

They looked at each other. "Easy does it," Kelly advised. "Getting up here in a long dress and heels is a lot easier than getting down."

"You first," Jill said.

When Kelly got to the bottom, there stood Luca bearing a silver tray holding four champagne flutes. His free hand went to his chest, and he sighed at Kelly. "Bella," he said in a breath. "*Magnifico! Mozzafiato!* You have never been more beautiful."

"Thank you, Luca," she said. Her dress was a creamy off-white strung with dark burnt-orange ribbon around the bodice and decolletage. The ribbon matched the satin dresses worn by bridesmaids Jill and Courtney, and they would all carry bouquets of mums, daisies and the most luxurious burnt-orange roses brought from San Francisco by Luca.

"You are all so delicious," Luca said. He lifted the champagne flutes one by one, passing them to the women, the last one his own. He put down the tray and raised the glass. "To the blending of two beautiful families," he said. "May God bless your households with great bounty and joy!"

"Thank you, Luca," Kelly said.

They sipped, and Courtney said, "I knew it. Cider."

"If you were in Italy, little bella, you would have the wine. Kelly, I should be the one to give you away to the groom. After all, were it not for me, you would not have found each other."

"Well, not exactly," she said with a laugh. "I believe we can give most of the credit to your wife. Besides, there's no giving away, only an escort to my groom. Colin has volunteered." She smoothed the starched white of his chef's jacket. "You are so beloved in the kitchen. That you would do this for me, Luca, is the greatest honor."

"I wouldn't let anyone else feed your guests on your wedding day, sweetheart. Are you almost ready? Because they're beginning to chew on the linens."

"Hey," Courtney said. "I get to stay up here while you and dad are gone, right?"

Kelly picked up a little lip gloss and leaned toward Courtney, giving her lips a little touch-up. "Sure. Whatever you and Jilly work out is fine with me."

"I don't know why I can't go with you. I've never been to Cabo."

"I draw the line there," Kelly said.

"It's not like I'd *bother* you," she said.

"I'll make a deal with you, chickie. You don't go on my honeymoon, I won't go on yours."

"You can come with me on my honeymoon," Courtney said.

"You look so beautiful today, Court," Kelly said, changing the subject.

"You're done talking about it, huh?"

Kelly nodded. Courtney looked at Jill and said, "Kind of hard to believe she's never done this mother thing before, isn't it?"

"It is," Jill agreed. "Now let's go get her married before the groom gets cold feet!"

"Are you and Colin ever going to get married?" Courtney asked.

"You look very beautiful today, Courtney," Jill said, changing the subject and smiling.

Luca threw an arm wide, indicating the women should precede him down the stairs. Courtney was last. To Jill and Kelly's backs she said, "I really think we're gonna have to work on our communication skills around here…"

The women had to pass through the kitchen to get to the back porch, and Kelly marveled at the industry—Luca brought his own staff and much of the food. She had suggested a buffet, but Luca wouldn't hear of it—they would serve. He said it wouldn't be too fancy—only five courses and two wines.

Colin was waiting by the back door. He took in the formally attired women and said, "Are you ready? Because Reverend Kincaid has herded everyone to their tables."

"Ready," Kelly said. "Is Lief there?"

"He's been there, his two brothers beside him. Muriel managed to get a table up front, though I think she had to negotiate it. And there are more Riordans here than expected at first. I hope there's plenty of food."

"Always plenty of food," Luca bellowed from behind them.

"Then let's do it," Colin said.

Courtney led the procession, followed by Jillian, followed by Kelly and Colin. They wound their way through the tables toward the trellis, toward the minister, as the strings played.

Kelly smiled when she saw that Lief leaned down to give Courtney a kiss before she stood in her place to the left of the men. He also leaned in to give Jill a kiss on the cheek before she took her place.

And then as Colin and Kelly neared, Lief's eyes grew dark and warm, and he smiled proudly, reaching out to her. Colin escorted Kelly right into Lief's hands. They gazed at each as the words that would begin a whole new family were spoken by Noah Kincaid.

"Dearly Beloved…"

* * * * *

Acknowledgments

Special thanks goes to Laura Osika, the Be in Virgin River Contest winner! Thanks for dropping in to visit us in Virgin River! As a part of the supporting cast, you were a fantastic addition to the story!

To my readers, your thousands of supportive letters and your amazing word-of-mouth recommendations have made this little town come alive, and I am eternally grateful for your encouragement and kindness.

For this story, as for almost every story I write, special thanks to Michelle Mazzanti for early reading and research assistance. I just couldn't get to the end of a book without your input and help.

Once again, Chief Kris Kitna, thanks for answering questions about hunting, fishing, local law and other details about the area.

I am indebted to Kate Bandy and Sharon Lampert. Without your continual loyalty and support I would be lost.

My heartfelt gratitude to Ing Cruz for creating

and managing Jack's Bar online, where hundreds of Virgin River readers exchange book news. (http://groups.yahoo.com/group/RobynCarr_Chatgroup/)

Thanks to Rebecca Keene for early readings of this and many manuscripts; your feedback is incredibly valuable.

Colleen Gleason and Kate Douglas, two women whose friendship is constant and filled with humor, affection and always stimulating writer talk, I am so grateful to have found you both.

Thanks to everyone at the Nancy Berland Public Relations Agency for the support and for always watching my back. Jeanne Devon of NBPR, thanks for the hours of creative work, for reading and critiquing. And special thanks to Cissy Hartley and the entire staff at www.writerspace.com for your wonderful work.

And as always, thank you to Liza Dawson of Liza Dawson Associates and to Valerie Gray, editorial director of Mira Books, two of the toughest readers in publishing. Thank you both for being relentless, tireless, devoted perfectionists. Every push makes each book a little better and I owe you. This is always a team effort, and I couldn't have a better team!

And my undying gratitude goes to the extraordinary opportunity given to me by the entire Harlequin team. Nobody does it better!